THE TALES OF THE HEIKE

translations from the asian classics

THE TALES OF THE HEIKE

Translated by Burton Watson

Edited, with an Introduction,
by Haruo Shirane

columbia university press   new york

Columbia University Press
Publishers Since 1893
New York   Chichester, West Sussex

Copyright © 2006 Columbia University Press
All rights reserved

Library of Congress Cataloging-in-Publication Data
Heike monogatari. English. Selections.
     The tales of the Heike/translated by Burton Watson ;
edited, with an introduction, by Haruo Shirane.
          p.   cm.   —   (Translations from the Asian classics)
     Includes bibliographical references.
     ISBN 978-0-231-13802-4 (cloth : alk. paper) — ISBN 978-0-231-13803-1 (pbk. : alk. paper)
     ISBN 978-0-231-51083-7 (electronic)
     1. Taira family—Fiction.   2. Japan—History—Gempei Wars, 1180–1185—Fiction.
     I. Watson, Burton.   II. Shirane, Haruo.   III. Title.   IV. Series.
PL790.H42   2006
895.632—dc22   2005034245

Designed by Chang Jae Lee

CONTENTS

PREFACE AND ACKNOWLEDGMENTS

The Tales of the Heike is one of the great literary classics of Japan, the subject of countless plays, narratives, and films, but it has not been as popular outside Japan as have such works as *The Tale of Genji*. One reason for the lack of attention is the difficulty in following the text, which is long and highly episodic and contains hundreds of names, places, and events. We hope to have overcome these hurdles with this abridged edition, concentrating on the most important and famous episodes while also linking them in such a way as to give the reader an overall vision of the extended narrative. The glossary, compiled by Michael Watson, should help identify the many minor and major characters and their relationships to both historical events and later reception. In addition, the bibliography of relevant primary and secondary sources in English, also compiled by Michael Watson, should be extremely useful to anyone teaching or studying *The Tales of the Heike* and related warrior tales.

My many thanks go to Burton Watson for agreeing to join me in this project, for his superb skill as translator, and for his patience. I am particularly indebted to Michael Watson, who helped me with the historical research and who volunteered to compile the glossary and the bibliography.

THE TALES OF THE HEIKE

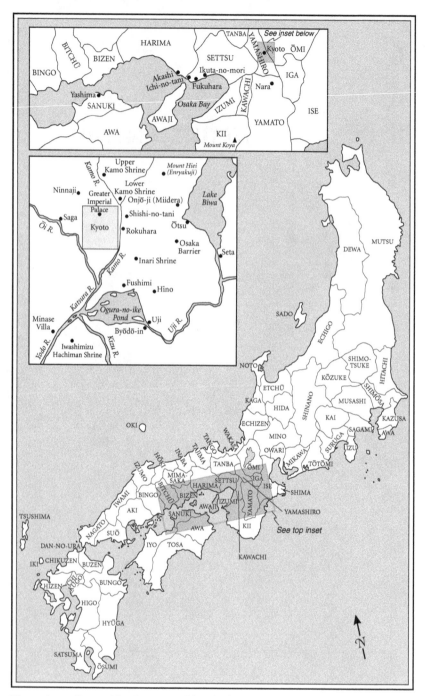

The provinces of Japan, with enlargements of the Inland Sea area and the Kyoto area. The circles indicate important battlegrounds.

INTRODUCTION

The Genre of Warrior Tales

The Tales of the Heike is the most famous example of a warrior tale (*gunki* or *gunki-mono*), a major genre in medieval Japanese literature. Warrior tales first became popular midway through the Heian period (794–1185) with the appearance of the *Record of Masakado* (*Shōmonki,* ca. 940) and the *Record of the Deep North* (*Mutsuwaki,* ca. 1062), both of which were written in *kanbun* (Chinese prose) by Buddhist monks or middle-rank intellectuals. The *Shōmonki* describes the uprising by Taira no Masakado (d. 940) and the attempt to save his spirit from hell.

The second major period of warrior tales, from the beginning of the medieval, or Kamakura, period (1185–1333) through the fourteenth century, begins with *The Tales of Heiji* (*Heiji monogatari,* 1221?), *The Tales of Hōgen* (*Hōgen monogatari,* 1221?), and *The Tales of the Heike* (mid-thirteenth century). During this period, the aristocratic court society changed into a warrior society. Both the *Hōgen monogatari* and the *Heiji monogatari* describe the military conflicts leading up to the Genpei war (1180–1185) and thus resemble the *Shōmonki* and the *Mutsuwaki* in being narratives about warriors who caused great disturbances. But in contrast to the *Shōmonki* and the *Mutsuwaki,* which are "records" (*ki*) written in *kanbun* with a documentary focus, the *Hōgen monogatari* and the *Heiji monogatari* have the quality of Heian vernacular tales (*monogatari*) in trying to re-create the participants' interior life. Unlike the *Shōmonki* and the *Mutsuwaki*, whose perspective is that of those at the center looking out at the rebels in the provinces, the military narratives in this second period are written from the perspective of those who had experienced the war personally or who sympathized with the defeated warriors. These texts also are written in the so-called mixed Japanese–Chinese style, which is a combination of Japanese prose and Chinese compounds and phrases, including allusions to Chinese classics and history.

The Rise and Fall of the Genji and the Heike (*Genpei seisuiki* or *Genpei jōsuiki*, thirteenth to fourteenth century), a Kamakura-period warrior tale, describes the *Hōgen monogatari* and the *Heiji monogatari* as "diaries [*nikki*] of the Hōgen and Heiji period," showing that in the Kamakura period they still were considered to be reliable records of events despite their *monogatari* character. Like other military narratives, the *Hōgen monogatari* and *Heiji monogatari* draw on *setsuwa*, or anecdotes, following a tradition dating back to the late-Heian-period *Tales of Times Now Past* (*Konjaku monogatari shū*, ca. 1120), which devotes one volume to warrior stories. Most of the military narratives are in three parts, describing the causes of the military conflict, the conflict itself, and the aftermath, with good examples being *The Tales of Hōgen* and *The Tales of Heiji*. The second period of warrior tales climaxed with the *Record of the Jōkyū Rebellion* (*Jōkyūki*, ca. 1222), which describes the failed attempt in 1221 (Jōkyū 3) by the retired emperor, GoToba (r. 1183–1198), to seize power from the Kamakura *bakufu* (military government), and the *Chronicle of Great Peace* (*Taiheiki*, 1340s–1371), which describes the collapse of the Kamakura bakufu in 1333 and the subsequent rule by the Ashikaga clan.

Although the military narratives in the second period are heavily influenced by the Heian *monogatari*, they differ in revealing the impact of various forms of recitation or oral performance practices (*katari*). The oral or musical performance of the military narratives had an important ritual function, to celebrate (*shūgen*) the preservation or restoration of order and to pacify the souls (*chinkon*) of those warriors who had died terrible deaths on the battlefield. To celebrate the restoration of order, the warrior tales affirmed those who had established or preserved order and peace; at the same time, they tried to console the spirits of the defeated, hoping to calm their angry and sometimes vengeful spirits and to offer them salvation by incorporating them into the new social order.

The third, late medieval, period of warrior tales produced texts that focus on war but are more about the fate of a single warrior or small group. For example, the *Record of Yoshitsune* (*Gikeiki*, 1411) describes Yoshitsune's flight to the Tōhoku region, concentrating on Yoshitsune, his family, and his retainers. *The Tales of the Soga Brothers* (*Soga monogatari*, mid-fourteenth century), which was recited by *goze*, or blind female singer-musicians, likewise tells the story of the Soga brothers as they avenge their father's death.

Many of these warrior chronicles have no identifiable authors but are the product of multiple writers. For example, *The Tales of the Heike* draw on numerous *setsuwa* and have many, greatly differing, variants. Likewise, the *Taiheiki* also had many editors. Because they did not know how the events were going to end, they had to make the *Taiheiki* into an open and unfinished work. Moreover, the authors of these military tales did not write the narratives from beginning to end; instead, they edited and rewrote the transmitted texts, much as the editors of *setsuwa* collections did, to suit their own needs. Another major characteristic of warrior chronicles like *The Tales of the Heike* and the *Taiheiki* is that they constantly refer to Chinese history and Chinese texts. They compare the disorder and dangers of the present with those of the past and draw lessons from this comparison or point to similarities. In this regard, they belong to a larger tradition of historical narrative.

The military narratives were transmitted in two fundamental ways: as "read texts" (*yomihon*), which could be used for sermons and other functions, and as "recited texts" (*kataribon*), performed by *biwa hōshi* (blind lute minstrels) or *monogatari sō* (storytelling monks) attached to armies. The *Hōgen monogatari*, the *Heiji monogatari*, and the *Heike monogatari* were recited by *biwa hōshi*, and the *Taiheiki* and the *Record of the Meitoku Rebellion* (*Meitokuki*, ca. 1394) were recited by *monogatari sō*. These warrior tales, which belonged to performative traditions, were later used and absorbed by other genres such as nō, *kōwaka-mai* (dramatic ballads), *otogi-zōshi* (Muromachi tales), *jōruri* (puppet plays), kabuki, Edo fiction, and modern novels.

About *The Tales of the Heike*

The Tales of the Heike (*Heike monogatari*) is about the Genpei (Genji–Heike) war (1180–1185), fought between the Genji, or Minamoto, clan, headed by Minamoto no Yoritomo, and the Heike, or Taira, clan, led by Taira no Kiyomori. The Taira's initial, rapid ascent to power was followed by an extended series of defeats, including their abandonment of the capital in 1183 (taking with them Antoku, the child emperor). By 1183 Yoritomo had gained control of the Kantō, or eastern, region; Kiso Yoshinaka, another Minamoto leader, had brought Kyoto under his power; and the Taira had fallen back to the Inland Sea. During an interlude of fighting within the Minamoto clan, Yoshinaka was defeated and eliminated by Yoritomo and his half brother (Minamoto) Yoshitsune in 1184. Then, in a decisive battle at Ichi-no-tani, also in 1184, near the present-day city of Kobe, Yoshitsune, leading the Minamoto forces, decisively defeated the Taira, driving them into the Inland Sea. Finally, in 1185, the last of the Taira forces were crushed at Dan-no-ura, in a sea battle on the western end of the Inland Sea. In the same year, Rokudai, the last presumptive heir of the Taira clan, was captured and eventually executed.

These wars between the Taira and the Minamoto, which mark the beginning of the medieval period, became the basis for *The Tales of the Heike*, which describes the lives of various warriors from both military houses, particularly those of the defeated Taira. The narrative also includes numerous non-samurai stories based on anecdotes (*setsuwa*), many of which deal with women and priests and were frequently transformed by the composers of the *Heike* into Buddhist narratives, much like the anecdotes in Buddhist *setsuwa* collections. So even though *The Tales of the Heike* is a military epic, it has strong Buddhist overtones, which are especially evident in the opening passage on the law of impermanence, in many of the stories of Buddhistic disillusionment and awakening (such as those of Giō and Koremori), and in the final "Initiates' Book" (Kanjō no maki) leading to the salvation of Kenreimon'in, the daughter of Kiyomori, who has a vision of the fall of her clan.

The first versions of *The Tales of the Heike* were probably recorded by writers and priests associated with Buddhist temples who introduced

Buddhist readings and other folk material into an earlier, chronological, and historically oriented narrative. These texts in turn were recited from memory and sung to a lute (*biwa*) by blind minstrels who entertained a broad commoner audience and in turn had an impact on subsequent versions of *The Tales of the Heike*, which combined both literary texts and oral material. Of the many variants of *The Tales of the Heike*, which differ significantly in content and style, the most famous today is the Kakuichi text, which is the one translated here. This text was recorded in 1371 by a man named Kakuichi, a *biwa hōshi* who created a twelve-book narrative of the decline of the Heike (Taira) clan. At some point, "The Initiates' Book," which gives the *Tales* unity and closure as a Buddhist text, was added, as were sections inspired by Heian *monogatari* and centering on women and the private life of the court.

Thanks largely to Kakuichi, the oral *biwa* performance of *The Tales of the Heike* eventually won upper-class acceptance and became a major performing art, its popularity peaking in the mid-fifteenth century. After the Ōnin war (1467–1477), the *biwa* version of *The Tales of the Heike* was performed less often, replaced by other performance arts such as nō and *kyōgen* (comic theater). Nonetheless, *The Tales of the Heike* continued to serve as a source for countless dramas and prose narratives. Indeed, most of the sixteen warrior pieces (*shuramono*) in today's nō drama repertoire are from *The Tales of the Heike*. Heike heroes appear in sixteenth-century ballad dramas (*kōwaka-mai*), and in the Tokugawa (Edo) period, stories from *The Tales of the Heike* became the foundation for a number of important kabuki and *jōruri* plays, thus making them one of the most influential works of premodern Japanese culture.

The first half of the *Heike*, books one through six, is centered on the history of Kiyomori, the head of the Taira (Heike) clan, who comes into conflict with the retired emperor GoShirakawa and then with various members of the Minamoto (Genji) clan. The second half, books seven through twelve, is dominated by three important Minamoto (Genji) leaders: Yoritomo, the head of the Genji in the east; Yoshinaka, who becomes the leader of the Genji farther to the west; and Yoshitsune, Yoritomo's brother. The real focus of the narrative, however, is not on the Genji victors (Yoritomo, the ultimate victor, plays almost a peripheral role) but on a series of defeated Taira figures: Shigemori, Shigehira, Koremori,

Munemori, and Kenreimon'in—all descendants of Kiyomori—who, bearing the sins of the forefather, suffer different fates on their way to death. In short, the first half of *The Tales of the Heike* centers on the Taira and Kiyomori, the clan's leader, and the second half is about the various defeated Taira, almost all of whom die or are executed. (Also important in the second half is the fall of the former Genji leader Kiso Yoshinaka, who is defeated by Yoritomo.) It is not until "The Initiates' Book" that the tragedy of the Taira becomes an opportunity for reconciliation, between Kenreimon'in (Kiyomori's daughter) and the retired emperor GoShirakawa, who was victimized by Kiyomori.

The translation is based on Ichiko Teiji, ed., *Heike monogatari*, 2 vols., in *Shinpen Nihon koten bungaku zenshū* (Tokyo: Shōgakukan, 1994), which is based on a variant of Kakuichi's text. This Kakuichi-bon is the main example of a "recited" lineage and owes its final form to Akashi no Kakuichi, the leader of the Ichikata school of reciters, who had a disciple write down an official version in 1371. The illustrations are from a 1656 Meireki woodblock edition, by permission of Shōgakukan.

Key Figures

Imperial Family

ANTOKU (r. 1180–1185): emperor and son of Emperor Takakura and Kenreimon'in; is held by the Taira clan and drowns at Dan-no-ura.

GoShirakawa (r. 1127–1192, 1155–1158): retired emperor, head of the imperial clan, and son of Retired Emperor Toba.

Kenreimon'in (1155–1213): daughter of Kiyomori and Tokiko (Nun of the Second Rank), consort of Emperor Takakura, mother of Emperor Antoku, and full sister of Munemori, Tomomori, and Shigehira; is taken prisoner at Dan-no-ura and dies a nun.

Mochihito, Prince (1151–1180): second son of Retired Emperor GoShirakawa and leader of an anti-Taira revolt in 1180; also called Prince Takakura.

Nun of the Second Rank: principal wife of Kiyomori and mother of Munemori, Shigehira, and Kenreimon'in; dies at Dan-no-ura.

Takakura: emperor and son of Retired Emperor GoShirakawa.

Toba: retired emperor and father of Retired Emperor GoShirakawa.

Taira (Heike) Head Family   Imperial Family

Tadamori (Taira clan head)   GoShirakawa

| | |

Kiyomori ══════════ Nun of the Second Rank (Niidono)

| | | | | |

Shigemori   Munemori   Shigehira   Kenreimon'in ══ Emperor Takakura   Mochihito

| |

Koremori   Emperor Antoku

|

Rokudai

Genealogy of key figures in *The Tales of the Heike*. For the identification of all the characters, see the glossary of characters.

Taira (Heike)

ATSUMORI: nephew of Kiyomori; dies at Ichi-no-tani.

KIYOMORI: son of Tadamori and, after his father's death, Taira clan head; dominates the court even after taking vows.

KOREMORI: eldest son of Shigemori; commits suicide after taking vows.

MUNEMORI: son of Kiyomori and Nun of the Second Rank and, after Shigemori's death, Taira clan head.

ROKUDAI: son of Koremori, grandson of Shigemori, and presumptive Taira clan head after Genpei war.

SHIGEHIRA: son of Kiyomori and Nun of the Second Rank; a Taira leader largely responsible for the burning of Nara; captured at Ichi-no-tani and later executed.

SHIGEMORI: eldest son of Kiyomori and, until his early death, a restraining influence on Kiyomori.

TADAMORI: father of Kiyomori and a former Taira clan head.

Minamoto (Genji)

YORITOMO: leader of the Minamoto in the east and founder of the
Kamakura shogunate after the Genpei war.

YOSHINAKA: cousin of Yoritomo and leader of the Minamoto in the
north; captures Kyoto and later is killed by Yoritomo's forces; also
called Lord Kiso.

YOSHITSUNE: younger half brother of Yoritomo and one of Yoritomo's chief commanders; defeats the Heike at Dan-no-ura.

Priests

MONGAKU: monk; incites Yoritomo to rebel against the Taira.

SHUNKAN: bishop and Shishi-no-tani conspirator.

BOOK ONE

The Bells of Gion Monastery (1:1)

The bells of the Gion monastery in India echo with the warning that all things are impermanent.[1] The blossoms of the sala trees teach us through their hues that what flourishes must fade.[2] The proud do not prevail for long but vanish like a spring night's dream. In time the mighty, too, succumb: all are dust before the wind.

Long ago in a different land, Zhao Gao of the Qin dynasty in China, Wang Mang of the Han, Zhu Yi of the Liang, and An Lushan of the Tang all refused to be governed by former sovereigns. Pursuing every pleasure, deaf to admonitions, unaware of the chaos overtaking the realm, ignorant of the sufferings of the common people, before long they all alike met their downfall.

More recently in our own country there have been men like Masakado, Sumitomo, Gishin, and Nobuyori, each of them proud and fierce to the extreme. The tales told of the most recent of such men, Taira no Kiyomori, the lay priest of Rokuhara and at one time the prime minister, are beyond the power of words to describe or the mind to imagine.

1. According to Buddhist legend, the Gion monastery, which was built by a rich merchant in a famous garden in India, was the first monastery in the Buddhist order. It also is said that the temple complex included a building known as Impermanence Hall, which contained four silver and four crystal bells.
2. The Buddha is said to have died under sala trees, at which time the trees' blossoms, ordinarily yellow, turned white to express their grief.

Kiyomori was the oldest son and heir of Taira no Tadamori, the minister of punishments, and the grandson of Masamori, the governor of Sanuki. Masamori was a ninth-generation descendant of Prince Kazurahara, a first-rank prince and the minister of ceremonies, the fifth son of Emperor Kanmu.

Night Attack at Courtiers' Hall (1:2)

While Tadamori was still governor of Bizen, he built a temple called Tokujōju-in to fulfill a vow taken by the retired emperor Toba. The main hall had thirty-three bays and enshrined one thousand and one Buddhist images. The dedication ceremony took place on the thirteenth day of the Third Month in the first year of the Tenshō era [1131]. In recognition of Tadamori's services, the retired emperor announced that he was assigning him to one of the currently vacant governorships, and Tadamori was accordingly granted the post of governor of the province of Tajima. As a further expression of the retired emperor's gratitude, he was given permission to enter the imperial palace. Thus at the age of thirty-six, Tadamori was able for the first time to enter the palace.

Persons of privilege that they were, the courtiers resented this move and plotted a night attack on Tadamori at the time the Gosechi Harvest Banquet was to be held on the evening of the twenty-third day of the Eleventh Month of that year. Upon learning of the plot, Tadamori declared, "I am not a civil official. I was born into a warrior family, and it would bring grief to both me and my family if I were to meet with unexpected humiliation. In the end, even the first thing they teach us is to defend ourselves so that we may serve our lord!"

Tadamori therefore made preparations to meet the attack. When he entered the palace, he carried with him a large dagger thrust casually under his court dress, and as he advanced toward the dimly lit interior of the chamber, he quietly drew out the dagger and held it up by his sidelocks. It glittered like ice. The courtiers' eyes were transfixed. In addition, among Tadamori's retainers was a man named Sahyōe-no-jō Iesada, the grandson of an assistant director of the Carpentry Bureau named Sadamitsu, a member of the Taira clan, and the son of Shinnosaburō Daifu Iefusa. This man, wearing a greenish yellow stomach guard under his light green hunting robe and carrying a sword with a bowstring bag under his arm, waited in attendance in a small courtyard by the hall.

Their suspicions aroused, the head chamberlain and his staff sent a chamberlain of the sixth rank to question him. "Who is this person in an unfigured hunting robe[3] behind the rain pipe by the bell pull?" he demanded. "You're causing a commotion! Get out!"

But Iesada replied, "I have been told that my liege lord, the governor of Bizen, is going to be attacked tonight. So I am waiting here to see what happens. I have no intention of leaving!"

Iesada held his ground, watchful as ever. As a result, the courtiers, perhaps concluding that the time was not right, did not attack that night.

But when Tadamori was summoned into the presence of the retired emperor and invited to dance, the courtiers, pretending to accompany his movements, sang out:

This Taira (wine jar) of Ise is a vinegar (squint-eyed) jar!

Although the members of the Taira clan were descended from Emperor Kanmu, they spent very little time in the capital, being of rather lowly rank, but they had close ties to the province of Ise. Hence they came to be known as the Ise Taira, or Heishi, which is pronounced the same as the word for "wine jar," a noted product of the Ise region. In addition, Tadamori happened to be squint eyed, which led the courtiers to make another pun.

Tadamori realized there was nothing he could do about this situation, and so before the dance performances had ended, he quietly prepared to withdraw. Proceeding to the rear of the Shishinden, the Palace Hall, he took out the dagger at his waist and, making sure that the others could see what he was doing, handed it over to one of the women attendants on duty and then left.

"How did it go?" asked Iesada, who was waiting outside.

Although Tadamori wanted to tell him, he was fearful that if he were to divulge everything, Iesada might rush in slashing. So he replied, "Nothing in particular." . . .

---

3.   Unfigured hunting robes are clothes worn by people of the sixth rank and below. With the exception of some chamberlains (tenjōbito), only those of the fifth rank or higher could enter the Seiryōden, the emperor's private residence.

Not surprisingly, no sooner had the Gosechi dances ended than all the courtiers began to complain to the retired emperor. "When people appear at official banquets with swords at their waists or go in and out of the palace with an armed guard, they all do so in accord with the rules laid down for such behavior. For a long time, imperial orders have regulated these matters. And yet Lord Tadamori, claiming that the person is a longtime retainer, summons this soldier in commoner's dress to wait in attendance in the palace courtyard and then to take his place at the Gosechi banquet with a sword slung at his waist. Both actions are a gross breach of etiquette that has rarely been seen in the past. He is guilty of a double fault and should not be let off lightly! We beg you to strike his name from the roster of those permitted in the palace and to relieve him at once of his post and duties!"

Much taken aback by their censures, the retired emperor sent for Tadamori and questioned him.

The courtiers are
surprised by the
presence of Iesada
(*bottom right*) in
the Palace Hall and
attempt to remove him,
but he does not budge.

Tadamori responded: "I did not know anything at all about my
retainer who was waiting in the courtyard. But recently there have
been indications that certain persons were plotting against me. This
man, who has been in my service for some time, got wind of this
and hoped to save me from possible embarrassment. Since he acted
on his own without informing me, I had no way of forestalling him.
If he has committed a fault, perhaps he should be summoned for
questioning.

"As for the weapon I carried, I already have handed it over to
a palace attendant. Perhaps it could be brought here so that you
may determine whether it is a real weapon and whether I am at
fault."

"That would seem reasonable," replied the retired emperor.

When the weapon was brought to him and the retired emperor
examined it, he discovered that although the hilt was lacquered black

like that of an ordinary dagger, the blade was made of wood coated with silver foil.

"In order to avoid possible humiliation, Tadamori had thought it best to provide himself with a weapon of some sort," the retired emperor pointed out. "But since he knew he was likely to meet with accusations later, he took the wise precaution of arming himself with a dagger made of wood. Such resourcefulness is precisely what one would expect from a warrior accustomed to carrying a bow and arrow with him. As for the retainer who stationed himself in the courtyard, he too behaved in a manner wholly appropriate to the retainer of a samurai, and therefore Tadamori is not to blame for the matter."

Thus the retired emperor ended by praising Tadamori's conduct, and the question of possible punishment was dropped.

The Sea Bass (1:3)

... After having risen to the office of minister of punishments, Tadamori died on the fifteenth day of the First Month in the third year of the Ninpei [1153] era at the age of fifty-eight. He was succeeded by his heir, Kiyomori.

It is said that the Taira family's unusual fortune and prosperity were due to the divine favor shown them by the deities of the Kumano Shrine.[4] Some years earlier, when Kiyomori was still governor of Aki, he made a pilgrimage to the Kumano Shrine by boat from the bay of Ise. During this time a large sea bass leaped into the boat.

"This is a mark of divine favor bestowed by the deities," announced the ascetic in charge of the pilgrimage. "You must hurry and eat it!"

"Long ago in China a white fish leaped into the boat of King Wu of the Zhou dynasty," Kiyomori remembered. "This must be a good omen!" Accordingly, although the members of the party had been observing the ten precepts of Buddhism and eating strictly vegetarian fare, Kiyomori had the fish cooked and fed to all his family members and samurai retainers.

---

4. Kumano Shrine is actually a grouping of three shrines on separate mountains in Kii Province. The shrines and their surroundings became an important site for both Shinto and Buddhism during the late Heian period and an important pilgrimage destination from the late Heian period until the present.

Perhaps because of this, he had one stroke of good fortune after another, until in the end he rose to the post of chancellor. Moreover, Kiyomori's sons and grandsons advanced in their official careers faster than dragons climbing up to the clouds. Such was Kiyomori's fortune that he outshone all his ancestors of the preceding nine generations.

Page-Boy Cuts (1:4)

No matter how wise a ruler may be or what policies his chief ministers may pursue, there always will be some worthless and insignificant fellows who, when others are not around, speak slanderously of the government; such is the way of the world. And yet when the lay priest Kiyomori was in his days of glory, not a soul dared to criticize him. The reason was this.

As part of his plans, the chancellor selected some three hundred boys aged fourteen, fifteen, and sixteen; had them cut their hair short and wear red battle robes; and go here and there around the capital. If someone spoke ill of the Heike, he might escape so long as his words were not detected. But if one of these boys heard about the matter, he would alert his companions and they would break into the person's house, confiscate his goods and belongings, tie him up, and drag him off to Rokuhara.[5] As a result, whatever people saw with their eyes or knew in their heart, they never dared express it in words. If "the Rokuhara lord's short-haired boys" were so much as mentioned, carriages and horsemen along the road would get out of the way. Even when the boys went in and out of the imperial palace, no one asked their names. For these reasons, the high officials of the capital looked the other way.

Kiyomori's Flowering Fortunes (1:5)

Not only did Kiyomori himself climb to the pinnacle of success, but all the members of his family enjoyed great good fortune as well.

5. Rokuhara, an area in Kyoto east of the Kamo River across Fifth to Seventh Avenues, was where the Taira situated their family's headquarters.

Kiyomori's eldest son, Shigemori, became a palace minister and a major captain of the left; his second son, Munemori, became a junior counselor and a major captain of the right; his third son, Tomomori, rose to the level of middle captain of the third court rank; and his grandson, Shigemori's heir Koremori, rose to that of lesser captain of the fourth court rank. In all, sixteen members of the family became high-ranking officials; more than thirty were courtiers; and a total of more than sixty held posts as provincial governors, guards officers, or officials in the central bureaucracy. It seemed as though there were no other family in the world but this one....

In addition, Kiyomori had eight daughters, all of whom fared well in life.... One of them was made the consort of Emperor Takakura and bore him a son who became crown prince and then emperor, at which time she received the title of Kenreimon'in. Daughter of the lay priest and the prime minister, mother of the ruler of the realm, nothing further need be said about her good fortune....

Giō (1:6)

As prime minister, Kiyomori now held the entire realm within the four seas in the palm of his hand. Thus ignoring the carpings of the age and turning a deaf ear to censure, he indulged in one caprice after another. An example was the case of Giō and Ginyo, sisters renowned in the capital at that time for their skillful performance as *shirabyōshi* dancers. They were the daughters of a *shirabyōshi* dancer named Toji. Giō, the older sister, had succeeded in winning extraordinary favor with Kiyomori. Thus the younger sister, Ginyo, also enjoyed wide repute among the people of that time. Kiyomori built a fine house for their mother, Toji, providing her with a monthly stipend of a hundred piculs of rice and a hundred strings of coins, so that the entire family prospered and lived a life of ease.

The first *shirabyōshi* dancers in our country were two women, named Shima-no-senzai and Waka-no-mai, who introduced this type of dancing during the time of the retired emperor Toba. Such dancers originally wore white jackets of the kind called *suikan* and tall black hats and carried silver-hilted daggers, pretending to be male dancers. Later they dropped the black hat and dagger and simply retained the *suikan* jacket, at which time they became known as *shirabyōshi*, or "white tempo," dancers.

As Giō became renowned among the *shirabyōshi* of the capital for the extraordinary favor she enjoyed, some people envied her and others spoke spitefully of her. Those who envied her would say, "What splendid good fortune this Lady Giō enjoys! Any woman entertainer would be delighted to be in her place. Her good fortune doubtless derives from the Gi element that makes up the first part of her name. We should have a try at that too!" Giichi, Gini, Gifuku, and Gitoku were some of the names that resulted.

The scorners took a different view. "How could fortune come from a name alone?" they asked. "It is due solely to good karma acquired in a previous existence!" and for the most part they declined to change their names.

After some three years had passed, another highly skilled *shirabyōshi* dancer appeared in the capital, a native of the province of Kaga named Hotoke, or "Buddha." She was said to be only sixteen. Everyone in the capital, high and low alike, exclaimed over her, declaring that among all the *shirabyōshi* dancers of the past, none could rival her.

Lady Hotoke thought to herself, "I have won fame throughout the realm, but I have yet to realize my true ambition, to be summoned by this prime minister of the Taira clan who is now at the height of power. Since it is the practice among entertainers, why should I hold back? I will go and present myself!" Accordingly she went and presented herself at Kiyomori's Nishi-hachijō mansion.

When Kiyomori was informed that the Lady Hotoke who enjoyed such renown in the capital at that time had come to call, he retorted, "What does this mean? Entertainers of that type should wait for a summons—they simply do not take it upon themselves to appear! I don't care whether she's a god or a buddha—I already have Giō in my service! Send her away!"

Refused admission in this summary manner, Hotoke was preparing to take her leave when Giō spoke to the prime minister. "It is quite customary for entertainers to present themselves in this way. Moreover, the girl still is young and just has happened to hit on this idea; it would be a shame to dismiss her so coldly. I, for one, would be greatly distressed. Because we are devotees of the same art, I cannot help feeling sympathy for her. Even if you do not let her dance or listen to her singing, at least admit her into your presence before you send her away. That would be the kind thing to do. Bend your principles a bit and call her in."

"If you insist," replied Kiyomori, "I will see her," and he sent word to have her admitted.

Having been rudely dismissed, Lady Hotoke was about to get into her carriage and leave, but at the summons she returned and presented herself.

"I had no intention of admitting you," Kiyomori announced when they met. "But for some reason Giō was so adamant that, as you see, I agreed to the meeting. And since you are here, I suppose I should find out what sort of voice you have. Try singing an *imayō* for me."

"As you wish," replied Lady Hotoke, and she obliged with the following song in the *imayō* style:

> Since I met you,
> I'm like the little pine destined for a thousand years!
> On turtle-shape isles of your pond,
> how many the cranes that flock there![6]

She repeated the song, singing it over three times while all the persons present listened and looked on in wonder at her skill.

Kiyomori was obviously much impressed. "You are very good at *imayō*," he said, "and I have no doubt that your dancing is of the same order. Let's have a look. Call in the musicians!"

When the musicians appeared, Hotoke performed a dance to their accompaniment. Everything about her was captivating, from her hairdo and costume to her appearance as a whole, and her voice was pleasing and artfully employed, so her dancing could not fail to make an impression. In fact, it far exceeded Kiyomori's expectations, and he was so moved by her performance that he immediately fell in love with her.

"This is somewhat troubling," said Hotoke. "Originally I was not to be admitted but was sent away at once. But through the kind offices of Lady Giō, I was allowed to present myself. Having done so, I would be most reluctant to do anything that would counter Lady Giō's intentions. I beg to be excused as soon as possible so that I may be on my way."

---

6. Pines, turtles, and cranes are symbols of longevity.

"There is no reason for that!" replied Kiyomori. "But if you feel uneasy in Giō's presence, I will see that she leaves."

"But how would that look?" objected Hotoke. "I was uneasy enough to find that the two of us had been summoned here together. If now, after all her kindness, she were dismissed and I were to remain behind, think how dreadful I would feel! If by chance you happen to remember me, perhaps you might summon me again at some future time. But for today I beg to take my leave."

Kiyomori, however, would not hear of this. "Nonsense!" he said. "You will do no such thing. Have Giō leave at once!"

Three times he sent an attendant with these instructions.

Giō had long been aware that something like this might happen, but she was not expecting it "this very day."[7] But faced with repeated orders to leave the house at once, she resigned herself to doing so and set about sweeping and tidying her room and clearing it of anything unsightly.

Even those who have only sought shelter under the same tree for a night or have merely dipped water from the same stream will feel sorrow on parting. How sorrowful, then, Giō's departure must have been from the place where she had lived these three years. Her tears, futile though they were, fell quickly. Since there was nothing she could do, however, she prepared to depart. But perhaps wanting to leave behind some reminder of herself, she inscribed the following poem on the sliding panel of the room, weeping as she did so:

Those that put out new shoots, those that wither are the same
grasses of the field—come autumn, is there one that will not fade?

Getting into her carriage, she returned to her home and there, sinking down within the panels of the room, began weeping.

"What has happened? What is wrong?" her mother and sister asked, but she did not reply. It was only when they questioned the maid who had accompanied her that they learned the truth.

Before long, the monthly stipend of a hundred piculs of rice and a hundred strings of coins ended, and for the first time Hotoke's friends and relations learned the meaning of happiness and prosperity. Among

7.   This is an allusion to Ariwara Narihira's death poem, which appears in both the *Kokinshū* (no. 861) and the final section of *The Tales of Ise*: "Although I have often heard of the path each must take in the end, I never thought it would come so soon."

high and low, word spread throughout the capital. "They say that Giō has been dismissed from the prime minister's service," people said. "We must go call on her and keep her company!" Some sent letters, others dispatched their servants to make inquiries. But faced with such a situation, Giō could not bring herself to receive visitors. The letters she refused to accept; the messengers she sent off without a meeting. Such gestures served only to deepen her mood of melancholy, and she passed all her time weeping. In this way the year came to an end.

The following spring Kiyomori sent a servant to Giō's house with this message: "How have you been since we parted? Lady Hotoke appears to be so hopelessly bored that I wish you would come and perform one of your *imayō* songs or your dances to cheer her up."

Giō declined to give any answer.

Kiyomori tried again. "Why no answer from you, Giō? Won't you come for a visit? Tell me if you won't come! I have ways of dealing with the matter!"

When Giō's mother, Toji, learned about this, she was very upset and, having no idea what to do, could only plead tearfully with her daughter. "Giō, at least send an answer," she begged. "Anything is better than being threatened!"

But Giō replied, "If I had any intention of going, I would have answered long ago. It is because I have no such intention that I'm at a loss as to how to reply. He says that if I do not respond, he has ways of dealing with the matter. Does this mean I will be banished from the capital? Or that I will be put to death? Even if I were expelled from the capital, I would have no great regrets. And if he wants to deprive me of my life, what of that? He once sent me away a despised person—I have no heart to face him again." She thus refused to send an answer.

But the mother continued begging. "As long as you continue to live in this realm, you cannot hope to defy the prime minister's wishes! The ties that bind man and woman are decreed from a past existence—they do not originate in this life alone. Those who vow to be faithful for a thousand or ten thousand years often end by parting, whereas those who think of this as merely an affair of the moment find themselves spending their whole lives together. In this world of ours there's no predicting how things will turn out between a man and a woman.

"For three whole years you enjoyed favor with the prime minister. That was a stroke of fortune hardly to be matched. Now if you refuse to answer his summons, it is scarcely likely you will be put to death.

Probably you will merely be banished from the capital. And even if you are banished, you and your sister are young and can manage to live even in the wildest and most out-of-the-way spot. But what about your mother? I am a feeble old woman—suppose I am banished too? Just the thought of living in some strange place in the countryside fills me with despair. Let me live out the rest of my days here in the capital. Think of it as being filial in this world and the next."

Much as it pained her, Giō did not feel that she could disobey these pleas from her mother, and so weeping all the while, she set out for the prime minister's mansion. But her heart was filled with foreboding. It would be too difficult to make the trip alone, Giō felt, and therefore she took her younger sister, Ginyo, with her, as well as two other *shirabyōshi* dancers, the four of them going in one carriage to Nishi-hachijō.

Upon her arrival, Giō was not shown to the seat she had previously been accustomed to occupy, but instead to a far inferior place where makeshift arrangements had been made. "How can this be?" she exclaimed. "Although I was guilty of no fault, I was driven out of the house. And now I find that even the seat I had occupied has been demoted! This is too heartless! What am I to do?" In an effort to hide her confusion, she covered her face with her sleeve, but the trickle of tears gave her away.

Moved to pity by the sight, Lady Hotoke appealed to Kiyomori. "What is the meaning of this?" she asked. "If this were someone who had never been summoned before, it might be different. But surely she should be seated here with us. If not, I beg your permission to go where she is."

"That will not be necessary!" replied Kiyomori, and Hotoke was thus helpless to move.

Later, Kiyomori, apparently quite unaware of Giō's feelings, asked how she had been faring since they met last. "Lady Hotoke seems so terribly bored," he remarked. "You must sing us an *imayō*."

Having come this far, Giō did not feel that she could disregard the prime minister's wishes. And so holding back her tears, she sang the following song in the *imayō* style:

> Buddha was once a common mortal,
> and we too one day will become buddhas.
> All alike endowed with the buddha nature,
> how sad this gulf that divides us!

Weeping all the while, she sang the song two more times. All the members of the Taira clan who were present, from the ministers of state, lords, and high-ranking courtiers down to the lowly samurai, were moved to tears. Kiyomori himself listened with keen interest. "A song admirably suited to the occasion," he commented. "I wish we could watch you dance, but unfortunately today there are other things to be attended to. In the future you must not wait to be summoned but come any time you like and perform your *imayō* songs and dances for Hotoke's amusement."

Giō made no answer but, suppressing her tears, withdrew.

Reluctant to disobey her mother's command, Giō had made the trip to the prime minister's mansion, painful as it was, and exposed herself a second time to callous treatment. Saddened by the experience and mindful that as long as she remained in this world similar sorrows likely awaited her, she turned her thoughts to suicide.

Ordered by Kiyomori to return to his residence, Giō (*left*) appears and performs for Kiyomori and Lady Hotoke (*right*).

"If you do away with yourself," said her sister, Ginyo, "I will do likewise!"

Learning of their intentions, their mother, alarmed, had no choice but to plead with Giō in tears. "You have every reason to be resentful," she said. "I forced you to go and thereby inflicted this pain, though I could hardly have known what would happen. But now, if you do away with yourself, your sister will follow your example, and if I lose both my daughters, then old and feeble as I am, I would do better to commit suicide myself rather than live alone. But by inducing a parent to carry out such an act before the destined time for death has come, you will be committing one of the Five Deadly Sins. We are mere sojourners in this life and must suffer one humiliation after another, but these are nothing compared with the long night of suffering that may await us hereafter. Whatever this life may entail, think how frightful it would be if you should condemn yourself to rebirth in one of the evil paths of existence!"

Faced with these fervent entreaties, Giō, wiping back her tears, replied, "You are right. I would be guilty of one of the Five Deadly Sins.[8] I will abandon any thought of self-destruction. But as long as I remain in the capital, I am likely to encounter further grief. My thought now is simply to leave the capital."

Thus at the age of twenty-two, Giō became a nun and, erecting a simple thatched retreat in a mountain village in the recesses of the Saga region,[9] she devoted herself to reciting the Buddha's name.

"I vowed that if you committed suicide, I would do likewise," said her sister, Ginyo. "If your plan now is to withdraw from the world, who would hesitate to follow your example?" Accordingly, at the age of nineteen she put on nun's attire and joined Giō in her retreat, devoting all her thoughts to the life to come.

Moved by the sight of them, their mother, Toji, observed, "In a world where my daughters, young as they are, have taken the tonsure, how could I, old woman that I am, cling to these gray hairs of mine?" Thus at the age of forty-five she shaved her head and, along with her two daughters, gave herself wholly to the recitation of Amida Buddha's name, mindful only of the life hereafter.

And so spring and the heat of summer passed, and as the autumn winds began to blow, the time came for the two star lovers to meet, the Herd Boy poling his boat across the River of Heaven, and people gazed up into the sky and wrote down their requests to them on leaves of the paper mulberry.[10]

As the nuns watched the evening sun sinking below the hills to the west, they thought to themselves that there, where the sun went down, was the Western Paradise of Amida. "One day we, too, will be reborn there and will no longer know these cares and sorrows," they said. Giving themselves up to melancholy thoughts of this kind, their tears never ceased flowing.

8. The Five Deadly Sins are killing one's father, killing one's mother, killing a Buddhist saint (*arhat*), injuring the body of a buddha, and harming the Buddhist ecclesiastical community.
9. Saga is an area to the immediate west of the capital.
10. The lovers, two stars known as the Herd Boy and the Weaving Maiden, are permitted to meet on only one night a year, when the Herd Boy crosses the River of Heaven, or the Milky Way, in his boat. Another version of the legend has him crossing over a bridge formed by sympathetic magpies. This occasion, known as Tanabata, takes place on the seventh night of the seventh lunar month, at which time celebrants write their wishes on leaves and dedicate them to the lovers.

When the twilight hour had passed, they closed their door of plaited bamboo, lit the dim lamp, and all three, mother and daughters, began their invocation of the Buddha's name.

But just then they heard someone tap-tapping at the bamboo door. The nuns started up in alarm. "Has some meddling demon come to interrupt our devotions, ineffectual as they are?" they wondered. "Even in the daytime, no one calls on us in our thatched hut here in the remote hills. Who would come so late at night? Whoever it is can easily batter down the door without waiting for it to be opened, so we may as well open it. And if it should be some heartless creature come to take our lives, we must be firm in our faith in Amida's vow to save us and unceasingly call his holy name. He is certain to heed our call and come with his sacred host to greet us. And then surely he will guide us to his Western Paradise. Come, let us take heart and not delay pronouncing his name!"

When they had thus reassured one another and mustered the courage to open the bamboo door, they discovered that it was no demon at all but Lady Hotoke who stood before them.

"What do I see?" said Giō. "Lady Hotoke! Am I dreaming or awake?"

"If I tell you what has happened, I may seem merely to be making excuses," said Lady Hotoke, straining to hold back her tears. "But it would be too unkind to remain silent, and so I will start from the beginning. As you know, I was not originally summoned to the prime minister's house but went of my own accord, and if it had not been for your kind intervention, I would never have been admitted. We women are frail beings and cannot always do as we wish. I was far from happy when the prime minister detained me at his mansion, and then when you were summoned again and sang your *imayō* song, I felt more than ever the impossibility of my position. I could take no delight in it because I knew that sooner or later my turn would come to fall from favor. I felt it even more when I saw the poem you wrote on the sliding panel with its warning that 'come autumn, all alike must fade!'

"After that, I lost track of your whereabouts. But when I heard that you and your mother and sister all had entered religious life, I was overcome with envy. Again and again I asked the prime minister to release me from service, but he would not hear of it.

"What joy and delight we have in this world is no more than a dream within a dream, I told myself—what could such happiness mean to me? It is a rare thing to be born a human being and rarer still to discover the teachings of the Buddha. If because of my actions now I were to be reborn in hell or to spend endless aeons transmigrating through the other realms of existence, when would I ever find salvation? My youth could not be counted on, that I knew, for neither young nor old can tell when death may overtake them. One may breathe one instant and then not live to breathe the next: life is as fleeting as the shimmering heat of summer or a flash of lightning. To revel in a moment's happiness and not be heedful of the life to come would be a pitiful course of action indeed! So this morning I stole away from the prime minister's mansion and have come here."

With these words she threw off the cloak that she had around her. She had assumed a nun's tonsure and habit.

"I have come dressed in this fashion," she told them, "because I wish to ask pardon for my past offenses. If you say you can forgive me, I would like to join you in your devotions, and perhaps we may be reborn on a single lotus leaf in the Western Paradise. But if you cannot bring yourself to forgive me, I will make my way elsewhere. Wherever I may settle, on a bed of moss or by the roots of a pine tree, I will devote what life is left to me to reciting the Buddha's name, hoping, as I have done for so long, for rebirth in his paradise."

Near tears, Giō replied, "I never dreamed you felt this way. In a world of sadness, we all are, no doubt, fated to endure such trials. And yet I could not help envying you, and it seemed that such feelings of envy would prevent me from ever achieving the salvation I yearned for. I was in a mean and merely half-resolved frame of mind, one suitable for neither this life nor the life to come.

"But now that I see you dressed in this manner, these past failings of mine fall away like so much dust, and at last I am certain of gaining salvation. Hereafter, all my joy will be to strive for that long-cherished goal. The whole world was puzzled when my mother and sister and I became nuns, deeming it an unprecedented step, and we too wondered in a way, and yet we had good reasons for doing what we did. But what we did was nothing compared with what you have done! Barely turned seventeen, with neither hatred nor despair to spur you on, you have chosen to cast aside the world of defilement and turn all your thoughts toward the Pure Land. How fortunate we are to meet such a fine guide and teacher! Come, we will work toward our goal together!"

So the four women, sharing the same hut, morning and evening offered flowers and incense to the Buddha, all their thoughts on their devotions. And sooner or later, it is said, each of the four nuns attained what she had so long sought, rebirth in the Western Paradise.

Thus, on the curtain that lists the departed in the Eternal Lecture Hall founded by the retired emperor GoShirakawa are found, inscribed in one place, the names of the four: "The honored dead, Giō, Ginyo, Hotoke, Toji."

Theirs was a moving story.

The stability in the capital gradually breaks down. Disagreements erupt within the imperial family as well as among temple-shrine complexes. In addition, tensions between Kiyomori, head of the now ascendant Taira clan, and the imperial court, led by the retired emperor GoShirakawa, peak in the Shishi-no-tani incident, in which Narichika, a Fujiwara courtier favored by GoShirakawa, becomes the principal conspirator in a plot to eliminate Kiyomori. He is joined by Shunkan, Yasuyori, and Saikō, a member of GoShirakawa's staff. A conflict breaks out between the court and Mount Hiei, a key Buddhist center, over a delayed court decision in which the warrior monks of Mount Hiei are routed. In 1177 a great conflagration consumes much of Kyoto and its cultural treasures.

BOOK TWO

KENREIMON'IN (Taira): daughter of Kiyomori; eventually gives birth to Emperor Takakura's child, the future Emperor Antoku.

KIYOMORI (Taira): Taira clan head.

NARICHIKA (Fujiwara): courtier favored by Retired Emperor GoShirakawa and principal Shishi-no-tani conspirator; executed by Kiyomori.

NARITSUNE (Fujiwara): son of Narichika; exiled for his father's involvement in the Shishi-no-tani conspiracy.

NORIMORI (Taira): son of Tadamori, brother of Kiyomori, and father-in-law of Naritsune; intervenes on Naritsune's behalf.

SAIKŌ: Shishi-no-tani conspirator; executed by Kiyomori.

SHUNKAN: bishop, high official at the Hosshō-ji temple, and Shishi-no-tani conspirator; exiled and never pardoned.

YASUYORI (Taira): minor member of the Taira clan and Shishi-no-tani conspirator.

The head abbot of Mount Hiei has been exiled by the court as punishment for the attack by the warrior monks. The monks are outraged at this unprecedented action and retaliate by recapturing their abbot on his way to his place of banishment. There is a rumor that Retired Emperor GoShirakawa is gathering troops to punish the temple center, but one of the lesser conspirators in the Shishi-no-tani plot mistakenly believes that the troops are moving against the Taira and reveals the plot to Kiyomori. Kiyomori arrests and then angrily executes Saikō, one of the conspirators. After Shigemori and Norimori intervene, Kiyomori agrees to the lesser punishment of banishment for the others.

The Admonition (2:6)

[handwritten: Taira Clan Head]

The lay priest and prime minister, Kiyomori, thus had a large number of persons arrested because of their involvement in the plot against him, but it still appeared that his mind was not at ease. Wearing a black-laced stomach guard with a tight-fitting silver-trimmed breastplate over a battle robe of red brocade, he carried under his arm a short halberd with a silver snake-coil handle, a weapon he kept constantly by his side even when he slept. (Some years earlier, when he was governor of Aki and visited the Itsukushima Shrine, the deity of the shrine, Daimyōjin, had spoken to him in a dream and presented him with the halberd.) As Kiyomori entered the corridor leading to the middle gate of his mansion, his face bore a darkly forbidding expression. He sent for Sadayoshi, the governor of Chikugo, who presently appeared, wearing a suit of armor with crimson lacing over a dark orange battle robe, and made his obeisance.

"Sadayoshi, tell me what you think!" said Kiyomori after a pause. . . . "Already I have several times put my life in jeopardy for the sake of Retired Emperor GoShirakawa. Whatever others may have told him, he should have remained faithful to the members of our family at least to the seventh generation!

"And yet, heeding the words of a worthless scoundrel like Narichika and that baseborn wretch Saikō, what does he do but plot to bring about the downfall of our entire clan! That was a terrible thing for him to do! In the future, if people should choose to speak slanderously of us, I suppose he will issue an edict calling for the destruction of our house. And once we've been branded enemies of the state, it will be too late to do a thing about it!

"Until these matters quiet down, I am considering moving the retired emperor to the Northern Palace in Toba or else bringing him here. What do you think of that? If I do that, the Northern Warriors, his personal guards, will probably shoot some arrows this way. You can pass the word along to our samurai to be prepared. I have finished performing services for the retired emperor! Saddle my horse and get out my full suit of armor!"

Police Lieutenant Morikuni raced by horse to the Komatsu mansion of Kiyomori's son, the palace minister Shigemori. "Things have taken a crucial turn!" he reported.

[handwritten: Shigemori = son of Kiyomori]

Not even waiting to hear him out, Shigemori exclaimed, "I knew it—they've cut off Lord Narichika's head!"

"No, not that," replied Morikuni. "But the prime minister has put on full armor. And all his samurai are preparing for an immediate attack on the retired emperor's Hōjū-ji residence. The prime minister says he is going to have the retired emperor placed in confinement in the Toba Palace, though I think his real intention is to banish him to Chinzei in Kyushu."

Shigemori could scarcely believe this. And yet when he visited him this morning, Kiyomori had indeed seemed as though he might be capable of some such madness. Shigemori drove his carriage as fast as he could to Kiyomori's Nishi-hachijō mansion.

Reaching the gate and getting out of his carriage, Shigemori entered to find his father attired in body armor. Several dozen high officials and courtiers of the Taira clan, all wearing various colored battle robes and dressed in different types of armor, were seated in two rows along the corridors leading to the middle gate. In addition, provincial officials, police officers, and other types of government officials overflowed the verandas and stood crowded together in the courtyard. Poles for banners had been passed around, horses' girths tightened, helmet cords tied, and it appeared that the whole company was just about to set out on an attack. Shigemori seemed strangely out of place as he entered the hall wearing a cap, an informal robe, and loose, large-pattern trousers, the last making a soft rustling sound as he walked.

Kiyomori waited with eyes lowered. "Shigemori is going to give me one of his customary scoldings," he thought to himself. "I will have to be stern with him!" But when he saw his son standing before him, his son who observed the Five Precepts of Buddhism[1] and valued compassion above all, who never violated the Five Standards of Confucian behavior[2] and was courteous and correct at all times, he felt ashamed to be confronting him in a suit of armor. Closing the partition slightly, he quickly threw a plain white monk's robe over his armor. But the metal breastplate of the armor still showed a little

---

1.   The Five Precepts are against killing, stealing, lasciviousness, lying, and drinking alcohol.
2.   The Five Standards are benevolence, righteousness, decorum, wisdom, and sincerity.

under the clerical robe, and in an effort to hide it, he kept adjusting the lapels of the robe first this way and then that.

Shigemori sat down in the seat above that occupied by his younger brother, Munemori. Kiyomori said nothing, and Shigemori likewise sat in silence. After some time, Kiyomori remarked, "Narichika's scheme to revolt was a matter of little importance. The whole thing was concocted by the retired emperor. Until the situation quiets down, I have decided to have the retired emperor moved to the Northern Palace at Toba or else bring him here. What would you say to such a move?"

Shigemori began to weep even before his father had finished speaking.

"What's the matter with you?" Kiyomori asked in perplexity.

Wiping back his tears, Shigemori replied, "When I hear you say such things, I think that your fortunes must be coming to an end. They say that when a person's fortunes are on the wane, he begins to think of doing evil. I can't believe you are in your right mind when I see you this way! This land of ours may be no bigger than a millet seed, a far-off border region. Yet ever since it has been ruled by descendants of the Sun Goddess Amaterasu[3] and the heirs of the august Amanokoyane[4] have aided them in ordering the state, donning armor has been deemed a violation of the code of decorum for one who has risen to the office of prime minister, has it not? And since you have taken clerical vows, how much worse this is in your case! To put aside your holy robes, symbols of the emancipation bestowed by the Buddhas of the past, present, and future, and to abruptly put on military dress and take up bow and arrow is not only to violate the Buddhist precepts and invite the punishment for an odious sin. It is likewise to turn against the Confucian virtues of benevolence, righteousness, decorum, wisdom, and sincerity. I am grieved to have to speak in this forthright manner, but I cannot hold back the feelings that are in my heart!

"In this world of ours, one has four debts: the debt to Heaven and Earth, the debt to one's sovereign, the debt to one's parents, and the debt to living beings as a whole. And of these four, the gravest is one's debt to one's ruler. As the saying goes, 'Of all the lands under

---

3. Amaterasu is the tutelary deity of the imperial family.
4. Amanokoyane is the tutelary deity of the Fujiwara clan, the most powerful aristocratic family for much of the Heian period.

Heaven, [there are] none that are not the king's.'[5] Xu You washed his ears in the Ying River after being asked by the ruler to take office, and after admonishing their ruler, the brothers Boyi and Shuqi retired to pick ferns on Mount Shouyang. Yet unconventional as they were, even these worthy men understood that the rules of decorum forbid one to go against their sovereign's command.

"And how much truer is this in our case! You have risen to the position of prime minister, a height never so much as glimpsed by our forebears. And I, Shigemori, ignorant and untalented as all know me to be, have nevertheless attained the rank of palace minister. Moreover, more than half the nation's provinces and districts are under the control of our clansmen, and we have a free hand in managing our country estates. The debt we owe the throne for such favors is truly extraordinary, is it not? If now, forgetting this vast debt we have incurred, we should even consider placing the retired emperor in confinement, a most culpable act, would we not be going against the divine will of the Sun Goddess Amaterasu and the bodhisattva Hachiman?[6] Japan is the land of the gods, and the gods will countenance no such breach of propriety.

"The steps that the retired emperor has considered taking are not entirely unreasonable. It is quite true that for generations our family has tried to conquer enemies of the court and to calm any waves of unrest that arise in the area within the four seas. And in doing so we have displayed unparalleled loyalty to the throne. And yet to become overly puffed up by the praise we have received would mark us as lacking sensitivity to others.

"Prince Shōtoku's Seventeen-Article Constitution states: 'For all men have hearts, and each heart has its own leanings. Their right is our wrong, and our right is their wrong. . . . How can any one lay down a rule by which to distinguish right from wrong? For we are all, one with another, wise and foolish, like a ring that has no end. Therefore, although others give way to anger, let us, on the contrary, dread our own faults.'[7]

---

5. This is an allusion to the *Book of Songs* (*Shijing*), the oldest collection of poetry in China and one of the Confucian classics.
6. Hachiman, who was worshiped as both a Japanese god (*kami*) and a bodhisattva, was the tutelary deity of warriors.
7. Prince Shōtoku (574–622), who served as regent during the reign of Empress Suiko (r. 592–628), was a figure renowned for both his political and his religious activities. His Seventeen-Article Constitution, which consists of injunctions for good government based on Confucian and Buddhist principles, was written in 604.

"However, the fortunes of our family have not run out, and the plot against us has come to light. And Lord Narichika, who was in consultation with the retired emperor, has already been taken into custody. Therefore, even if the retired emperor had had some questionable aim in mind, there now is no longer anything to fear. When crimes have been committed, you should see that appropriate punishment is handed out. Other than that, you need only keep the throne informed of the state of affairs. Strive to be even more loyal and circumspect in your service of the retired emperor; seek in your exercise of government to show even more compassion for the common people. Then the gods will surely protect you, and you will in no way contradict the buddhas' unseen wishes. And when the gods and buddhas bestow their blessings and approval, the retired emperor will have to amend his thinking. Sovereign or subject—which has first claim on our allegiance? There can be no dispute, just as when choosing between reason and error, we cannot do other than follow reason."

Signal Fires (2:7)

"And in this case," Shigemori continued, "reason is on the side of the retired emperor. Therefore I must do what I can to protect the retired emperor's residence at Hōjū-ji. Ever since I was first promoted to the fifth rank at court until I reached my current position of palace minister and commander in chief, every step in my advancement has been due to the kindness of the retired emperor. The debt I owe him is heavier than a thousand, ten thousand jewels, deeper than once-dyed or twice-dyed crimson. So I must go and shut myself up where he is. When I do so, probably a few samurai who are willing to fight on my behalf and risk their lives for me will respond to my summons and help me guard the retired emperor's Hōjū-ji residence. But what dire and unforeseen events may follow thereafter!

"How lamentable—that in order to remain loyal in the service of my sovereign, I must thereby forget the debt I owe my own father, a debt that towers higher than the eighty-thousand-foot summit of Mount Sumeru![8] How painful—that if I disregarded the sin of unfilial

---

8. According to Buddhist mythology, Mount Sumeru, which rises in the center of this universe, is the highest mountain in the world.

conduct, I would have to be faithless to the ruler and become a traitor to him! Forward or backward, my way is blocked! Right or wrong—how am I to judge? Come, then—behead me at once! If you do, then I will not be able either to help defend the retired emperor or to take part in my father's action against him. . . ."

Such were the lengthy words he spoke as he wept into the sleeve of his robe. And all his clansmen, the callous along with the tender-hearted, wet the sleeves of their armor with tears.

After being addressed in this manner by the son in whom he put such trust, Kiyomori spoke in a much subdued tone. "No, no," he said. "I had no such extreme measures in mind. I merely feared that some misunderstanding might arise if evil-minded men should get the ear of the retired emperor."

"Even if a misunderstanding should arise," Shigemori answered, "you must not think of taking action against the retired emperor!"

Shigemori abruptly rose from his seat and went to the middle gate. As he did so, he addressed the samurai there. "You all have heard what I said just now, have you not? I came here this morning in hopes of preventing any such action, but there was such a commotion that I returned to my own home. If you still intend to move against the retired emperor, then do so only after you have seen my head fall! Those in my party, let us be off!"

So saying, he returned to his Komatsu mansion. . . .

After many warriors follow Shigemori's call to arms, a chastened Kiyomori acquiesces to his son's wishes and Shigemori sends his men home. After he tells the Chinese story of the "signal fires," the narrator praises Shigemori for his actions. Narichika, whom the monks of Mount Hiei had cursed because of an incident involving one of his subordinates, is taken away to a miserable island off the coast of Bizen.

The Death of the Senior Counselor (2:10)

And so the Hosshō-ji[9] administrator, Bishop Shunkan; the police commissioner, Yasuyori; and the Tanba lesser captain, Naritsune,

---

9. The Hosshō-ji temple, which was founded in 1077 by Emperor Shirakawa, was the first and largest of a group of temples known as the Six Victory Temples (because each contained the character for "victory" in its name). They were built to the immediate east of the capital and had strong ties to various retired emperors until the thirteenth century.

three men in all, were banished to the island of Kikai-ga-shima off the southern coast of Satsuma.

The island is situated very far from the capital and can be reached only by a wearisome journey over the waves. In ordinary times no ships call there, and its inhabitants are few. A certain number of natives live there, but they scarcely resemble the people of our country, as they are as dark in color as oxen. They have hair all over their bodies and do not understand the words spoken to them.

The men wear no caps; the women do not let their hair hang down; and since neither have regular clothing, they hardly seem like human beings. Because nothing edible grows on the island, the people must depend first of all on what they can get by hunting and fishing. No farmers till the fields, and so rice and other grains are unknown; there are no groves of mulberry for feeding silkworms, hence no cloth is to be had.

In the middle of the island stands a tall mountain that continually sends forth flames. The area around it is rich in sulfur, and for this reason the island is often called Sulfur Island. Thunder constantly rumbles up and down the mountainside, and rain falls in torrents on the foothills. In such a place, one could hardly hope to survive for even a day or an hour. . . .

Although Narichika takes the tonsure, he is executed without ever being able to see his son Naritsune again. He has a final communication with his wife, who then becomes a nun to pray for him. The story of how Fujiwara Sanesada rose by praying at the shrine of the Taira tutelary deity at Itsukushima is held up in contrast to the fates of Narichika and the other conspirators. A fight breaks out between Mount Hiei and the Onjō-ji temple in Ōmi Province over the location of an esoteric Buddhist initiation ceremony for Retired Emperor GoShirakawa. The narrator wonders whether this and other similar incidents foreshadow the "latter age of the Buddhist law."

Yasuyori's Prayer (2:15)

The existence of the men exiled to Kikai-ga-shima is as precarious as dew on a leaf tip; their lives are worth little. Nevertheless, because the Taira minister Norimori, father-in-law of the Tanba lesser captain Naritsune, continued to send supplies of food and clothing from one of his properties, the estate of Kase in Hizen Province, both Shunkan and Yasuyori, as well as Naritsune, managed to stay alive.

Of these three, Yasuyori, when on his way into exile, had taken vows as a Buddhist priest at Murozumi in Suō, assuming the religious name Shōshō. He had long desired to take such a step, as he indicated in this poem:

> A world only to be renounced in the end —
> how hateful, that I did not cast it aside sooner!

In the past, the Tanba lesser captain Naritsune and the newly ordained priest Yasuyori had been devotees of the Kumano Shrine. "If only we could find a suitable place on this island to worship the three Kumano deities," they complained. "We could offer prayers there for our return to the capital!"

Shunkan, who by nature had not a particle of religious feeling, showed no interest in their plans. But the other two, of one heart in their faith, began searching here and there around the island in hopes of finding a place that resembled the Kumano area. They found a wonderful spot of woodland and water, festooned here and there with tree leaves the color of crimson brocade or embroidery; of splendid cloud-topped peaks, seeming as though draped in various shades of blue green gauze; with the mountain scenery, the stands of trees far surpassing anything found elsewhere. Gazing south one could see a vast expanse of ocean, its waves deeply shrouded in clouds and mist, while to the north, from the soaring mountain crags, a hundred-foot waterfall came cascading down. The awesome thundering of its waters and the pine winds imparting an aura of holiness made it seem like the mountain waterfall of Nachi, the seat of one of the Kumano deities. They decided at once to call this place the mountain shrine of Nachi.

One of the peaks they labeled the Shingū, or New Shrine, another the Hongū, or Original Shrine, and various spots approaching these they called the such-and-such lesser shrine, giving them names taken from the subsidiary shrines of the Kumano area. And then each day, with Priest Yasuyori as the leader and the Tanba lesser captain accompanying him, they would carry out their "pilgrimage to Kumano," praying for a return to the capital. "Hail to the Gongen Kongō Dōji," they intoned in supplication. "We implore you, take pity on us! Permit us once more to go back to our old homes and see our wives and children again!"

BOOK THREE

KENREIMON'IN (Taira): daughter of Kiyomori; eventually gives birth
to Emperor Takakura's child, the future Emperor Antoku.

KIYOMORI (Taira): Taira clan head.

NARITSUNE (Fujiwara): son of Narichika; exiled for his father's involvement in the Shishi-no-tani conspiracy.

NORIMORI (Taira): son of Tadamori, brother of Kiyomori, and father-
in-law of Naritsune; intervenes on Naritsune's behalf.

SHUNKAN: bishop, high official at the Hosshō-ji temple, and Shishi-
no-tani conspirator; exiled and never pardoned.

YASUYORI (Taira): minor member of the Taira clan and Shishi-no-tani
conspirator.

The Pardon (3:1)

On the first day of the first month of the second year of the Jishō
era [1178], New Year's felicitations were offered at the palace of the
retired emperor, and on the fourth day Emperor Takakura paid
a ceremonial visit to the retired emperor, his father. These ritual
activities were carried out in the customary manner. But the retired
emperor had not yet gotten over his anger at the fact that the preceding summer the senior counselor Narichika and many other of his
intimates had been executed or sent into exile. He took little interest
in government affairs and appeared to be in a disgruntled mood. As

[handwritten: viewed retired emperor w/ suspicion]

for Prime Minister Kiyomori, ever since Yukitsuna[1] had informed him of the plot against him, he had viewed the retired emperor with great suspicion. Although on the surface his relations with the retired emperor remained unchanged, behind the forced smiles lurked an attitude of deep distrust.

On the seventh day of the First Month a comet appeared in the eastern sky. It was of the type called Chi You's Banner or Red Breath.[2] On the eighteenth day the comet increased in brilliance.

Meanwhile, it was learned that Kiyomori's daughter (later Kenreimon'in), who at this time was still called empress, had taken ill, a fact that greatly upset the members of the court and the populace as a whole. Sutra recitations for her recovery were initiated at various temples, and government officials were dispatched to present offerings at shrines here and there. The physicians brought out all their medicines; the yin-yang diviners plied their skills; and every sort of exoteric and esoteric Buddhist ritual was performed. Then it became known that this was no ordinary illness but that in fact the consort was pregnant. Emperor Takakura was eighteen at the time and the consort was twenty-two, but until now they had not been blessed with either son or daughter. How splendid if a prince should be born! thought the members of the Heike clan, and they displayed such jubilation that one would suppose the happy event had already taken place. The comment of the other clans was "Now the Heike will really be in their glory—the child is sure to be a boy!" . . .

[left margin handwritten: Buddhism]

When Norimori heard the reports of the consort's continued illness, he said to Shigemori, the lord of the Komatsu mansion, "Many different types of prayers have been offered for the consort's well-being. But I cannot help feeling that a general pardon at this point would be the most effective. If the men who have been exiled to Kikai-ga-shima were recalled, the blessings and benefits would surely be greater than those that could be achieved by any other means."

[left margin handwritten: Brother of Kiyomori]

Shigemori thereupon approached his father Kiyomori on the matter. "Norimori keeps pleading with me to recall his son-in-law Naritsune from exile, and I am much moved by his appeals. If these reports of the consort's continued illness are true, her troubles must

___

ına is a minor character who was party to the Shishi-no-tani plot.
)u was a rebellious warrior of ancient China. Comets, particularly of this type, were
ed as evil portents.

have been caused by the angry spirit of the deceased Narichika. And if you hope to placate his angry spirit, then above all you should recall his son Naritsune from exile while the latter is still alive. Once these doubts and pleadings of others are appeased, our own affairs will go smoothly. By granting their wishes, we will ensure the swift fulfillment of our own wishes; the consort will give birth to a male child, as we all hope she will; and our family will enjoy even greater glory than in the past!"

Kiyomori replied in a tone much milder than that he recently had been accustomed to use. "In that case," he said, "what should we do about Shunkan and Yasuyori?"

"If you recall Naritsune, you should recall the others as well. To leave any one of them behind would surely invite blame."

"I have no objection to recalling Yasuyori," said Kiyomori. "But Shunkan owes everything he has attained in life to my help and intervention. And yet he turns around and uses his own Shishi-no-tani villa as a base of operations, seizing every chance he can to plot his nefarious schemes. I could never think of pardoning Shunkan!"

Shigemori returned home and summoned his uncle Norimori. "Your son-in-law Naritsune will be pardoned. You need have no more worry on that score."

Norimori pressed his palms together in a gesture of joy and thanksgiving. "When Naritsune was sent into exile, he kept pleading with me and asking tearfully why I couldn't intercede for him. It was a heartrending sight!"

"I can well imagine how you felt," replied Shigemori. "Anyone is bound to feel deeply concerned when a son is involved. I will do all I can for you when I speak to my father." With that, he withdrew to an inner room.

So at last it was decided that the exiles in Kikai-ga-shima should be recalled, and Kiyomori issued a letter of pardon and dispatched it by messenger from the capital. Norimori was so overjoyed that he sent a private messenger of his own to accompany the official envoy on his way. They had orders to proceed as rapidly as possible, traveling day and night. But the sea-lanes were not always favorable to their progress, and they had to battle adverse winds and waves. Thus although they left the capital in the last third of the Seventh Month, they did not arrive at Kikai-ga-shima until around the twentieth of the Ninth Month.

The Foot-Drumming (3:2)

The messenger dispatched with the letter of pardon was Tan Zaemon-no-jō Motoyasu. As he and his men stepped ashore from the boat, they began inquiring here and there. "Are the men who were exiled from the capital here?—the Tanba lesser captain, the Hosshō-ji administrator, the Taira police commissioner?"

Naritsune and Yasuyori had gone as usual to worship at the Kumano Shrine they had built and were not around. Only Shunkan was there and when he heard these inquiries, he exclaimed, "Have I longed so much that now I'm dreaming? Or is this the Devil of the Sixth Heaven[3] come to play tricks on my mind? I can't believe this is true!" Stumbling, staggering, he scrambled forward as fast as his feet would take him. "What do you want? My name is Shunkan and I was exiled from the capital!" he announced.

The messenger took the prime minister's letter of pardon out of the pouch that was hanging around the neck of one of his servants and handed it to Shunkan.

Opening the letter, Shunkan read: "The grave offense for which exile to a distant island was imposed is hereby pardoned. Prepare to return to the capital with all possible speed. Because of the prayers for the imperial consort's safe delivery, a general pardon has been issued. Accordingly, Lesser Captain Naritsune and Priest Yasuyori are granted pardon."

That was all the letter contained—no mention whatsoever of Shunkan. He thought that perhaps his name was on the outside cover of the document, but he could not find it there. He read the letter over from beginning to end, from end to beginning, but he could find only two names, no trace of a third.

After a while, Naritsune and Yasuyori appeared. But whether Naritsune read the letter of pardon or Yasuyori read it, they could find only two names, never three. Perhaps the whole thing is a dream, they thought, and yet it seemed real. Surely it must be real—yet it was still like a dream. Moreover, although the messenger brought

---

3. According to Buddhist cosmology, the Devil of the Sixth Heaven is the lord of the highest of the Six Realms of Desire and, together with his followers, keeps people from adhering to Buddhism.

with him various letters for Naritsune and Yasuyori that had been entrusted to him by persons in the capital, there was not so much as a note of inquiry addressed to Bishop Shunkan. Have all the people I know somehow vanished from the capital? thought Shunkan, more distressed than ever.

"All three of us were accused of the same crime and sentenced to exile in the same place!" he exclaimed. "Why, then, when a pardon is issued, should only two men be recalled and the other left behind? Have the Heike suffered some lapse of memory? Or did the scribe who wrote the letter make a mistake? What is the meaning of this?" he demanded, gazing up at the heavens, flinging himself on the ground, weeping and moaning, little as such antics could help him.

"The fact that I'm here like this is all because of your father's poisonous schemes!" cried Shunkan in agony, clinging desperately to Naritsune's sleeve. "You can't pretend my troubles are no concern of yours! Even if I can't return to the capital without a pardon, at least take me in the boat as far as Kyushu. While you two were here, just as the swallows come in spring and the wild geese visit the paddy fields in autumn, so from time to time I received word of what was happening in the capital. But now if you leave me, how can I ever hope for such news?"

In an effort to comfort him, Naritsune replied, "I understand exactly how you must feel. And happy as I am that we two have been recalled to the capital, I hardly have the heart to make the journey when I see you in this distraught condition. But the envoy has said that it is impossible to take you with us. And if word should get abroad that three men left the island when there was not a pardon for three, I'm afraid there might be real trouble. It's best if I go back to the capital first and talk to people. I will see what sort of mood the prime minister is in and then send someone to fetch you. Meanwhile, you must wait here patiently as you have in the past. The important thing is to look after your health. You've been skipped over this time, but sooner or later you are certain to be pardoned!" To these words of assurance, Shunkan responded only with tears, without caring who saw.

A bustle of activity signaled that the boat was about to depart, whereupon Shunkan began frantically scrambling aboard, only to be put off, and having been put off, scrambling aboard once more, determined to be taken along. But he was left behind with the bed quilt that Naritsune had given him as a parting gift and a memento from Priest Yasuyori, a copy of the Lotus Sutra. When the hawser was untied and the boat started to pull away from the shore, Shunkan seized hold of the hawser, clinging to it until he had been dragged into water up to his waist, up to his armpits, up to the point where he could barely stand. And when he could no longer keep his footing, he grasped hold of the gunwale, crying, "What are you doing! Do you really mean to go off and leave me? I never thought you could be so cruel! Where is the kindness you once showed me? Just take me along, wrong as it may be! Take me at least as far as Kyushu!"

But to his frantic pleas the envoy only replied, "That is quite impossible!" And when he had pried Shunkan's fingers loose from the gunwale, the boat at last rowed off.

At a loss to know what else to do, Shunkan returned to the shore and, flinging himself down, began beating his legs on the ground in the sort of tantrum small children indulge in when their nurse or mother has gone off and left them. "Let me come on board! Take me with you!" he screamed.

But the boat merely rowed away from the shore, leaving behind its customary trail of white waves. Although it had not yet gone far into the distance, Shunkan could no longer see it through the confusion of his tears. Rushing to a nearby hilltop, he waved to the boat in the offing. When Lady Sayo of Matsura in ancient times waved her scarf in longing at the boat that carried her husband to a far-off land, her despair could hardly have been greater than Shunkan's.

Even after the boat had disappeared from sight and evening had fallen, Shunkan did not return to his humble dwelling, but with the salt of the waves still on his legs and the night dews wetting him, he remained where he was until dawn.

Nonetheless, he thought to himself, Naritsune is a man of great kindness, and he will surely take steps to rescue me! Leaning heavily on this hope, he put aside for the moment all thought of drowning himself, fragile though such hopes might be. Now he could understand just how the brothers Sōri and Sokuri must have felt long ago when they were cast away on the desert island of Kaigakusen.[4]

---

4. According to Buddhist mythology, Sōri and Sokuri were the sons of a powerful man in southern India. Abandoned by their stepmother to starve to death on an island when their father was absent, the two were later reborn as the bodhisattvas Kannon and Seishi.

Many Buddhist rituals are performed throughout the realm to ensure the safe birth of Kenreimon'in's child. The rites have an effect, and the empress gives birth to a son. But blunders and improprieties mar the rituals and celebrations following the birth. On his return from Kikai-ga-shima to the capital, Naritsune stops at the hut in Narichika's place of exile and at his father's villa in the capital before going to see his remaining family and servants.

Ariō (3:8)

So of the three men who had been exiled to the island of Kikai-ga-shima, two were recalled to the capital. The third, Bishop Shunkan, was left to be sole guardian of the dismal island, a bitter fate indeed.

From the time Shunkan was a young man, he had in his service a boy named Ariō whom he treated with great kindness. When word reached the capital that the exiles from Kikai-ga-shima would be arriving in the city that very day, Ariō journeyed as far as Toba in the outskirts of the capital to welcome them, but he could see no sign of his old master. Asking the reason for this, he was told, "That man's crimes were so terrible that he's been left behind on the island."

Ariō was stunned by the news. For a while he spent all his time loitering around Rokuhara, where the Heike had their headquarters, hoping to learn something more about his master's fate. But there did not appear to be any possibility of a pardon for Shunkan.

He then went to visit Shunkan's daughter at the place where she was living in hiding. "Your father was not included among those who were pardoned and will not be returning to the capital. I must somehow make my way to the island and see for myself how he is faring. I wonder whether you would write a letter that I can take with me." Weeping as she did so, Shunkan's daughter wrote the letter and gave it to him.

Ariō would like to have taken leave of his father and mother, but he was afraid they would not approve of the journey and so he did not do so. A ship was leaving for China around the Fourth or Fifth Month, but he felt he could not delay his departure until the beginning of summer. Instead, he left the capital around the end of the Third Month and, after enduring the numerous hardships of a sea voyage, arrived at the bay of Satsuma in Kyushu.

From Satsuma he went to the port from which he would take a boat to Kikai-ga-shima. There the local people, suspicious of what he was up to, stripped him of his clothing, but he never for a moment regretted having made the trip. So that they would not rob him of the letter from Shunkan's daughter as well, he hid it in his topknot.

He boarded a merchant vessel that took him to the island. But even though he had heard vague stories about it when he was in the capital, he was utterly unprepared for what he found. The island had no rice paddies, no vegetable fields, no villages, and no hamlets, and although a few persons were living there, he could barely understand a word they said.

Ariō addressed one of them: "Excuse me . . ."

"What is it?" was the answer.

"The Hosshō-ji administrator who was exiled here from the capital—do you know where he is?"

If the words "Hosshō-ji" and "administrator" had meant anything to the man, he might have answered, but as it was, he merely shook his head. "I don't know."

One of the natives, however, seemed to understand something of the matter. "Let me see . . ." he said. "There were three men in all, but two were recalled to the capital. I used to see the one who was left behind wandering around here and there, but I don't know where he is now."

Concerned that Shunkan might have wandered into the mountains, Ariō started off in that direction, pushing deep into the area, climbing peaks, descending into valleys. But white mists hid the path he had come by and the trail ahead was uncertain; winds in the dense foliage woke him from his dreams before he could catch so much as a dream glimpse of his master.

Having found no trace of Shunkan in the mountains, he tried looking along the shore. But there, except for the gulls who left their footprints in the sand or the plovers flocking around the white sandbars in the offing, he could see no sign of life.

One morning Ariō spied someone approaching him from the shore in the distance, a lean, emaciated figure as thin as a dragon-fly, tottering along alone. The person seemed at one time to have been a Buddhist priest, for his hair grew straight up as though the head had formerly been shaved. Various bits of seaweed clung to his head, looking like a veritable forest of growth. His joints stuck out, his skin hung in folds, and it was impossible to tell whether the garments he wore were made of silk or hemp. In one hand he held a piece of edible seaweed, in the other, a fish, and although he was trying to walk, he staggered from side to side and made little progress.

I have seen many beggars in the capital, Ariō thought, but never one that looked like this! The Buddha tells us that the asura[5] demons live on the shores of the great sea and that beings in the Three Evil Paths[6] and the Four Lower Realms of Existence[7] dwell deep in the mountains or by the vast ocean. Perhaps I have somehow stumbled on the realm where the hungry ghosts[8] live!

As he drew nearer to the figure, he began to wonder whether the person might know something about his master's whereabouts. "Pardon me," he said.

"What is it?"

"The Hosshō-ji administrator who was exiled from the capital — would you happen to know where he is?"

Ariō may have been unable to recognize his old master, but how could Shunkan make a similar mistake?

"That's me!" he exclaimed, but the words were scarcely out of his mouth when he dropped the things he had in his hands and fell to the ground in a faint. Now at last Ariō knew what had become of his master.

Ariō gathered up Shunkan's unconscious form, cradling it on his knees. "It's Ariō! I'm here!" he said, his tears raining down. "Was it for nothing that I endured the many hardships of the sea voyage, coming all the way here to look for you, only to be confronted by a pitiful sight like this?"

After a while, Shunkan began to regain consciousness. As Ariō helped him sit up, he observed, "How amazing—that you should want to come all this way to look for me! Day and night I have thought of nothing but those in the capital. Sometimes the faces of my loved ones come to me in dreams; at other times I think I see

5.   Asura are godlike beings who are constantly fighting.
6.   The lowest of the Ten Paths of Existence, the Three Evil Paths are the paths of beasts, hungry ghosts, and hell dwellers.
7.   The Four Lower Realms of Existence are the worlds of the asura, beasts, hungry ghosts, and hell dwellers.
8.   Hungry ghosts (J. *gaki*) are beings who suffer from insatiable hunger and thirst.

them standing right before me. And since my body has become so weak and feeble, I can no longer tell dream from reality. Even your coming here now seems to be no more than a dream. And if it is a dream, what am I to do when I wake?"

"No—I am really here!" said Ariō. "And seeing you this way, I can only marvel that you've been able to keep alive until now!"

"Ah, the hopelessness and desolation in my heart since Naritsune and Yasuyori abandoned me—I wonder whether you can even imagine what it was like? I thought then of drowning myself. But, foolish as I was, I put my trust in those worthless promises that Naritsune made, trying to reassure me by saying, 'Just wait till I send word from the capital!' There's nothing at all on this island for a person to eat. So while I still had my strength, I used to go to the mountains and gather sulfur, which I would trade to the merchants from Kyushu in exchange for food. But I've grown weaker day by day, and I can't do that anymore. Now, when the weather is mild like this, I go down to the shore, get on my knees and press my palms together, begging fish from the men who are fishing or hauling in nets there. Or when the tide goes out, I gather shellfish or pick up bits of edible seaweed. I've depended on the very moss on the sea rocks to sustain this dewdrop life of mine until today. You can scarcely imagine the measures I've resorted to in order to keep alive in this uncertain world of ours. I want to tell you more about it, but now let's go to my house."

How could anyone who looked the way Shunkan did possibly have a house? Ariō wondered in bewilderment. But when they had walked a little while, they came to a grove of pines. There, using bamboo that had washed up on the shore for supports and bundles of reeds for beams and lintels, Shunkan had put together a hut of sorts. Although it was covered from top to bottom with layers of pine needles, it hardly looked as though it could withstand the wind and rain.

In earlier times, when Shunkan was administrator of the temple called Hosshō-ji, he was charged with managing more than eighty landed estates that belonged to the temple. He lived in a mansion adorned with grand and imposing gates and was surrounded by four or five hundred servants and retainers. How strange, then, that he should end his days in such a miserable condition!

Various kinds of karma or past actions affect a person's life—the karma that calls forth retribution within one's present lifetime, the karma whose effects are not seen until one's next existence, and that whose effects appear only in future existences. All the funds and goods that Shunkan used in his lifetime were the property of the great temple with which he was affiliated, goods that belonged to the Buddha. Because he sinned by using such goods, the donations of the faithful, in an utterly shameless manner, he was suffering retribution while still in this life.

The Death of Shunkan (3:9)

By this time convinced that Ariō's visit was a reality and not a dream, Shunkan announced, "Last year when the messenger came from the capital for Naritsune and Yasuyori, he brought me no letters at all. And now you say nothing about news from the capital—does this mean that you too have no messages for me?"

Ariō, choked with tears, for a while merely hung his head and made no answer. When some time had passed, he lifted his head and, brushing back the tears, replied, "After you went off to the Nishi-hachijō mansion, the officials came around at once to make arrests. They seized your retainers, grilled them about their connection with the plot against the Heike, and put them to death. Your wife, fearful that she would not be able to conceal your little son from them, went into hiding in the mountains beyond Kurama.[9] I was the only one who knew their whereabouts and used to go from time to time to see if I could be of help. Your son in particular longed so for his father that whenever I would go there, he would tease and beg, saying, 'Ariō, please take me with you to that island where my father is!' In the Second Month of this year he died of smallpox. This sorrow, added to what she had already suffered on your account, seemed to be too much for your wife to bear. She grew weaker with each day that went by, and on the second day of the Third Month she died. So only your daughter is left, living with her aunt in Nara. I've brought you this letter from her."

Taking the letter and opening it, Shunkan found that all that Ariō had told him was true. At the end, the letter said, "Why, when three men were exiled, have two been called back to the capital and you

9.   Kurama is an area north of Kyoto and east of Mount Hiei.

have yet to return? Whether she is highborn or low, a girl's lot is a sorrowful thing! If only I were a boy, I could surely find some way to go to the island where you are, couldn't I? Please come home with Ariō, come as soon as you can!"

Shunkan held the letter pressed against his face and for a while remained silent. Then at last he said, "See, Ariō—see what a foolish thing she writes! Poor thing—she says I am to hurry back to the capital with you. If I had been free to do any such thing, why would I have spent three springs and autumns on this island? My daughter must be twelve now. And with no one to look out for her, how can she find a husband or go into service in the palace or get along in the world at all?"

With these words, he broke down in tears. Observing him, Ariō could well understand why people say that as clear as a father's understanding may be in all other matters, love blinds him when it comes to his own child.[10]

"Since I was banished to this island," Shunkan continued, "I have had no calendar and no way to keep track of the days and months. But when I see the spring blossoms scattering or the leaves falling in the autumn, I know that the seasons are passing. When the cicada's cry signals the end of the wheat harvest, I know that summer has begun, and the piles of snow tell me it's winter. I observe the waxing and waning of the moon and understand that thirty days have gone by. And now I learn that my son—I've counted on my fingers, he must be six by now—has gone before me! When I was called to the Nishi-hachijō mansion, he wanted to go along and begged me to take him. I tried to comfort him, telling him I would be right back. It seems only a moment ago I left him—if I'd thought that was the last time we'd be together, I'd have lingered a while longer to look at him!

"The bond between parent and child, the vows that join husband and wife together—all these are ties that transcend a single lifetime. And now my wife and little boy have preceded me in death—I am surprised that some dream or vague imagining did not bring me a hint of their passing! The reason I've continued to drag out my life, shameless in the eyes of others, was simply that I hoped I might see them once

10. An almost direct quotation of a poem by Fujiwara no Kanesuke (877–933), in *Gosenshū* (no. 1102).

more. Now only my concern for my daughter remains to weigh on my heart, but sad as her lot may be, she will surely be able to manage somehow. And if I prolong my existence any further, I'll merely be a burden to you, something that is too bitter to contemplate!"

From this time on, Shunkan refused to eat even the meager fare on which he had subsisted until now. Instead, devoting himself solely to the invocation of Amida's name, he prayed that he might die with his thoughts fixed on being reborn in the Pure Land.

On the twenty-third day following Ariō's arrival in the island, Shunkan breathed his last in the little hut he had built. He was thirty-seven years of age.

Clinging to the body of his master, Ariō looked up to the heavens and threw himself on the ground, weeping bitter tears, useless as they were. And when he could weep no more, he said, "By rights I should go to serve you in the world beyond. But your daughter is still in this world, and she and I are the only ones who can offer proper prayers for your welfare in the next life. So for the time being I will remain alive and pray for your enlightenment!"

He left the deathbed as it was, dismantled the hut, gathered up the dried pine branches and bundles of dead reeds and, piling them on the corpse, cremated it, the smoke rising as from a salt maker's fire of seaweed. Then he gathered up the whitened bones, placed them in a bag around his neck, and, once more borrowing passage on a merchant vessel, went with them to the Kyushu mainland.

Hastening back to the capital, he proceeded to where Shunkan's daughter was living and gave her a detailed account of all that had happened.

"When your father read your letter, he was more deeply moved than ever," said Ariō. "But on that island there was no such thing as an inkstone or paper, so he could not write an answer. It must have pained him to think he could not convey to you all that was in his heart. And now, no matter how many rebirths we may undergo, no matter how many kalpas may pass, we will never hear his voice or see him again!"

On hearing these words, Shunkan's daughter fell prostrate, her voice lifted in unbridled weeping. Immediately, at the age of twelve, she became a nun, carrying out religious practice at the Hokke-ii nunnery in Nara, her sad life devoted to praying for the repose of h father and mother in the other world.

As for Ariō, he climbed Mount Kōya,[11] still carrying Shunkan's remains in the bag around his neck, and laid them to rest in the Oku-no-in cemetary.[12] Then he became a Buddhist priest at the Rengedani settlement nearby. Thereafter, he traveled around the various provinces and outlying areas of the country, carrying out religious practices and praying for his master's well-being in the afterlife.

And so the grief and sorrows piled up, a portent of the fearful end that awaited the Heike.

A typhoon strikes the capital, and an oracle says it presages a breakdown of Buddhist law and kingly law. While on a pilgrimage to Kumano, Kiyomori's son Shigemori asks for a long life if the Taira's prosperity is to last or a quick death should the Taira's end be near. Almost immediately, Shigemori falls ill and dies. Kiyomori, no longer restrained by his exemplary son, settles his accounts with the imperial family and places Retired Emperor GoShirakawa under house arrest.

11. Mount Kōya is a mountain in the northeastern part of present-day Wakayama Prefecture where Kūkai (774–835), a noted Shingon priest, established the Kongōbu-ji temple in 816. It is a sacred site for the Shingon school of esoteric Buddhism.
12. Oku-no-in is the name of the famous cemetery on Mount Kōya where Kūkai supposedly waits in deep meditation for the coming of Miroku, the next Buddha of this world.

BOOK FOUR

MOCHIHITO, PRINCE: second son of Retired Emperor GoShirakawa; also called Prince Takakura.
YORIMASA (Minamoto): elderly warrior.

The Taira reach the height of their glory. Having driven Emperor Takakura from the throne, Kiyomori installs his own grandson (Antoku) as emperor. Another attempt is made to overthrow the Taira. Prince Mochihito, as the son of Retired Emperor GoShirakawa, has a strong claim to the imperial succession and is persuaded by Minamoto no Yorimasa to lead a revolt against the Taira. The plot is discovered, and Mochihito is forced to flee the capital and take refuge at Mii-dera temple in Ōmi Province. Mii-dera temple thereupon forms an alliance with the Kōfuku-ji temple in Nara. The monks of Mii-dera prepare for a surprise attack on the Taira headquarters at Rokuhara, but they are delayed by an ally of the Taira. Abandoning the plan for an offensive battle, Yorimasa and the Mii-dera monks try to hold the Taira forces at the Uji River in order to give Prince Mochihito time to flee south to Kōfuku-ji.

The Battle at the Bridge (4:11)

While riding from Mii-dera[1] to Uji, Prince Mochihito fell off his horse six times. "It's because he got no sleep last night!" his men said.

---

1. Mii-dera temple, also known as the Onjō-ji temple, was a center for Tendai school esotericism in Ōmi Province. Mii-dera and Mount Hiei had a long, and often violent, history of disagreements.

After ripping the planks off three sections of the Uji Bridge, they took him into the nearby Byōdō-in[2] so he could get a short rest.

Meanwhile, those back in Rokuhara exclaimed, "What's that? The prince is trying to escape to the southern capital at Nara! Go after him and strike him down!"

The Taira forces were headed by Commander of the Military Guards of the Left Tomomori, Middle Captain Shigehira, Director of the Stables of the Left Yukimori, and Satsuma Governor Tadanori, as well as by the samurai commanders, Kazusa Governor Tadakiyo, his son Tadatsuna, Hida Governor Kageie, his son Kagetaka, Takahashi no Hangan Nagatsuna, Kawachi no Hangan Hidekuni, Musashi no Saburōzaemon Arikuni, Etchū no Jirō Moritsugi, Kazusa no Gorōbyōe Tadamitsu, and Akushichibyōe Kagekiyo. The entire force, numbering more than twenty-eight thousand riders, crossed Mount Kohata and raced to the foot of the Uji Bridge.

When they saw that their adversaries were holed up in the Byōdō-in, they challenged them three times, and the prince's forces responded with battle cries of their own.

The riders in the Taira vanguard shouted, "Watch out—the bridge planks have been torn off! Watch out—the bridge planks have been torn off!" But those in the rear, unable to hear the warning, pressed forward, each eager to take the lead. As a result, more than two hundred mounted men in the vanguard were pushed into the water, where they drowned and were washed downstream.

Drawn up at opposite ends of the bridge, the two forces exchanged the volley of arrows that marked the start of hostilities. On the prince's side, Shunchō, Tajima, Habuku, Sazuku, and Tsuzuku no Genta let fly a rain of arrows that pierced the shields and helmets of their opponents.

Yorimasa, wearing a heavy silk battle robe and indigo-laced armor with a white fern-leaf design, had dispensed with a helmet, as though anticipating that this day would be his last. His son and heir Nakatsuna wore a red brocade battle robe and armor laced in black. So that he could handle his bow more effectively, he did not wear a helmet either.

2.   The Byōdō-in was a large temple complex located next to the Uji River that was built in the mid-eleventh century by Regent Fujiwara no Yorimichi on the site of a villa owned by his father, Michinaga.

Drawing his great spear, Tajima strode forward alone over the bridge. Catching sight of him, the Taira forces shouted, "Now, men, shoot him down!" Using their strongest bows and their most skilled archers, they aligned their arrowheads and sent volley after volley flying; one arrow no sooner sped on its way than another was fitted into place. But Tajima, wholly unperturbed, nimbly dodged the high-flying ones, leaped over the low ones, and, with his spear, struck down those that came straight at him while friend and foe looked on in wonder. From that day on, he became known as Tajima the Arrow-Downer.

Among the warrior monks in the prince's party was Jōmyō Meishū of Tsutsui. He was dressed in black-laced armor over a dark blue battle robe, and a five-plate helmet. He carried a sword with black lacquer fittings and, on his back, a quiver containing twenty-four arrows fledged with black eagle-wing feathers. Grasping a lacquered, rattan-wrapped bow and his favorite long, plain-handle spear, he made his way over the bridge, calling out his name in a loud voice.

"You've heard of me from times past—now have a look! Everyone in Mii-dera knows me—Jōmyō Meishū of Tsutsui, warrior monk, one fighter who's a match for a thousand! Anyone who thinks he's up to it, come forward—I'll take him on!"

From his quiver of twenty-four he drew one arrow after another, fitting them to his bow and sending them winging. Twenty men dropped dead at once, and eleven others suffered wounds, until only one arrow was left in the quiver.

Then he tossed his bow aside with a clatter, undid his quiver, and threw that away too. Throwing off his fur boots, he scampered barefoot over the crossbeams of the bridge. Anyone else would have been too terrified for such a feat, but Jōmyō made his way forward as blithely as though he were sauntering down one of the avenues of the capital.

He used his spear to batter his enemies, mowing down five of them. When he struck at a sixth, his spear broke in the middle. Hurling it aside, he went on fighting with his sword, slashing in every direction at the crowd of attackers, employing the spider-leg thrust, the spiraling stroke, the T-shape attack, the somersault, the water-wheel. In no time he had felled eight men, but as he brought his sword down on the helmet of a ninth, it struck with such force that the blade broke at the hilt, slipped away, and fell with a splash into the river. Left with nothing to wield but the dagger at his waist, he went right on with his frenzied assault.

Among the warrior monks was one named Ichirai, a man of great strength and agility who served the Reverend Master Keishū of the Jōen Cloister. He had followed Jōmyō's lead and was battling away just behind him. He wanted to push past Jōmyō, but the crossbeam was so narrow he could not get by. Seizing the rear flap of Jōmyō's helmet, he called out, "By your leave, Jōmyō!" and vaulted deftly over Jōmyō's shoulder. Then he went on battling.

Although Ichirai died in the fighting, Jōmyō somehow managed to crawl back to the Byōdō-in. There, on the grass in front of the temple gate, he stripped off his battle gear and threw it aside. Examining his helmet, he counted sixty-three marks where arrows had struck, five where the arrow had actually pierced the helmet. He was not badly wounded, however, and so after treating his wounds with moxa to stanch the blood, he wrapped a cloth around his head and put on a white monk's robe. Then he broke a bow in half to use as a staff, put on plain clogs, and, intoning the name of the Buddha Amida, set off in the direction of Nara.

Followed by Ichirai (*right*), Jōmyō guards the bridge at the Uji River while Tadatsuna (*left*) leads the Heike troops across it.

Taking note of how Jōmyō did it, the warrior monks of Mii-dera and the men of the Watanabe League came scrambling over the bridge beams, vying with one another to be the first across. Some seized an enemy head or a battle trophy and then returned to the Byōdō-in side; others, mortally wounded, ripped open their bellies and threw themselves into the river. So the melee at the bridge raged on like a blazing fire.

Observing the situation, one of the Taira samurai commanders, Kazusa Governor Tadakiyo, hurried to the side of the Taira leaders. "Look there!" he said. "See how fierce the fighting on the bridge is! We want to get to the other side. But right now the river is swollen with the Fifth Month rains. If we try to wade across, we'll lose a lot of men and horses. We'd better go by way of Yodo or Imoarai, or perhaps by Kawachi Road."[3]

3.   All these are areas to the southwest, where the river is more shallow.

But Ashikaga no Matatarō Tadatsuna, a native of the eastern province of Shimotsuke, came forward and spoke up. "Yodo, Imoarai, Kawachi—are we going off to India or China to look for allies? We're the ones who have to do the job! The enemy is right before our eyes—if we don't attack but let them escape to Nara, reinforcements from Yoshino and Totsugawa will come swarming around to aid them, and then we'll have a real fight on our hands!

"There's a big river in the east called the Tone that marks the boundary between Musashi and Kōzuke provinces. In the past the Chichibu and Ashikaga clans had a falling-out and were constantly battling each other at the river. Once the Ashikaga planned to launch a main attack by the ford at Nagai and send rear forces by the Koga and Sugi fords. An ally of the Ashikaga, Priest Nitta of Kōzuke, had prepared boats for their use at Sugi Ford, but the Chichibu managed to destroy them all. When the Ashikaga discovered what had happened, they decided, 'If we don't get across the river now, our name as fighting men will be forever disgraced. If we drown, we drown—we've got to make a try at it!' And they got across, probably because they used the horse-raft formation.

"With the enemy in sight and a battle waiting for us across the river, we eastern warriors aren't in the habit of fussing over the depth of the water. This river can hardly be deeper or swifter than the Tone—so, gentlemen, follow me!" And with these words he rode his horse straight into the water.

Some three hundred or more riders followed him, led by Ōgo, Ōmuro, Fukazu, Yamagami, Naha no Tarō, Sanuki no Hirotsuna, Onodera Zenji Tarō, and Heyako no Shirō, along with the retainers Ubukata no Jirō, Kiriu no Rokurō, and Tanaka no Sōda.

"Put the strong horses on the upstream side and the weaker ones downstream!" shouted Ashikaga in a loud voice. "While the horses still have their footing, ease up on the reins and walk them. Once they start to lose their footing, tighten the reins and let them swim. If it looks like someone's going to wash away, have him grab the tip of your bow. Grip each other's hands and go across shoulder to shoulder. Get a firm seat in the saddle and press down on the stirrups. If your horse's head starts to go under, pull him up, but don't pull so hard that he goes under again. If the water starts coming over you, slide back until you're sitting on the horse's rump. Let the water hold you up, and put as little weight as possible on your horse. Don't try to use your bows in the middle of the river. Even if the enemy shoots at you, don't shoot back. Keep your neck guard down at all times, but don't duck your head so low that an arrow can hit the top of your helmet. Go straight across the river, don't get washed aside. Don't fight the water, just cross it! Cross it!"

Thanks to these instructions, the three hundred or more riders were able to cross over and bound up the opposite bank without losing a single man.

> Yorimasa's forces are crushed by the Taira. He commits suicide in the Byōdō-in temple after reciting a poem. Despite the time afforded for his escape, Prince Mochihito is killed by the Taira forces within a few miles of his destination. Although Kiyomori originally ordered all the prince's sons to be executed, he relents and allows them to become monks instead. Mii-dera temple is burned down by the Taira forces.

BOOK FIVE

The Burning of Nara (5:14)

In the capital, people were saying, "When Prince Takakura went to Onjō-ji, the monks of Kōfuku-ji in Nara not only expressed sympathy with his cause but even went to Onjō-ji to greet him. In doing so they showed themselves to be enemies of the state. Both Kōfuku-ji and Onjō-ji will surely be attacked!"

When rumors of this kind reached the monks of Kōfuku-ji, they rose up like angry hornets. Regent Fujiwara no Motomichi assured them that "if you have any sentiments you wish to convey to the throne, I will act as your intermediary on whatever number of occasions may be required." But such assurances had no effect whatsoever.

Motomichi dispatched Tadanori, the superintendent of the Kangaku-in, to act as his emissary, but the monks met him with wild clamor, shouting, "Drag the wretch from his carriage! Cut off his topknot!" Tadanori fled back to the capital, his face white with terror. Motomichi then sent Assistant Gate Guards Commander Chikamasa, but the monks greeted him in similar fashion, yelling, "Cut off his topknot!" He dropped everything and fled back to the capital. On that occasion, two lackeys from the Kangaku-in had their topknots cut off.

In addition, the Nara monks made a big ball, of the kind used in New Year's games, dubbed it "Prime Minister Kiyomori's head," and yelled, "Hit it! Stomp on it!" Easy talk is the midwife of disaster, and incautious action is the highway to ruin, people say.[1] This prime minister, Kiyomori, as the maternal grandfather of the reigning emperor, was someone to be spoken of with the utmost respect. It seemed as though only the Devil of the Sixth Heaven could have inspired the Nara monks to use such language in referring to him.

When news of these events reached Prime Minister Kiyomori, he began making plans to deal with the situation. In order to bring an immediate halt to the unruly doings in Nara, he appointed Senoo Kaneyasu as the chief of police of Yamato Province, where Nara is situated, and sent him with a force of five hundred horsemen under his command. "Even if your opponents resort to violence, you must not retaliate in kind!" he warned the men when they set off. "Do not wear armor or helmets, and do not carry bows and arrows!"

But the Nara monks were not, of course, aware of Kiyomori's private instructions, and, seizing some sixty of Kaneyasu's men who had become separated from the main force, they cut off their heads and hung them in a row around the border of Sarusawa Pond.

Enraged at this, Kiyomori commanded, "Very well, then, attack Nara!"

He dispatched a force of more than forty thousand horsemen to carry out the attack, with Shigehira as commander in chief and Michimori as second in command. Meanwhile more than seven thousand monks, both old and young, had put on helmets and

---

1. This is a reference to *Chengui*, a Tang-period ethical text.

dug trenches across the road at two places, one at the slope called
Narazaka and the other at the Hannya-ji temple, and fortified
them with barricades of shields and thorned branches. There they
awaited the attackers.

The Heike, their forty thousand men split into two parties, swept
down on the two fortified points at Narazaka and Hannya-ji, shouting their battle cries. All the monks were on foot and armed with
swords. The government forces, being mounted, could thus charge
back and forth among them, chasing some this way, driving others
that, showering arrows down on them until countless numbers had
been felled. The ceremonial exchange of arrows signaling the start
of hostilities took place at six in the morning, and the battle continued throughout the day. By evening, both the fortified points at
Narazaka and Hannya-ji had been captured....

The fighting continued into the night. Darkness having fallen,
the Heike commander in chief, Shigehira, who was standing in

Monk soldiers and the Heike clash near the Hannya-ji temple in Nara (*right*). The temples, which have been set on fire by the Heike, burn while the monk soldiers flee (*left*).

front of the gate of the Hannya-ji temple, called for torches to be lit. A certain Tomokata, a minor overseer of the Fukui estate in Harima, broke his shield in two and, using it as a torch, set fire to one of the commoners' houses in the area. It was the twenty-eighth night of the Twelfth Month and a strong wind was blowing. Although only one fire had been set, it was blown by the wind this way and that until it had spread to many of the temples in the vicinity.

By this time, those monks who were ashamed to be thought cowardly and who cared what kind of name they left behind them had died in the fighting at Narazaka or Hannya-ji. Those who could still use their legs fled in the direction of Mount Yoshino and Totsukawa. The older monks who were unable to walk any great distance, along with the special students in training at the temples, the acolytes, and the women and children all fled as fast as they could to Kōfuku-ji or Tōdai-ji, some thousand or more persons climbing up to the second story of the latter temple's Hall of the Great Buddha. To prevent any of their pursuers from reaching them, they then threw down the ladders by which they had ascended. When the flames from the fire came roaring down on them, their shrieks and cries could hardly have been surpassed by even those of the sinners being tortured in the Hell of Scorching Heat, the Great Hell of Scorching Heat, or the Hell of Never-Ceasing Torment.

Kōfuku-ji was founded at the behest of Lord Tankai, Fujiwara no Fuhito,[2] and thereafter served generation after generation as the temple of the Fujiwara clan. Its Eastern Gold Hall contained an image of Shakyamuni Buddha brought to Japan when Buddhist teachings were first introduced. The Western Gold Hall contained an image of the bodhisattva Kannon that, on its own accord, had risen out of the earth. These, along with the corridors strung like emerald gems surrounding them on four sides, the two-story hall with its vermilion and cinnabar trimmings, the two pagodas with their nine-ring finials shining in the sky, all went up in smoke in the space of an instant.

In Tōdai-ji was enshrined the one-hundred-and-sixty-foot gilt-bronze image of the Buddha Vairochana—burnished by the hand and person of Emperor Shōmu[3] himself—the representation of the Buddha who abides eternally, never passing away, as he manifests his living body in the Land of Actual Reward and the Land of Eternally Tranquil Light. The protuberance on the top of his head towering on high, half-hidden in the clouds; the tuft of white hair between his eyebrows, an object of veneration:[4] this hallowed figure was as perfect as the full moon. Now amid the flames, the head fell to the ground, and the body melted and fused into one mountainlike mass. The eighty-four thousand auspicious marks of the Buddha were suddenly obscured like an autumn moon by the clouds of the Five Cardinal Sins; the garlands of jewels adorning the forty-two stages of bodhisattva practice were blown away like stars in the night sky by the winds of the Ten Evil Actions.[5] Smoke rose to blanket the sky, flames filled every corner of the empty air. Those who witnessed with their own

---

2.   By becoming the father of an empress, Fujiwara no Fuhito (659–720) was one of the first of his clan to rise to great power in the aristocracy.

3.   Emperor Shōmu (701–756, r. 724–749) was famous for his acts of Buddhist piety.

4.   The protuberance and the tuft of hair are two of the thirty-two distinguishing marks of the body of the Buddha.

5.   The Ten Evil Actions are killing, stealing, committing adultery, lying, using duplicitous language, slandering, equivocating, coveting, becoming angry, and holding false views.

eyes what was happening turned their gaze aside; those far off who heard reports of the disaster felt their spirits quail. All the doctrines and sacred writings of the Hossō and Sanron schools of Buddhism were lost, with not one scroll remaining.[6] Never before in India or China, it seemed, to say nothing of our land of Japan, had the Buddhist law suffered such terrible destruction.

King Udayana fashioned an image of fine gold, and Vishvakarman carved one out of red sandalwood, but these Buddha figures were merely life-size.[7] How could they compare with the Buddha of Tōdai-ji, unique and without equal anywhere in the entire continent of Jambudvipa in which we humans live? Yet this Buddha, who no one thought would ever suffer injury or decay whatever ages might pass, had now become mingled with and defiled by worldly dust, leaving behind only a legacy of unending sorrow. Brahma, Indra, the Four Heavenly Kings, the dragons, spirits, and others of the eight kinds of guardian beings, the wardens of the underworld, all those who lend divine protection to Buddhism must have looked on with alarm and consternation. The god Daimyōjin of the nearby Kasuga Shrine, who guards and protects the Hossō sect—what could he have thought? Little wonder, then, that the dew that fell on Kasuga meadow now had a different color, and the storm winds over Mount Mikasa sounded with a vengeful roar.

When the number of persons who perished in the flames was tallied up, it was found that more than seventeen hundred had died in the second story of the Hall of the Great Buddha, more than eight hundred at Kōfuku-ji, more than five hundred at this hall, more than three hundred at that hall—a total, in fact, of more than three thousand, five hundred persons. Of the thousand or more monks who died in the fighting, some had their heads cut off and exposed by the gate of Hannya-ji, while the heads of others were carried back to the capital.

On the twenty-ninth day of the month that the commander in chief, Taira no Shigehira, having destroyed the Southern Capital of Nara, returned to the Northern Capital of Heian, only Prime Minister Kiyomori, his anger now appeased, delighted in the outcome. But the

6. The Kōfuku-ji temple and the Tōdai-ji temple were centers for Hossō school and Sanron school studies, respectively.
7. According to Buddhist mythology, King Udayana was the creator of the first Buddhist statue. Vishvakarman is the patron god of artisans.

empress, Retired Emperor GoShirakawa, Retired Emperor Takakura, Regent Motomichi, and the others below them in station all deplored what had happened, declaring, "It was one thing to punish the evil monks, but what need was there to destroy the temples?"

The heads of the monks killed in battle were originally intended to be paraded through the main streets of the capital and then hung on the tree in front of the prison, but those in charge were so shocked at the destruction of Tōdai-ji and Kōfuku-ji that these orders were never issued. Instead, the heads were simply discarded here and there in the moats and drainage ditches.

In a document written in his own hand, Emperor Shōmu had declared, "When these temples prosper, the entire realm shall prosper. When these temples fall to ruin, the realm, too, shall fall into ruin." It thus appeared that without doubt these events must presage the downfall and ruin of the nation.

Thus this terrible year [1180] came to an end, and the fifth year of the Jishō era began.

BOOK SIX

GoSHIRAKAWA: retired emperor and head of the imperial clan.
KIYOMORI (Taira): lay priest, prime minister, and retired Taira clan head.
MUNEMORI (Taira): son of Kiyomori and Taira clan head.
NUN OF THE SECOND RANK (Taira): wife of Kiyomori.
YORITOMO (Minamoto): leader of the anti-Taira forces in the east.
YOSHINAKA (Minamoto): cousin of Yoritomo and leader of the anti-Taira forces in the north; also called Lord Kiso.

The New Year's ceremonies are shortened and do not have their normal luster owing to the burning of Nara. The gloom is deepened by the death of Retired Emperor Takakura. Yoshinaka of Kiso, working to overthrow the Taira, begins to gather allies in the north. The Taira's rule continues to weaken, and rebellions break out in Kyushu, Shikoku, and elsewhere.

The Death of Kiyomori (6:7)

After this, all the warriors of the island of Shikoku went over to the side of Kōno no Michinobu. Reports also came that Tanzō, the superintendent of the Kumano Shrine, had shifted his sympathies to the Genji side, despite the many kindnesses shown him by the Heike. All the provinces in the north and the east were thus rebelling against the Taira, and in the regions to the west and southwest of the capital the situation was the same. Report after report of uprisings in the outlying areas came to startle the ears of the Heike, and word repeatedly reached them of additional impending acts of rebellion. It seemed as though the "barbarian tribes to the east and west"[1] had suddenly risen up against them. The members of the Taira clan were not alone in thinking that the end of the world was close at hand. No truly thoughtful person could fail to dread the ominous turn of events.

On the twenty-third day of the Second Month, a council of the senior Taira nobles was convened. At that time Lord Munemori, a former general of the right, spoke as follows: "We earlier tried to put down the rebels in the east, but the results were not all that we might have desired. This time I would like to be appointed commander in chief to move against them."

"What a splendid idea!" the other nobles exclaimed in obsequious assent. A directive was accordingly handed down from the retired emperor appointing Lord Munemori commander in chief of an expedition against the traitorous elements in the eastern and northern provinces. All the high ministers and courtiers who held military posts or were experienced in the use of arms were ordered to follow him.

When word had already gotten abroad that Lord Munemori would set out on his mission to put down the Genji forces in the eastern provinces on the twenty-seventh day of the same month, his departure was canceled because of reports that Kiyomori, the lay priest and prime minister, was not in his customary good health.

On the following day, the twenty-eighth, it became known that Kiyomori was seriously ill, and people throughout the capital and at Rokuhara whispered to one another, "This is just what we were afraid of!"

From the first day that Kiyomori took sick, he was unable to swallow anything, not even water. His body was as hot as though there were a fire burning inside it: those who attended him could scarcely come within twenty-five or thirty feet of him so great was the heat. All he could do was cry out, "I'm burning! I'm burning!" His affliction seemed quite unlike any ordinary illness.

Water from the Well of the Thousand-Arm Kannon on Mount Hiei was brought to the capital and poured into a stone bathtub, and Kiyomori's body was lowered into it in hopes of cooling him. But

---

1.   A phrase used in China to refer to provinces in all four directions.

the water began to bubble and boil furiously and, in a moment, had all gone up in steam. In another attempt to bring him some relief, wooden pipes were rigged in order to pour streams of water down on his body, but the water sizzled and sputtered as though it were landing on fiery rocks or metal, and virtually none of it reached his body. The little that did so burst into flames and burned, filling the room with black smoke and sending flames whirling upward.

Long ago, the eminent Buddhist priest Hōzō was said to have been invited by Enma, the king of hell, to visit the infernal regions. At that time he asked if he might see the place where his deceased mother had been reborn. Admiring his filial concern, Enma directed the hell wardens to conduct him to the Hell of Scorching Heat, where Hōzō's mother was undergoing punishment. When Hōzō entered the iron gates of the hell, he saw flames leaping up like shooting stars, ascending hundreds of yojanas into the air. The sight must have been much like what those attending Kiyomori in his sickness now witnessed.

Kiyomori's wife, the Nun of the Second Rank, had a most fearful dream. It seemed that a carriage enveloped in raging flames had entered the gate of the mansion. Stationed at the front and rear of the carriage were creatures, some with the head of a horse, others with the head of an ox. To the front of the carriage was fastened an iron plaque inscribed with the single word *mu*, "never."

In her dream the Nun of the Second Rank asked, "Where has this carriage come from?"

"From the tribunal of King Enma," was the reply. "It has come to fetch His Lordship, the lay priest and prime minister of the Taira clan."

"And what does the plaque mean?" she asked.

"It means that because of the crime of burning the one-hundred-and-sixty-foot gilt-bronze image of the Buddha Vairochana[2] in the realm of human beings, King Enma's tribunal has decreed that the perpetrator shall fall into the depths of the Hell of Never-Ceasing Torment. The 'Never' of Never-Ceasing is written on it; the 'Ceasing' remains to be written."

The Nun of the Second Rank woke from her dream in alarm, her

2.   This refers to the Great Buddha of the Tōdai-ji temple.

body bathed in perspiration, and when she told others of her dream, their hair stood on end just hearing about it. She made offerings of gold, silver, and the seven precious objects to all the temples and shrines reputed to have power in such matters, even adding such items as horses, saddles, armor, helmets, bows, arrows, long swords, and short swords. But no matter how much she added as accompaniment to her supplications, they were wholly without effect. Kiyomori's sons and daughters gathered by his pillow and bedside, inquiring in anguish if there were something that could be done, but all their cries were in vain.

On the second day of the second intercalary month, the Nun of the Second Rank, braving the formidable heat, approached her husband's pillow and spoke through her tears. "With each day that passes, it seems to me, there is less hope for your recovery. If you have anything you wish to say before you depart this world, it would be good to speak now while your mind is still clear."

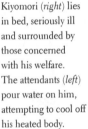

Kiyomori (*right*) lies in bed, seriously ill and surrounded by those concerned with his welfare. The attendants (*left*) pour water on him, attempting to cool off his heated body.

In earlier days the prime minister had always been brusque and forceful in manner, but now, tormented by pain, he had barely breath enough to utter these words. "Ever since the Hōgen and Heiji uprisings, I have on numerous occasions put down those who showed themselves enemies of the throne, and I have received rewards and acclaim far surpassing what I deserve. I have had the honor to become the grandfather of a reigning emperor and to hold the office of prime minister, and the bounties showered on me extend to my sons and grandsons. There is nothing more whatsoever that I could wish for in this life. Only one regret remains to me—that I have yet to behold the severed head of that exile to the province of Izu, Minamoto no Yoritomo! When I have ceased to be, erect no temples or pagodas in my honor, conduct no memorial rites for me! But dispatch forces at once to strike at Yoritomo, cut off his head, and hang it before my grave—that is all the ceremony that I ask!" Such were the deeply sinful words that he spoke!

On the fourth day of the same month, the illness continuing to torment him, Kiyomori's attendants thought to provide some slight relief by pouring water over a board and laying him on it, but this appeared to do no good whatsoever. Moaning in desperation, he fell to the floor and there suffered his final agonies. The sound of horses and carriages rushing about seemed to echo to the heavens and to make the very earth tremble. Even if the sovereign of the realm himself, the lord of ten thousand chariots, had passed away, there could not have been a greater commotion.

Kiyomori had turned sixty-four this year. He thus was not particularly advanced in age. But the life span decreed him by his actions in previous existences had abruptly come to an end. Hence the large-scale ceremonies and secret ceremonies performed on his behalf by the Buddhist priests failed to have any effect; the gods and the Three Treasures of Buddhism[3] ceased to shed their light on him; and the benevolent deities withdrew their guardianship.

And if even divine help was beyond his reach, how little could mere human beings do! Although tens of thousands of loyal troops stationed themselves inside his mansion and in the grounds around it, all eager to sacrifice themselves and to die in his place, they could not, even for an instant, hold at bay the deadly devil of impermanence, whose form is invisible to the eye and whose power is invincible. Kiyomori went all alone to the Shide Mountains of death, from which there is no return; alone he faced the sky on his journey over the River of Three Crossings to the land of the Yellow Springs. And when he arrived there, only the evil deeds he had committed in past days, transformed now into hell wardens, were there to greet him. All in all, it was a pitiful business.

Since further action could not be postponed, on the seventh day of the same month Kiyomori's remains were cremated at Otagi in the capital.[4] The Buddhist priest Enjitsu placed the ashes in a bag hung around his neck and journeyed with them down to the province of Settsu, where he deposited them in a grave on Sutra Island.

Kiyomori's name had been known throughout the land of Japan, and his might had set men trembling. But in the end his body was

---

3.   The Three Treasures of Buddhism are the Buddha, the Buddhist law, and the community of Buddhist priests.
4.   Otagi is a famous crematorium and cemetery in the eastern part of Kyoto.

no more than a puff of smoke ascending in the sky above the capital, and his remains, after tarrying a little while, in time mingled with the sands of the shore where they were buried, dwindling at last into empty dust.

The Taira are able to beat back a Minamoto advance but cannot press the attack into the Minamoto strongholds in the east. Several obvious signs—the death of the leader of a Taira campaign, the deaths of priests praying for Taira victory and prosperity—foreshadow defeat for the Taira. Nevertheless, Munemori, the leader of the Taira clan and commander in chief of their armies, spends his time solidifying his position in the court bureaucracy.

BOOK SEVEN

MUNEMORI (Taira): son of Kiyomori and Taira clan head.
SANEMORI (Taira): elderly warrior.
TADANORI (Taira): brother of Kiyomori.
YOSHINAKA (Minamoto): cousin of Yoritomo and leader of the anti-
   Taira forces in the north; also called Lord Kiso.

*The Taira summon warriors from all the provinces, but those who gather
are mainly from the west. This army goes north to attack Yoshinaka and
his troops. Yoshinaka traps and crushes the Taira army at both Kurikara
Valley and Shinohara. Sanemori, an elderly Taira vassal, had pledged to
die fighting during the battle at Shinohara.*

Sanemori (7:8)

Although all his fellow warriors on the Taira side had fled,
Sanemori of the province of Musashi, one lone horseman, kept
turning back again and again to engage the enemy and block their
advance.

Purposely hoping to pass as a young man, he put on armor laced
with greenish yellow leather over a battle robe of red brocade. He
wore a horned helmet and carried a sword with gilt fittings, arrows
fledged with black and white eagle feathers, and a rattan-wrapped
bow. He was seated in a gold-rimmed saddle astride a gray horse with
white markings.

Tezuka Mitsumori, one of the warriors under Lord Kiso, spotted Sanemori and, thinking he would make a worthy opponent, called out to him, "What valiant man is that who goes there? I admire you for fighting on alone when all your comrades have fled. Tell me your name!"

"And who may you be?" asked Sanemori in return.

"Tezuka Mitsumori of the province of Shinano!" came the reply.

"Then we are well matched," Sanemori answered. "With all due respect to you, however, I have reasons for not wanting to reveal my name. Come on now, Tezuka. Let's see what you can do!"

As the two men prepared to lock in combat, one of Tezuka's retainers, rushing up from behind in order to protect his lord from attack, threw himself at Sanemori.

"Ho there, little fellow! Would you presume to grapple with the bravest man in all Japan?" said Sanemori. Dragging the retainer to his side, he pressed the man's head against the pommel of his saddle, cut it off, and tossed it aside.

His retainer cut down before his eyes, Tezuka wheeled around to Sanemori's left side and, lifting up the lower fringe of his armor, struck him two blows with his short sword. As Sanemori faltered under the impact, Tezuka seized him and dragged him from his horse.

Still fierce enough in spirit, Sanemori was by this time exhausted from the battle, and moreover, he was an old man. Thus Tezuka was able to overpower him. When another of Tezuka's retainers arrived late on the scene, Tezuka ordered him to cut off Sanemori's head, and then he galloped off to show it to Lord Kiso.

"I have met up with a very strange adversary!" said Tezuka. "I took him for an ordinary samurai, but he was wearing a brocade battle robe. He might be a commanding general, I thought, but he had no troops. I asked him repeatedly to reveal his name, but he refused to do so. He spoke with an eastern accent."

"Aha," said Lord Kiso. "This must be Sanemori of Musashi. I met him once when I was visiting Kōzuke Province. I was only a boy then, and he already had flecks of gray in his hair. By now he should be completely white headed. But this man's beard and side-locks are black—something strange is going on. Higuchi Jirō is well acquainted with Sanemori; send for Higuchi!"

The moment that Higuchi Jirō laid eyes on the head, he said, "Ah, how pitiful! Yes, this is Sanemori."

"If so," said Lord Kiso, "then he must be at least seventy by now. He should be completely white haired. Why are his beard and side-locks still black?"

The tears streaming down his face, Higuchi replied, "You're right. I should have explained about that, but I was so touched by the sight that before I knew it these tears overcame me. Even on less than momentous occasions, a man of arms should be able to say some-thing worth remembering. And Sanemori could do that, because I recall how he always used to tell me, 'If you're over sixty when you go into battle, you should dye your beard and sidelocks black so you'll look like a younger man. It may be childish to try to compete with the young ones to be the first to attack, but at least you won't be treated with contempt just because you're old!' So I'm sure he must have dyed his beard and sidelocks. Wash them and see."

"You may be right," said Lord Kiso. And when he had the beard and sidelocks washed, they did indeed turn out to be white.

As to the fact that Sanemori was dressed in a brocade battle robe, when he took his final leave of the Taira leader, Lord Munemori, in the capital, he stated, "Last year when we rode east to attack the Genji, I did not shoot a single arrow. So timid I was that I shied at the sound of a water bird taking wing. And then with the others I fled back to the capital from Kanbara in Suruga Province. I was not the only one who did so, and yet I regret it deeply as a shameful blot on my old age. Now that we are setting out to attack the northern prov-inces, I am determined to die in battle.

"I originally was a native of the province of Echizen in the north. In later years, because a domain was bestowed on me there, I had occasion to live in Nagai in Musashi Province. The old saying has it that when you return to your native land, you should do so wear-ing brocade.[1] So I would like permission to wear a battle robe of brocade."

"Nobly spoken!" said Munemori. And thus, we are told, he gave Sanemori permission to wear brocade.

In ancient times Zhu Maichen in China brandished his brocade sleeves in triumph when he returned to his home at Mount Kuaiji. And in our own time Sanemori has won renown for himself among the populace of the northern provinces. But how sad to reflect that

---

1.   This is an allusion to the *Shiji* (*Records of the Historian*).

imperishable as his fame may be, he himself is now no more than an empty name, his mortal remains gone to dust by the roadside to Echizen!

On the seventeenth day of the Fourth Month, when a hundred thousand or more Heike horsemen rode out from the capital, one might have supposed that no one could stand up against them. And yet now when they returned in the latter part of the Fifth Month, they had been reduced to slightly more than twenty thousand!

Try to catch all the fish in the stream and you'll get plenty of fish this year, but no fish next year. Burn down the whole forest and you may shoot lots of game this year, but none the year after. As some people have pointed out, it is not wise to use up all your resources at one time.

Having crushed the Taira, Yoshinaka heads for the capital. Not knowing that Yoshinaka has already enlisted the help of the temple at Mount Hiei, the Taira petition the temple for help, only to be turned down. The Taira are then forced to flee west with Emperor Antoku and the three imperial regalia. Retired Emperor GoShirakawa also flees from the city but in a different direction.

Tadanori Leaves the Capital (7:16)

Taira no Tadanori, the governor of Satsuma, returned once more to the capital, although where he had been in the meantime is uncertain. Accompanied by five mounted warriors and a page, a party of seven horsemen in all, he rode along Gojō Avenue to the residence of Fujiwara no Shunzei.[2] The gate of Shunzei's mansion was closed and showed little sign of opening.

When Tadanori announced his name, there was a bustle inside the gate, and voices called out, "Those men who fled from the city have come back!" Tadanori dismounted from his horse and spoke in a loud voice. "There is no cause for alarm. I have come back merely because I have something I would like to say to His Lordship. You need not open the gate—if you could just have him come here a moment. . . ."

---

2.   Fujiwara no Shunzei (1114–1204) was a famous poet, scholar, and judge of *waka* contests.

"I was expecting this," said Shunzei. "I'm sure he won't make any trouble—let him in."

The gate was opened and Shunzei confronted his caller, whose whole bearing conveyed an air of melancholy.

"You have been good enough to give me instruction for some years," said Tadanori, "and I hope I have not been entirely unworthy of your kindness. But the disturbances in the capital in the last two or three years and the uprisings in the provinces have deeply affected all the members of my clan. Although I have not intended in any way to neglect my poetry studies, I fear I have not been as attentive to you as I should have been.

"The emperor has already left the capital, and the fortunes of my family appear to have run out. I heard some time ago that you were going to compile an anthology of poetry at the request of the retired emperor. I had hoped that, if you would be so kind as to give your assent, I might have perhaps one poem included in it in fulfillment of my lifelong hopes. But then these disorders descended on the world and the matter of the anthology had to be put aside, a fact that grieves me deeply.

"Should the state of the world become somewhat more settled, perhaps work on the anthology can be begun. I have here a scroll of poems. If in your kindness you could find even one of them to be worthy of inclusion, I will continue to rejoice long after I have gone to my grave and will forever be your guardian in the world beyond."

Reaching through the opening in his armor, Tadanori took out a scroll of poems and presented it to Lord Shunzei. From among the poems he had composed in recent years, he had selected some hundred or so that he thought were of superior quality and had brought them with him now that he was about to take final leave of the capital.

As Shunzei opened the scroll and looked at it, he said, "Since you see fit to leave me with this precious memento of your work, you may rest assured that I will not treat it lightly. Please have no doubts on that score. And that you should present it to me now, as a token of your deep concern for the art of poetry, makes the gesture more moving than ever—so much so that I can scarcely hold back the tears!"

Overjoyed at this response, Tadanori replied, "Perhaps I will find rest beneath the waves of the western ocean; perhaps my bones will be left to bleach on the mountain plain. Whatever may come, I can now take leave of this uncertain world without the least regret. And so I say good-bye!"

With these words he mounted his horse, knotted the cords of his helmet, and rode off toward the west. Shunzei stood gazing after until the figure had receded far into the distance. And then it seemed that he could hear Tadanori reciting in a voice loud enough to be heard from afar:

> Long is the journey before me—my thoughts race
> with the evening clouds over Wild Goose Mountain.

Deeply grieved at the parting, Shunzei wiped back the tears as he turned to reenter his house.

Later, after peace had been restored and Shunzei had begun compiling the anthology known as the *Senzaishū* [*The Collection of a Thousand Years*],[3] he recalled with deep emotion his farewell meeting with Tadanori and the words that the latter had spoken on that occasion. Among the poems that Tadanori had left behind were several that might have been included in the anthology. But since the anthology was being compiled by imperial command, Shunzei did not feel that he could refer to Tadanori by name. Instead, he selected one poem entitled "Blossoms in the Old Capital" and included it with the notation "author unknown." The poem read:

> In ruins now, the old capital of Shiga by the waves,
> yet the wild cherries of Nagara still bloom as before.

Because Tadanori was among those branded as enemies of the sovereign, perhaps less might have been said about him. And yet there is great pathos in his story.

The Flight from Fukuhara (7:20)

Palace Minister Munemori and the other Heike leaders, with the exception of Lord Koremori, took their wives and children with them

---

3. *Senzaishū* (1187) is the seventh imperial waka collection, edited by Shunzei.

when they left the capital. But for persons of less exalted station, such a course of action was impossible. They had to leave behind all their loved ones, never knowing when they might meet again. Even when the time of reunion is fixed, when promises have been made to return on such-and-such a day, at such-and-such an hour, how long is the interval of waiting! How much harder was it, then, for these people, this day their last together, the hour of parting even now at hand—little wonder that those departing and those left behind alike should wet their sleeves with tears.

Some followed the Heike leaders because they recalled how for generations their families had served under them, others because they could not forget great kindnesses bestowed in more recent years or days. But whether young or old, now they had nothing but backward glances, barely able to tear themselves away. Some would go to spend their days on distant sea paths or sleep by wave-lapped beaches, others to journey far afield over steep mountain passes, whipping their horses onward, manning the rudders of their boats, each with his own thoughts, his own memories as he made his way in flight.

When Palace Minister Munemori arrived at Fukuhara, the site of the former capital, he summoned the more important samurai who served under him, several hundred men both young and old, and addressed them as follows: "Blessings imparted to us through good deeds piled up in the past have now run out; misfortunes born of accumulated evil press down on us. And so the gods have turned against us, and the retired emperor has cast us aside. We have left the imperial city and now are travelers on the highway, with nowhere to turn.

"But they say that even those who lodge for one night beneath the same tree are bound by karma from a former existence and that those who dip water from the same stream do so because of deep ties from other lifetimes. And how much deeper are the ties in our case! You are no mere one-day sojourners at our gate but retainers who have served our family for generation after generation. Ties of kinship link some of us, making us anything but strangers; generations of service in other cases have forged profound bonds between us. The prosperity of our clan in past times brought wave after wave of bounty to you, enabling you to fulfill your personal needs. Now, should you not consider how best to repay that debt of gratitude? The emperor, who gained his throne through observance of the Ten Good Precepts[4] in a previous existence, has departed from the capital, taking with him the three imperial regalia.[5] Wherever he may venture, to whatever faraway wilderness, to whatever remote mountain recess, should we not wait for and attend him?"

The warriors, young and old alike in tears, replied, "Even lowly birds and beasts know how to repay a debt of kindness and show gratitude to those who have favored them. Why, then, should we, who are human beings, not be aware of what duty demands? For twenty years and more you have looked after our wives and children and tended to the wants of your followers—we owe everything to our lord's beneficence. Moreover, we are fighting men, bearers of arms, trained to life in the saddle—would we not count it a disgrace to be double-hearted? Therefore, wherever the ruler may go, be it beyond Japan to the lands of Silla or Paekche, Koguryo, or Pohai,[6] to the end of the clouds or the end of the sea, we will never cease to attend him!"

In different voices but speaking with one intent, they made their declaration, and all the Heike lords seemed heartened by their response.

The Heike spent one night at Fukuhara, their former home. It was the beginning of autumn and the moon was a waning crescent. In the late hours of the night, when the moon had set, all was quiet, and in the travelers' beds, mere makeshifts of grass, tears mingled with the dew, for everything around them moved them to sadness.

Not knowing when they might return here again, they gazed about them at the various spots where the late prime minister Kiyomori had built his capital.

For spring there had been the Flower-Viewing Knoll, for autumn, the Moon-Viewing Strand. The Hall of the Bubbling Spring, the Pine-Shaded Hall, the Riding Ground Hall, the two-story Viewing Stand Hall, the Snow-Viewing Palace, the Reed-Thatched Palace, the mansions of the nobles, the Temporary Imperial Palace built on orders from Lord Kunitsuna—their roof tiles in the shape of mandarin ducks, their terraces of precious stone—all had in the course of three years fallen into ruin. Old moss covered the pathways, autumn grasses

---

4. The Ten Good Precepts are the avoidance of killing, stealing, adultery, lying, duplicitous language, slandering, equivocating, coveting, anger, and false views.
5. The regalia are a sword, a mirror, and a curved jewel.
6. These all are places in what is now Korea and northeastern China.

blocked the gates. Pine seedlings sprouted from the roof tiles, vines had overgrown the walls. Tall buildings leaned to one side, encrusted with moss; only pine winds passed there now. Window blinds had rotted away, leaving the sleeping rooms exposed to view, but only the moon looked in.

When dawn came, the Heike set fire to the imperial palace at Fukuhara, and Emperor Antoku and those accompanying him all took to the boats. Even though their departure was perhaps not as painful as that when they left the capital, it nevertheless filled them with regret.

The evening smoke rising up from the seaweed fires of the fisherfolk, the dawn cries of deer on the hillcrest, the sound of the waves washing ashore in cove after cove, the moon reflected in the tears on their sleeves, the crickets chirping in a thousand autumn grasses—all that they saw, all that they heard seemed to overwhelm them with feeling, leaving nothing that did not wound their spirits.

The more than one hundred thousand horsemen who only yesterday had set out bridle to bridle from the foot of Ausaka Barrier today

After staying overnight at Fukuhara, the Heike set fire to the palace (*right*) and prepare to depart for Kyushu by boat (*left*).

were a mere seven thousand souls casting off their mooring lines amid the waves of the western ocean. The cloud-strewn sea was calm and still now, the bright day drawing to a close. The lone islands were veiled in evening mist, and the moon's rays floated on the water.

Cleaving the waves of distant inlets, drawn on by sea tides as they sped forward, the boats seemed to mount the clouds in mid-sky. By now the capital was even farther away than the clouds, so many were the mountains and rivers that had come between. "What a long way we've journeyed!" they thought, and there was no end to their tears.

Spying a flock of white birds resting on the waves, they exclaimed, "Ah yes! Ariwara no Narihira saw birds like these on the Sumida River and asked what they were called." They were called "capital birds," a name to stir sad memories in all who heard it.[7]

The Heike departed from the capital on the twenty-fifth day of the Seventh Month, in the second year of the Juei era [1183].

7.   This is an allusion to *The Tales of Ise*, sec. 9.

BOOK EIGHT

Retired Emperor GoShirakawa chooses his fourth son to be the new crown prince and installs him as emperor, a rival to the Taira's sovereign, Antoku. No longer able to muster an army, the Taira are forced to take to the sea. Yoritomo is appointed shogun by Emperor GoShirakawa and subsequently requests an order to subjugate Yoshinaka, whose men have been plundering the capital. After Yoshinaka commits other excesses, Yoritomo is given permission to move against him and sends an army westward under the command of his brother Yoshitsune.

BOOK NINE

Yoshitsune's punitive army arrives just as Yoshinaka's forces are at their weakest. Yoshinaka tries to set up defensive positions at Seta and Uji, outside the capital, but Yoshitsune is able to enter the capital and rescue Emperor GoShirakawa. Yoshinaka, who had earlier entered the capital with fifty thousand warriors, is forced to flee on horseback with six other riders.

The Death of Lord Kiso (9:4)

Lord Kiso had brought with him from Shinano two women attendants, Tomoe and Yamabuki. Yamabuki had remained in the capital because of illness. Of these two, Tomoe, fair complexioned and with long hair, was of exceptional beauty. As a fighter she was a match for a thousand ordinary men, skilled in arms, able to bend the stoutest bow, on horseback or on foot, ever ready with her sword to confront any devil or god that came her way. She could manage the most unruly horse and gallop down the steepest slopes. Lord Kiso sent her into battle clad in finely meshed armor and equipped with a sword of unusual size and a powerful bow, depending on her to perform as one of his leading commanders. Again and again she emerged unrivaled in feats of valor. And this time too, even though so many of Lord Kiso's other riders had fled from his side or been struck down, Tomoe was among the six who remained with him.

Certain reports claimed that Yoshinaka was heading toward Tanba by way of Long Slope; others, that he had crossed over Ryūge Pass and was proceeding to the northern provinces. In fact he was fleeing west toward Seta, anxious to discover where Imai Kanehira and his men were. Meanwhile, Imai had been defending his position at Seta with the eight hundred or more men under him. But when his forces had been reduced by fighting to a mere fifty riders, he furled his banners and started back toward the capital, thinking that his superior in command, Yoshinaka, must be wondering about him. In Ōtsu, at a place on the Lake Biwa shore called Uchide, he met up with Lord Kiso as the latter was headed west.

While still some distance apart, Lord Kiso and Imai recognized each other and spurred their horses forward in anticipation of the meeting. Seizing Imai's hand, Lord Kiso exclaimed, "I had intended to die in the fighting in the riverbed at Rokujō, but I wanted so much to find out what had become of you. That's why I dodged my way through all those enemy troops and slipped off so I could come here!"

"Your words do me great honor," replied Imai. "I, too, had fully expected to die in the encounter at Seta, but I hastened here in hopes of finding out how you were faring."

"The bonds that link us have not come to an end yet!" said Lord Kiso. "My own forces have been broken up and scattered by the enemy, but they have most likely taken shelter in the hills and woods hereabouts and are still in the vicinity. Unfurl those banners you are carrying and raise them high!"

When Imai hoisted the banners, more than three hundred friendly horsemen, spotting them, gathered around, some having escaped from the capital, others from the troops that had fled from Seta.

Yoshinaka was overjoyed. "With a force this size, there's no reason we can't fight one last battle!" he said. "Whose men are those I see massed there in the distance?"

"I believe they're under the command of Lord Ichijō Tadayori of Kai."

"How many men would you say there are?"

"Some six thousand or more, I would judge."

"They will make an excellent opponent. If we are to die in any case, let's confront a worthy foe and meet death in the midst of a great army!" With these words, he spurred his horse forward.

That day Yoshinaka was wearing a red brocade battle robe and a suit of finely laced armor. He had a horned helmet on his head and carried a sword of forbidding size. On his back was a quiver containing the arrows left from the day's fighting, fledged with eagle tail-feathers, their tips projecting above his head, and in his hand he grasped a bow bound with rattan. He rode his famed horse Oniashige or Demon Roan, a powerful beast of brawny build, and was seated in a gold-rimmed saddle.

Raising himself up in his stirrups, he called out his name in a loud voice. "From times past you've heard of him: Kiso no Kanja. Now take a look at him! Minamoto no Yoshinaka, director of the Imperial Stables of the Left, governor of Iyo, the Rising Sun Commander! And you, I hear, are Ichijō of Kai. We are well matched. Come attack me and show that man in Kamakura—Yoritomo—what you can do!" Shouting these words, he galloped forward.

Ichijō of Kai addressed his troops. "The one who just spoke is the commander. Don't let him get away, men! After him, you young fellows! Attack!" Vastly superior in number, Ichijō's troops surrounded Yoshinaka, each man eager to be the first to get at him.

Encircled by more than six thousand enemy horsemen, Yoshinaka's three hundred galloped forward and backward, left and right, employing the spider-leg formation and the cross-formation in their efforts to escape from the circle. When they finally succeeded in breaking through to the rear, only fifty of them were left.

Free at last, they then found their path blocked by more than two thousand horsemen under the command of Toi no Jirō Sanehira. Battling their way through them, they confronted four or five hundred of the enemy here, two or three hundred there, a hundred and fifty in another place, a hundred in still another, dashing this way and that until only five riders, Yoshinaka and four of his followers, remained. Tomoe, still uninjured, was among the five.

Lord Kiso turned to her. "Hurry, hurry now! You're a woman—go away, anywhere you like!" he said. "I intend to die in the fighting. And if it looks as though I'm about to be captured, I'll take my own life. But I wouldn't want it said that Lord Kiso fought his last battle in the company of a woman!"

But Tomoe did not move. When Lord Kiso continued to press her, she thought to herself, "Ah! If only I had a worthy opponent so I could show him one last time what I can do in battle!"

While she was hesitating, they encountered thirty horsemen under the command of Onda no Moroshige, a warrior of the province of Musashi who was renowned for his strength. Tomoe charged into the midst of Onda's men, drew her horse up beside his, and, abruptly dragging him from his seat, pressed his head against the pommel of her saddle. After holding him motionless for a moment, she wrenched off his head and threw it away. Then she threw off her helmet and armor and fled somewhere in the direction of the eastern provinces.

Of the other remaining horsemen, Tezuka Tarō was killed in the combat and Tezuka no Bettō fled. Only two men, Lord Kiso and Imai, remained.

"Up until now I never gave a thought to my armor, but today it seems strangely heavy!" said Lord Kiso.

"You can't be tired yet, my lord," said Imai, "and your horse is in good shape. A few pounds of choice armor could not weigh on you that heavily. It's just that your spirits are flagging because we have so few men left. You still have me, though, and you should think of me as a thousand men. I still have seven or eight arrows, and I'll use them to keep the enemy at bay. Those trees you see there in the distance are the pine groves of Awazu. Go over among those trees and make an end of things!"

As they spurred their horses onward, they spied a new group of some fifty mounted warriors heading toward them. "Hurry over to that grove of pines! I'll hold off these men!" he repeated.

"I ought to have died in the fighting in the capital," said Lord Kiso, "but I've come this far because I wanted to die with you. Rather than dying one here and the other there, it's better that we die together!"

When Lord Kiso insisted on galloping at his side, Imai leaped to ie ground, seized the bit of Lord Kiso's horse, and declared, "No matter how fine a name a warrior may make for himself at most times, if he should slip up at the last, it could mean an everlasting blot on his honor. You are tired and we have no more men to fight with us. Suppose we become separated in combat and you are surrounded and cut down by a mere retainer, a person of no worth at all! How terrible if people were to say, 'Lord Kiso, famous throughout the whole of Japan—done in by so-and-so's retainer!' You must hurry to that grove of pines!"

"If it must be—" said Lord Kiso, and he turned his horse in the direction of the Awazu pines.

Imai, alone, charged into the midst of the fifty enemy horsemen. Rising up in his stirrups, he shouted in a loud voice, "Up to now you've heard reports of me—now take a look with your own eyes! Imai no Shirō Kanehira, foster brother of Lord Kiso, thirty-three years of age. Even the lord of Kamakura has heard of me. Come cut me down and show him my head!"

Then, fitting his eight remaining arrows to his bow in rapid succession, he sent them flying. With no thought for his own safety, he proceeded to shoot down eight of the enemy riders. Then, drawing his sword, he charged now this way, now that, felling all who came within reach of his weapon, so that no one dared to face him. He took many trophies in the process. His attackers encircled him with cries of "Shoot him! Shoot him!" But although the arrows fell like rain, they could not pierce his stout armor or find any opening to get through, and so he remained uninjured.

Meanwhile, Lord Kiso galloped off alone toward the Awazu pine grove. It was the twenty-first day of the first lunar month, and evening was approaching. The winter rice paddies were covered with a thin layer of ice, and Lord Kiso, unaware of how deep the water was, allowed his horse to stumble into one of them. In no time the horse had sunk into the mud until its head could not be seen. He dug in with his stirrups again and again, laid on lash after lash with his whip, but could not get the animal to move.

Wondering what had become of Imai, he turned to look behind him, when one of the enemy riders who had been pursuing him, Ishida Tamehisa of Miura, drew his bow far back and shot an arrow that pierced the area of Lord Kiso's face unprotected by his helmet. Mortally wounded, he slumped forward, the bowl of his helmet resting on the horse's head, whereupon two of Ishida's retainers fell on

him and cut off his head. Ishida impaled the head on the tip of his sword and, raising it high in the air, shouted, "Lord Kiso, famed these days throughout all of Japan, has been killed by Ishida no Jirō Tamehisa of Miura!"

Although Imai had continued to battle the enemy, when he heard this, he asked, "Who is left now to go on fighting for? You lords of the eastern provinces, I'll show you how the bravest man in all Japan takes his life!" Then he thrust the tip of his sword into his mouth and flung himself down from his horse in such a way that the sword passed through his body, and so he died. Thus there was no real battle at Awazu.

As the Genji fight among themselves, the Taira return to the old capital at Fukuhara and establish a stronghold at Ichi-no-tani near the shore (of what is now the city of Kobe), protected to the north by steep mountains and to the south by the Inland Sea. Yoshitsune prepares to attack, but the Taira's position at Ichi-no-tani seems impervious to a direct assault.

Lord Kiso's horse (*left*)
is caught in a frozen
field, where Kiso is
shot down by Ishida.
When Kanehira (*right*)
hears of his death,
he places a sword in
his mouth and kills
himself.

The Old Horse (9:9)

Palace Minister Munemori dispatched Yoshiyuki of Aki as his spokes-man to the other Heike lords with this message: "Word has come that Yoshitsune has attacked and overcome our forces at Mikusa and is pushing his way into the Ichi-no-tani area. It is imperative that the mountain approach be defended. All of you will favor me by pro-ceeding there!" But the Taira lords unanimously declined to heed his request.

Munemori then approached Noritsune, the governor of Noto. "I hesitate to keep turning to you for help, but will you be good enough to go to the mountain area?"

Noritsune replied, "Military actions go well only when you think of nothing else. If you go about it as you would in hunting or fishing, looking for a comfortable spot, trying to avoid a position that is in any way unfavorable, you will never win the battle. You may request my help as often as you like—I am quite willing to take on a difficult assignment. And in my sector at least, I will defeat the enemy—you may rest assured of that!"

Highly pleased with the confident tone of this reply, Munemori sent Noritsune a force of more than ten thousand riders headed by Etchū no Zenji Moritoshi. Moritoshi's elder brother Michimori, the governor of Echizen, joined the expedition, and together they went to strengthen the Heike defenses in the mountain region. By the mountain region is meant the foothills in the region of Hiyodori Pass.

Michimori sent for his wife and had her brought to Noritsune's encampment so he could say good-bye to her. Noritsune, greatly angered by this, observed, "This is a crucial position and I have been sent to guard it. Our situation here is extremely precarious. At any moment the Genji could swoop down on us from the hilltops, and if that happens there'll be no time for preparations. If you grab a bow it will be useless if you don't have time to fit an arrow to it; if you fit an arrow, it won't do any good if you have no time to draw the bow. And how much worse if you go about things in the leisurely way that you are doing! You'll be no use to us at all!"

Michimori evidently realized that Noritsune's censures were reasonable, for he quickly began arming himself properly and had his wife sent away.

Around evening of the fifth day, the Genji left their camp at Koyano and began slowly advancing in the direction of the Heike encampment at Ikuta-no-mori. Watching from their position toward Suzume-no-matsubara, Mikage-no-mori, and Koyano, the Heike could see the Genji confidently building camps here and there and setting beacon fires. As the night advanced, the fires glowed like the moon rising from behind the hills. "In that case, we'll build beacon fires, too!" said the Heike, and they began to light fires of their own in Ikuta-no-mori. As the night came to a close, the fires shone like stars in the gradually brightening sky. The onlookers understood then what the poet had in mind when he spoke of distant fires resembling fireflies on the riverbank.[1]

---

1.   An allusion to a poem by Ariwara no Narihira in *The Tales of Ise*, sec. 87.

The Genji went about their business is an unhurried manner, resting their horses in a camp set up here, feeding their horses fodder in a camp set up there. But the Heike were anxious and ill at ease, anticipating an attack at any moment.

At dawn on the sixth day, Yoshitsune divided his ten thousand horsemen into two parties, placing seven thousand of them under the command of Toi Sanehira and sending them off to attack Ichi-no-tani from the west. He himself took the remaining three thousand and went around by way of the Tanba road, intending to attack from the rear in the area of Hiyodori Pass.

"That area is a notoriously bad spot!" his men grumbled. "We are willing enough to die fighting the enemy, but nobody wants to get killed by falling down a cliff! Isn't there someone who knows these mountains and can guide us?"

Hirayama Sueshige of the province of Musashi came forward and announced, "I'll be your guide!"

"You're from the eastern provinces," said Yoshitsune. "How could you know anything about these western mountains when you've only set eyes on them for the first time today!"

"I'm not sure I agree with that," Sueshige replied. "Poets know all about the cherry blossoms at Yoshino or Hatsuse, whether or not they've been there. And a brave man knows well enough how to come up from behind on an enemy stronghold!" He did not seem to care how brash his words sounded.

Next to come forward was Beppu no Kotarō, also from Musashi, a young man of eighteen. "My father, the monk Yoshishige, used to tell me, 'Whether you're pursued by an enemy or hunting in the passes, if you lose your way deep in the mountains, toss the reins over the back of an old horse and drive him ahead of you. He's sure to find the way out!'"

"Well spoken!" said Yoshitsune. "An old horse knows the way even when the fields are blanketed with snow—there've been cases to prove it." He accordingly gave orders that an old roan with white markings be fitted with a gold-trimmed saddle and white-polished bit. The reins were then thrown over its back, and it was driven ahead to lead the party through the unknown depths of the mountains.

It was the beginning of the Second Month, and patches of snow lingered on the peaks, looking like white blossoms in the distance. At times the party was visited by bush warblers from the valleys; at other times they lost their way in mist. Climbing up, they found themselves among gleaming peaks that soared into the white clouds; descending, they came on green wooded hills with craggy cliffs that dropped off steeply. Even the snow on pine tops had yet to melt, and moss all but buried the few faint trails. When storm winds blew, one might have taken the snow flakes for plum blossoms.[2]

Flailing whips to left and right and urging their mounts onward, the men, finding that evening had overtaken them on the mountain path, dismounted and made camp for the night.

Musashibō Benkei appeared with an old man in tow. "Who is this?" asked Yoshitsune.

"A hunter who lives in these mountains," Benkei replied.

"Then he must know the region. Have him tell us what he knows!"

"Why would I *not* know the area?" said the old man.

"We are on our way to attack the Heike stronghold at Ichi-no-tani."

"You will never get there!" said the old man. "There are three-hundred-foot gorges, cliffs jutting out more than a hundred feet, and places a man on foot can't even get by, much less men on horses! What's more, the Heike have dug pits and set up spiked barricades—you'd have to deal with them as well!"

"Can deer make their way through these places you speak of?"

"Yes, deer can get through. As soon as the weather warms up, the deer from Harima go north to Tanba to bed down in the deep grass. And when it gets cold, the Tanba deer cross over to Inamino in Harima where there's less snow and it's easy to forage."

"Then there's our riding path!" said Yoshitsune. "If deer can get through, there's no reason horses can't! Hurry and show us the way!"

"I'm afraid it's too much for an old man like me."

"You must have a son, don't you?"

"I do," replied the old man, and brought forward a boy of eighteen named Kumaō. Yoshitsune immediately had the boy's hair put up in manly fashion and, since the father's name was Washio no Takehisa, gave him the name Washio no Yoshihisa and ordered him to take the lead and guide the party through the mountains.

Years later, after the Heike had been defeated and Yoshitsune had a falling-out with his brother Yoritomo and was attacked in the

---

2.   All the natural images mentioned are associated in Japanese poetry with early spring.

region of Ōshū, this same Washio no Yoshihisa was among the warriors who died at his side.

Several Minamoto warriors attempt to be the first to enter the Taira's main defenses on the shore. One of the first to do so is Kumagae Naozane, who withdraws when his son Kojirō is wounded. Later, a large Minamoto force attacks the Taira positions to the east but is beaten back.

The Attack from the Cliff (9:12)

After this, the other Genji warriors charged into the fray, the Chichibu, the Ashikaga, the Miura, the Kamakura, and the Inomata, Kodama, Noiyo, Yokoyama, Nishitō, Tsuzukitō, and Shinotō leagues, until all the Genji and Heike forces had closed in combat. The two sides repeatedly dashed into each other's ranks, calling out their names back and forth, shouting and clamoring until the hills resounded with their cries, the din of their charging horses echoing like thunder. The arrows whizzing back and forth resembled nothing so much as torrents of rain. Some warriors, a wounded comrade on their backs, struggled to make their way toward the rear; others, despite being wounded, continued to fight while the mortally wounded fell dead where they were. Men rode side by side, grappling together and slashing at each other until one delivered a fatal stab to the other. Some held their foe down while they cut off his head; others, pinned down, had their heads lopped off in a like manner. Neither side revealed any weakness that its attackers could turn to advantage, and the Genji forces through their frontal attack alone did not seem to be able to gain victory.

Meanwhile, Yoshitsune had circled around to the rear and by dawn of the seventh day had climbed up to the region of Hiyodori Pass, preparing to swoop down on the Heike position at Ichi-no-tani. Just then, two stags and a doe, perhaps startled by the Genji horsemen, fled downhill in the direction of the Heike stronghold at Ichi-no-tani.

Catching sight of them, the Heike soldiers in the fort below exclaimed excitedly, "All the deer around here must have been so frightened of us that they fled far off into the mountains. That these deer would deliberately come toward a large force like ours seems highly peculiar! It must mean that the Genji are getting ready to charge down on us from above!"

Takechi Kiyonori, a man from Iyo Province, came forward. "Whatever it means," he said, "if they come from the direction of the enemy, we shouldn't let them by!" and he proceeded to fell the two stags with his bow and arrows, though he let the doe get away.

"What's the good of your shooting at deer!" objected Moritoshi of Etchū. "With just one of those arrows, you could have held off ten of the enemy. Killing is a sin to begin with, and then you waste arrows!" he grumbled.

Yoshitsune looked down over the Heike stronghold in the distance. "Try sending some of the horses down," he ordered. A few of the saddled horses were accordingly sent galloping down the slope. Some broke their legs and fell along the way, but others managed to reach the bottom without mishap. Three of them pulled up near the roof of Etchū Moritoshi's encampment and stood there trembling with fright.

Observing this, Yoshitsune announced, "If the riders are careful enough, the horses can get down without injury. Look lively, now—I'll show you how it's done!" Leading a force of thirty horsemen, he plummeted down the slope. The rest of the force followed, the incline so steep that the stirrups of the men in the rear clattered against the armor and helmets of those ahead of them. The ground was sandy, with scatterings of small rocks and stones, so that the riders fairly slid down for a distance of some seven hundred feet until they reached a shelflike stretch that halted their fall.

Peering down below, they could see only huge moss-shrouded rocks, a sheer drop of some hundred and forty or fifty feet. No way to go back where they had come from, no way to go forward that they could see, the men were utterly baffled, exclaiming, "This is the end!"

Just then, Sawara Yoshitsura came forward. "In Miura where I come from, we think nothing of galloping day and night over places like this just to get at a bird on the wing. This is a Miura-style racecourse!" he declared and led the way by plunging down the slope. The rest of the men followed. "Ei! Ei!" they cried in muffled voices, encouraging their horses on, the descent so terrifying that they kept their eyes closed as they went down. It seemed a feat impossible for mere human beings to accomplish, instead a performance by devils or spirits.

Halfway down, they began calling out their battle cries, and as the voices of the three thousand horsemen came echoing back from the surrounding hills, they sounded like the shouts of one hundred thousand.

The men under Murakami Yasukuni began setting fires and before long had burned down all the Heike barracks and makeshift buildings. By chance, a strong wind was blowing and black smoke billowed through the air, throwing the Heike soldiers into such panic that they scrambled toward the beaches fronting the encampment, certain that in that direction lay their only hope for escape.

A number of boats were drawn up in readiness along the shore, but the fleeing troops were in such haste to board them that at times four or five hundred or even a thousand men, all fully armed, struggled to get into a single boat, impossible as that was. After advancing no more than three hundred and fifty yards from shore, three large vessels sank before the eyes of the onlookers.

Thereafter, the order went out: "Persons of rank are to be allowed aboard, underlings are not!" and swords and halberds were used to enforce it. But even after the order became known, men continued to cling to the boats that refused to take them, trying to climb aboard. As a result, a hand was cut off here, an arm severed at the elbow there, until the waters along the Ichi-no-tani shore turned crimson and the bodies floated side by side.

The Heike warrior Noritsune, the governor of Noto, had fought many battles and had never once been defeated, but what must have been his thoughts now? Mounted on his steed Usuguro, Gray Black, he fled westward. At the Akashi shore in Harima he boarded a boat and made his way across the straits to Yashima in Sanuki.

The Death of Tadanori (9:14)

Taira no Tadanori, the governor of Satsuma, served as commanding general of the western flank at the battle of Ichi-no-tani. Dressed in a battle robe of dark blue brocade and armor laced with black silk, he rode a sturdy black horse fitted with a lacquer saddle flecked with gold. Surrounded by some hundred horsemen under his command, he was retiring from the engagement in a calm and unhurried manner, halting his horse now and then to parry with one of the enemy.

Okabe no Rokuyata, a member of the Inomata group of Genji warriors, spotted Tadanori and galloped after him in pursuit, urging his horse forward with spurs and whip and shouting, "Who goes there? Declare your name!"

"I'm a friend!" replied Tadanori, but as he turned to speak, he revealed enough of his face to make it apparent that his teeth were blackened.

"Ha!" thought Rokuyata. "No one on our side looks like that! This must be one of the Taira lords." Overtaking Tadanori, he began to grapple with him. On seeing this, the hundred horsemen under Tadanori, fighting men recruited from other provinces, fled as fast as they could, not one of them coming to his aid.

"Wretch!" exclaimed Tadanori. "You should have believed me when I said I was a friend!" Brought up in Kumano, a powerful man trained to act with lightning speed, Tadanori drew his sword and struck three blows at Rokuyata, two while the latter was still seated in the saddle and a third after he had unhorsed him. The first two glanced off Rokuyata's armor and did no harm. The third pierced his face, though not with sufficient force to kill him.

Tadanori pinned his attacker to the ground and was about to cut off his head when Rokuyata's page, rushing up from behind, drew his long sword and with one blow cut off Tadanori's arm at the elbow.

Tadanori realized this was the end. "Give me time enough for ten invocations of the Buddha!" he said. Gripping Rokuyata, he flung him a bow's length to the side. Then he faced west and, in a loud voice, recited these words: "His bright light illumines the worlds in the ten directions. Without fail He gathers up all living beings who recite His name!" He had scarcely concluded his recitation when Rokuyata approached from behind and struck off his head.

Rokuyata felt that the man had died like a true commanding general, but he still did not know his name. He found a slip of paper fastened to Tadanori's quiver, however, on which was written a poem entitled "On a Journey, Lodging Beneath the Blossoms." It read:

Evening drawing on, I'll take lodging in the shade of this tree,
    and make its blossoms my host for the night.

The poem was signed "Tadanori."

Having thus learned who his opponent was, Rokuyata impaled the head on the tip of his long sword and, lifting it high up, declared in a loud voice, "You have heard much these days of this Taira lord, the governor of Satsuma—I, Okabe no Rokuyata Tadazumi, have killed him!"

When they heard Tadanori's name, the Taira and Genji warriors alike exclaimed, "What a pity! A man skilled both in arms and the practice of poetry, a true commanding general!" And there were none who did not wet their sleeve with tears.

The Capture of Shigehira (9:15)

Middle Captain Shigehira was second in command at the Heike encampment at Ikuta-no-mori, but all the men under his command had fled, leaving only Shigehira and one of his retainers.

On that day Shigehira was dressed in a battle robe of dark blue with a pattern of flocks of plovers embroidered in yellow. He wore armor with purple-shaded lacing and rode his famous horse Dōji Kage, Boy Fawn. The retainer with him was his foster brother Gotōbyōe Morinaga, who wore a battle robe of tie-dyed silk and crimson-laced armor and rode one of Shigehira's prize steeds, a cream-color horse called Yomenashi, No-Night-Eyes.[3]

As they were making their way toward the shore, the Genji warriors Kajiwara Kagesue and Shō no Takaie, spotting Shigehira as one of the enemy commanders, flailed their whips and spurred their horses forward in swift pursuit. Several escape boats were drawn up on the beach, but the enemy riders pressed forward so rapidly from behind that Shigehira and his retainer had no time to embark. Instead, they raced over the Minato and Karumo rivers, galloped onward with Hasu Pond on their right and Koma Woods on their left, rode past Itayado and Suma, and fled off toward the west.

Shigehira and Morinaga were mounted on superlative horses, and their pursuers, whose horses were by now exhausted from the strained pace, had little hope of overtaking them. As the distance between the two parties grew greater, Kajiwara, rising up in his stirrups, drew back his bow and let fly an arrow on the chance that he might manage a hit. The arrow buried itself in the haunch of Shigehira's horse.

As the horse faltered, Morinaga, fearful that he would be ordered to change mounts with his master, whipped up his horse and fled from the scene.

---

3. A horse with a white node, or "night eye," behind its front knee was believed to be able to run fast at night. Presumably, this horse could run even faster.

Looking after him, Shigehira called out, "Morinaga, what are you doing? After all those vows you made in past days, are you going to desert me?"

But Morinaga, pretending not to hear, merely ripped the red Heike badge from his armor and flung it aside, galloping away as fast as he could.

The Genji riders pressing closer, his horse weakened, and Shigehira rode into the sea, but by chance the water was so shallow at that spot that he realized it would be impossible to drown himself. Dismounting, he cut the straps of his armor, undid his shoulder cord and, slipping out of his helmet and other fittings, prepared to cut open his stomach.

Shō no Takaie, who was riding ahead of Kajiwara, spurred his mount forward with whip and stirrups and, leaping from the horse's back with all possible speed, shouted, "Don't try anything like that! From now on I'll be right beside you wherever you go!" Then he hoisted Shigehira onto his own horse and tied him tightly to the pommel of the saddle, while he himself mounted another horse and led Shigehira off in the direction of the Genji encampment.

Meanwhile, Morinaga, mounted on a superb horse noted for its stamina, was able to make a rapid getaway. Later, he took refuge with a Buddhist priest of Kumano known as the Hokkyō (Dharma Bridge) of Onaka. But after the priest's death, his widow, a nun, journeyed to the capital in connection with a lawsuit, and at that time Morinaga accompanied her. Because he was Shigehira's foster brother, people of both high and low station in the capital recognized him. "How shameless, that Morinaga!" they said, wagging their fingers in reproval. "After all the kindness he received, to refuse to die with his lord! And now, to add to the outrage, he comes here in the company of a nun!"

Even Morinaga, they say, could not help feeling a sense of shame, and he kept his face hidden behind a fan.

The Death of Atsumori (9:16)

The Heike had lost the battle. "Those Taira lords will be heading for the shore in hopes of making their getaway by boat!" thought Kumagae Naozane to himself. "Fine! I'll go look for one of their generals to grapple with!" and he turned his horse in the direction of the beach.

As he did so, he spotted a lone warrior riding into the sea, making for the boats in the offing. He was wearing a battle robe of finely woven silk embroidered in a crane design, armor of light green lacing, and a horned helmet. He carried a sword with gilt fittings and a quiver whose arrows were fledged with black and white eagle feathers and held a rattan-wound bow in his hand. He was seated in a gold-rimmed saddle, astride a gray horse with white markings.

The lone warrior's horse had swum out about two hundred feet from the shore when Kumagae, waving with his fan, called out, "Ho there, General! I see you. Don't shame yourself by showing your back to an enemy. Come back!"

The rider, acknowledging the call, turned toward the beach. As he was about to ride up out of the waves, Kumagae drew alongside and grappled with him, dragging him from his horse. Pinning him down so as to cut off his head, Kumagae pushed aside his helmet. The face he saw was that of a young man of sixteen or seventeen, lightly powdered and with blackened teeth.

Gazing at the boy's handsome face, Kumagae realized that he was just the age of his own son Kojirō, and he could not bring himself to use his sword. "Who are you? Tell me your name and I'll let you go!" he said.

"Who are you?" asked the young man.

"No one of great importance—Kumagae Naozane of the province of Musashi."

"Then there's no need for me to tell you my name," the young man replied. "I'm worthy enough to be your opponent. When you take my head, ask someone who I am—they will know all right!"

"Spoken like a true general!" thought Kumagae. "But simply killing this one man can't change defeat into victory or victory into defeat. When my son Kojirō has even a slight injury, how much I worry about him! Just think how this boy's father will grieve when he hears that he's been killed! If only I could spare him."

But as he glanced quickly behind him, he saw some fifty Genji horsemen under Toi and Kajiwara coming toward him. Fighting back the tears, he said, "I'd like to let you go, but our forces are everywhere in sight—you could never get away. Rather than fall into someone else's hands, it's better that I kill you. I'll see that prayers are said for your salvation in the life to come."

"Just take my head and be quick about it!" the boy said.

Kumagae was so overcome with pity that he did not know where to strike. His eyes seemed to dim, his wits to desert him, and for a moment he hardly knew where he was. But then he realized that, for all his tears, no choice was left him, and he struck off the boy's head.

"We men who bear arms—how wretched is our lot!" he said. "If I had not been born of a warrior family, would I ever have faced a task like this? What a terrible thing I have done!" Again and again, he repeated the words as he raised his sleeve to brush the tears from his face.

After some time, aware that he must get on with the business, he removed the boy's armor and battle robe and wrapped the head in them. As he was doing so, he noticed a brocade bag with a flute in it that had been fastened to the boy's waist. "Ah, how pitiful!" he said. "Those people I heard at dawn this morning playing music in the enemy stronghold—he must have been one of them! Among all the ten thousand troops from the eastern provinces fighting on our side, is there anyone who carries a flute with him into battle? These highborn people—how gentle and refined they are!"

Later, when Kumagae's battle trophies were presented to Yoshitsune for inspection, there were none among the company who did not weep at the sight.

It was subsequently learned that the young man slain by Kumagae was Atsumori, the seventeen-year-old son of the master of the Palace Repair Office, Taira no Tsunemori. From that time onward, Kumagae's desire to become a Buddhist monk grew even stronger. The flute in question had been presented by Retired Emperor Toba to Atsumori's grandfather, Tadamori, who was a skilled player. From him it had been passed down to the son, Tsunemori, and in turn had been given to Atsumori because of his marked aptitude for the instrument. It was known by the name Saeda, Little Branch.

It is moving to think that for all their exaggerated phrases and flowery embellishments, even music and the arts can in the end lead a man to praise the Buddha's way.

After a resounding defeat, the Taira forces scatter in their attempt to flee by sea.

BOOK TEN

HŌNEN: Buddhist priest and one of the founders of Pure Land Buddhism in Japan.

KOREMORI (Taira): son and heir of Shigemori; seeks salvation.

SHIGEHIRA (Taira): son of Kiyomori; accused of the crime of burning Nara.

TAKIGUCHI: son of a courtier; later becomes a priest at Mount Kōya.

YOKOBUE: woman of lesser birth.

In the aftermath of the battle of Ichi-no-tani, the captured commander, Shigehira, and the heads of the slain Heike are paraded in the capital. The retired emperor offers to spare Shigehira's life in exchange for the imperial treasures held by the Heike. The request is denied, and rumors persist that Shigehira will be punished for his role in burning Nara.

Regarding the Precepts (10:5)

When Middle Captain Shigehira heard the Heike response to his request, he replied, "It was only to be expected. The people of my clan must think very badly of me!" He regretted ever having made such a request, useless as regrets now were. The Heike were hardly likely to return the three imperial regalia, the sacred treasures of the nation, just to save the life of one man, Shigehira. He thus had expected an answer like this all along, although before it was delivered, he had been in a mood of anxious suspense. Now that the reply had arrived and it was certain that he would be sent to the east, he became deeply despondent, convinced that all avenues of escape had finally been cut off. The thought of parting from the capital this time was more painful than ever.

He sent for Toi no Sanehira and told him, "I am considering becoming a monk. Would that be possible?"

Sanehira reported this to Yoshitsune, who passed on the request to Retired Emperor GoShirakawa. "After he has been handed over to Yoritomo, perhaps something can be arranged," replied the retired emperor. "But it cannot be permitted at the present time."

"In that case," said Shigehira when he received word of this, "I would like to meet once more with a holy man who has been my teacher for many years so that I may discuss with him the matter of my life hereafter. Would that be possible?"

"Who is this holy man?" asked Sanehira.

"He is known as Priest Hōnen of Kurodani."

"I see no objection," said Sanehira, and gave his consent.

Overjoyed at this, Shigehira asked the holy man to visit him. Speaking through his tears, he said, "I was destined to meet with you once more—that must have been why I was taken prisoner alive! What should I do about my life in the world to come? In the past, when I was a person of some consequence, I was immersed in government affairs, tangled in official duties, my mind too often prone to pride and arrogance, so I had no time to think what fate might await me in a future life. And how much worse things have been since the fortunes of our clan ran out and we entered this era of confusion! Fighting battles here, wrangling and contending there, one finds one's mind wholly taken up with evil thoughts of how to destroy others and save one's own skin, making it impossible for goodness of heart to come forth.

"In particular, regarding the burning of Nara, I had orders from the sovereign, orders from the military, duties to the ruler, and obligations to society that I could hardly avoid. But when we went there to stop the nefarious actions of the monks, events took a totally unexpected turn that ended in the destruction of the temples. There was nothing we could do about it, and yet, since I was commander in
f at the time, I suppose it must be viewed as the evil deed of one
alone, for as the saying goes, responsibility rests with the one on
And I have come to feel that all the many humiliations I have

suffered recently, often of a nature hardly apparent to others, are nothing other than retributions for that deed.

"Now I would like to shave my head, begin observing the religious precepts, and devote myself entirely to the practice of the Buddhist way. But as you see, I am a prisoner and my mind is no longer mine to command freely. I cannot tell what fate awaits me from one day to the next. Is there some religious practice that might have the power to cancel out even one of my sinful actions?—to my great regret, I hardly know. For as I look back over my life up to now, I see that my transgressions pile up higher than Mount Sumeru and that my good deeds count for less than a handful of dust. Should the end come while I am in this hopeless state, my fate would doubtless be rebirth in one of the Three Evil Paths of hell dwellers, hungry spirits, and beasts. I therefore entreat you, holy man that you are, to show pity and compassion, and if there is some way by which an evil person such as I can find salvation, teach me what it is!"

For a while Hōnen was choked with tears and did not reply. After some time, he said, "Because you have been fortunate enough to be born in human form, a state so difficult to achieve, it is unspeakably sad to think that in your next existence you might be reborn in one of the Three Evil Paths. But since you, weary of this sordid realm we live in and longing to attain rebirth in the Pure Land, are now determined to cast aside your evil mind and cultivate a mind of goodness, the Buddhas of the past, present, and future must surely rejoice.

"There are many different ways to achieve this separation from the mundane world. But for those of us born in the Latter Day of the Law, this age of foulness and disorder, the invocation of the Buddha's name is the one most highly recommended. There are nine grades to achieve within the Pure Land, and the religious practice to be carried out consists of merely reciting the six characters that make up the *nenbutsu, Namu Amida butsu,* or 'Hail to Amida Buddha!'

"Even the most stupid person, the most dull and benighted, can benefit from this recitation. Never think yourself contemptible because your offenses are grave. Even those who have committed the Ten Evil Acts or the Five Cardinal Sins can, if their heart is truly repentant, achieve rebirth in the Pure Land. Never give up hope because you feel your meritorious acts are too few. If in your mind you perform no more than one recitation or ten recitations of the *nenbutsu,* the Buddha will come to welcome you to his land. 'Solely by reciting his name will you reach the Western region,' says the commentary by the Chinese priest Shandao. 'Moment by moment calling the name constitutes constant repentance,' Shandao teaches us, by which he means that when we invoke Amida's name moment by moment, we are performing an act of repentance. While we intone the words 'A sharp sword is Amida's name!' no devils can come near us. While we bear in mind that 'one voice reciting the *nenbutsu* banishes all sin,' all our transgressions will be expiated.

"I have tried to summarize the essential doctrines of the Pure Land sect and to concentrate on the most important points. But whether or not you actually attain rebirth in the Pure Land depends entirely on the mind of faith. Just be completely sincere in your faith and set aside all doubt! If you have deep faith in the teaching, if at all times and places, whatever the circumstances, whether walking, standing, sitting, or lying down, whether performing actions of the body, mouth, or mind, you never forget to concentrate on the *nenbutsu* and intone the sacred name, then, when your life has come to a close, you will, without the slightest doubt, leave this world of suffering and attain rebirth in a land from which you will never regress."

Shigehira listened to these instructions with great joy. "I would like to observe the Buddhist precepts," he said. "Is it possible to do so without becoming a monk?"

"It is very common for persons to observe the precepts even when they do not take formal monastic vows," replied Hōnen. He then took a razor and touched it to Shigehira's forehead, making motions as though shaving, and in this way administered to him the ten precepts for correct conduct. Weeping tears of joy, Shigehira signified that he would accept and obey them. Sensitive always to the deeper import of all things, Hōnen was momentarily quite overcome with emotion and cried as he explained the content of the precepts to Shigehira.

To signify his gratefulness, Shigehira had Tomotoki bring an inkstone that Shigehira had left at the house of a certain samurai that he had frequently visited in the past. Presenting it as an offering to Hōnen, he said, "Do not give this away, but keep it somewhere within sight, and when you recall to whom it once belonged, think that I myself am there and recite a *nenbutsu* for my sake. And if you should find time," he said through his tears, "recite a passage of scripture to aid me in my life hereafter."

The inkstone had originally been a gift from the emperor of the Song court in China, to whom Shigehira's father, Kiyomori, had sent a present of gold dust. It was inscribed with the words "To the Taira Prime Minister of Wada in Japan." It was known by the name Matsukage, Pine Shade.

> Shigehira is sent east to Kamakura to face Yoritomo. On his trip, which evokes numerous poetic places, he exchanges poetry with a courtesan at a traveler's inn.

Senju-no-mae (10:7)

Since Shigehira had been responsible for the destruction of the temples in Nara, it was only to be expected that the monks of Nara would demand that he be handed over to them so they could exact their revenge. Accordingly, he was placed in the custody of Kano no Suke Munemochi, a native of the province of Izu. His lot resembled that of a wrongdoer who, upon his death, must go before the ten kings of hell, passing from one to another every seven days and being judged for his crimes, a pitiable process indeed!

Munemochi, however, was a kind and understanding man and showed no trace of harshness or severity in his treatment of Shigehira. Among his various acts of thoughtfulness, he had a special bathing apartment prepared and invited Shigehira to bathe there. "After getting all grimy and sweaty from the journey here, I suppose they want me to clean myself up before they do away with me," thought Shigehira to himself. Just then, a young lady-in-waiting of around twenty, pale in complexion and strikingly beautiful, wearing a tie-dyed single robe and a figured bath apron, opened the door of the bathroom and slipped in. Some moments later, a maid of fourteen or fifteen wearing a blue-dyed single robe, her hair hanging down to her waist, appeared carrying a wash basin and combs. The lady-in-waiting tended to Shigehira's needs while he bathed in a leisurely manner and washed his hair.

When she was ready to take her leave, the lady said, "My master, Lord Yoritomo, sent me because he thought it might seem unmannerly to send a man when a woman might serve you better. He said that if there was anything you desired, I was to inform him of your wishes."

"Since I am now his prisoner, how could I make requests?" replied Shigehira. "My only wish at this point is to be allowed to become a monk!"

When the lady returned and reported these words to Yoritomo, he said, "That is out of the question! If he were merely a personal enemy of mine, something might be done. But he has been turned over to me as an enemy of the state. His wishes cannot possibly be granted!"

Later, Shigehira made inquiries among the warriors who were assigned to guard him. "That was a very refined young woman who waited on me just now," he said. "I wonder what her name is."

"She is the daughter of the brothel keeper of Tegoshi," they replied, "a person of quite exceptional beauty and refinement of character. She has been in his lordship's service for around two or three years now. Her name is Senju-no-mae."

When evening came and a little rain had fallen, shedding an air of melancholy over the scene, the lady-in-waiting came to Shigehira's rooms, bringing with her a *biwa* and a *koto*.[1] Munemochi ordered that rice wine be served, and accompanied by ten or more of his family members and retainers, he took a seat near Shigehira. Senju-no-mae served the wine, but Shigehira took only a sip, appearing to be in a very dispirited mood.

"I may have mentioned it before," said Munemochi, "but the lord of Kamakura has ordered me to see that all measures are taken for your comfort. If I am lax in doing so, he says he will be most angry with me! I am originally from Izu, so I am only a sojourner here in Kamakura, but I would like to do whatever I can to serve you." Then addressing Senju-no-mae, he suggested, "Sing us something before you serve more wine."

Senju-no-mae set aside the wine bottle and sang the following verses once or twice:

These sheer gauze robes are so weighty—
how could the weaving woman who made them be so heartless!

"Ah—these verses were composed by Sugawara no Michizane, the deity of the Kitano Shrine," said Shigehira. "He swore that when

1.   The *biwa* is a member of the lute family. The *koto*, or "zither," as it sometimes is translated, is a larger instrument.

anyone recited them, he would fly through the air three times in one day to protect him. But in my present existence, I have been cast aside by the god. Even if I were to join in the recitation, what good would it do? But perhaps I might do so if they were the sort of verses that could help lighten my sins."

Senju-no-mae immediately chanted the line:

> Though you commit the Ten Evil Acts, he will save you!

She followed this with a song in the *imayō* style:

> All you who long for the Pure Land,
> raise your voice in invocation of Amida's name!

After she had sung this four or five times with feeling, Shigehira finally tipped his wine cup.

Senju-no-mae then offered the cup to Munemochi. While he was drinking, she played an engaging air on the *koto*.

"That music," said Shigehira, "is usually referred to as the Five Constant Joys. But in my case, I must think of it as the Joy of the Life Hereafter. May it accompany me quickly to a favorable finale!" he said in a joking manner. Then, picking up the *biwa* and retuning it, he played the closing section of the piece called Ōjō, whose title suggests the word "rebirth."

As the night advanced, Shigehira, now calmer and his mind more at ease, declared, "I would never have expected to find persons of such refinement here in the eastern region. Perhaps you could sing us something more..."

Senju-no-mae then chanted a *shirabyōshi*-style passage in a highly intriguing and expressive fashion:

> Those who merely stop one night under the same tree,
> who merely dip the waters of the same stream—
> all are bound by ties from a past existence!

Then Shigehira recited the lines:

> The lamp grows dimmer, Lady Yu's tears stream down

The lines refer to a time long ago in China when Gaozu, the founder of the Han dynasty, and Xiang Yu battled each other for mastery of the empire. In seventy-two encounters Xiang Yu emerged victorious, but at last he was defeated. He had a horse named Dapple, so fast it could run a thousand miles in one day, and his thought was to flee on this horse with his consort, Lady Yu. But the horse—who knows why?—stood firm and refused to move. "My strength has deserted me, there is nowhere now to flee!" Xiang Yu lamented. "I care nothing for the enemy's assaults, but how it pains me to part with my Yu!"

So he grieved as the night wore on. The lamp grew dimmer, Lady Yu wept tears of despair, while from all four sides in the deepening night came the din of the enemy soldiers. Councillor Tachibana Hiromi[2] composed a poem in Chinese on the subject, which Shigehira now remembered and quoted. It was a truly apt allusion.

With the hour growing late, the warriors attending Shigehira took their leave, and Senju-no-mae returned to her quarters as well.

The next morning, as Yoritomo was reciting from the Lotus Sutra before his Buddhist altar, Senju-no-mae came to wait on him. Turning to her with a smile, he said, "I paired you up with someone very interesting last night, don't you think?"

"What happened?" asked Saiin Chikayoshi, who was sitting nearby writing something.

"I always used to think that these Heike men were ignorant of anything other than bows and arrows and battle gear," said Yoritomo. "But I stood outside for a long time last night listening to this Middle Captain Shigehira play the *biwa* and recite lines of poetry—it was a truly remarkable performance!"

"I should have been there with the others," said Chikayoshi, "but I was not feeling well. From now on, though, I'll surely be among the listeners. For generations the Taira family has been known for its poets and persons of literary talent. People used to compare the various members of the family to flowers, and they said that Shigehira was like a peony." For some time afterward, Yoritomo continued to talk of how fine Shigehira's *biwa* playing and poetry recitations had been. "A man of true refinement!" he said.

Senju-no-mae, too, found the events of that night lingering long in her memory. Later, when she heard that Shigehira had been handed

2. Tachibana Hiromi (836–890) was a scholar and courtier.

over to the monks in Nara and beheaded, she took off her customary
attire, put on the dark black robe of a nun, and devoted herself to
religious practice at the Zenkō-ji in Shinano. There she prayed that
Shigehira might attain enlightenment in the life hereafter, and she
herself, it is said, in time fulfilled her long-cherished hope for rebirth
in the Pure Land.

*The story of Koremori, the eldest son of Shigemori and the grandson of
Kiyomori, who struggles to seek salvation, is foreshadowed by that of Takiguchi, a priest at Mount Kōya, and Yokobue, a woman of lesser social status. Yokobue became a legendary figure in the Muromachi period.*

Yokobue (10:8)

Middle Captain Koremori of the Komatsu mansion was, in a physical sense, residing in the Heike headquarters at Yashima, but his
mind constantly journeyed to the capital. His wife and the young
ones he had left behind there were forever in his thoughts, their faces
alone haunting him. Not for a moment could he forget them, and to
go on living like this seemed to him utterly meaningless.

In the Third Month of the first year of the Genryaku era [1184],
at dawn on the fifteenth day, he made his way stealthily out of his
Yashima quarters. Accompanied by Yosōbyōe Shigekage, a young
boy named Ishidōmaru, and a retainer named Takesato who had
some knowledge of boats—three men only—he set out in a small
vessel from the harbor of Yūki in the province of Awa. Rowing across
the straits of Naruto, they reached the province of Kii, passing Waka,
Fukiage, the Myōjin Shrine of Tamatsushima where the goddess
Sotoorihime[3] made her divine appearance, and the shrines at Nichi-
zen and Kokuken, and thus arrived at the harbor at Ki-no-minato.

"If only I could follow these mountain paths and journey to the
capital to see my loved ones once more!" thought Koremori. "But it is
bad enough that my uncle Shigehira was taken captive and paraded
through the avenues of the capital, subjected to humiliation there
and in Kamakura. If I too were taken captive, think what ignominy
I would heap on the name of my deceased father!" Thus, while his

---

3.   Sotoorihime is one of the tutelary deities of Japanese poetry.

thoughts warred with one another, his heart hesitating a thousand times, he set off at last in the direction of Mount Kōya.

At Mount Kōya lived a holy man whom Koremori had known for many years. His name was Saitō Tokiyori, the son of Saitō Mochiyori, a courtier of Sanjō. He had originally been a samurai in service at the Komatsu mansion, but at the age of thirteen he was selected to serve in the Takiguchi guard of the imperial palace. There he fell very much in love with a young woman named Yokobue, a lesser maid-in-waiting to Empress Kenreimon'in. When his father learned about this, he berated Tokiyori angrily. "I had meant for you to marry into some influential family so you could easily pursue an official career. But instead you take up with a person of no worth!"

Tokiyori thought to himself, "The fabulous queen mother of the West may have existed long ago, but she's not here today. The immortal Dong-fang Shuo is a mere name—no one's ever laid eyes on him. In this world where neither young nor old know what fate awaits them, life is briefer than a spark from a flint. Even the long-lived seldom last more than seventy or eighty years, and of those, hardly twenty or more years are lived in good health. In this dream-like, this phantom world of ours, why should I marry someone who is ugly? But if I go on seeing the one I love, I will be disobeying my father's command. Let this dilemma, then, be a good friend for what it teaches me. Better to forsake this world of sorrow and embark on the true path of religion!" Thus at the age of nineteen he cut off his topknot and retired to the Ōjō-in cloister in Saga to devote himself entirely to the religious life.

"It was one thing for him to have abandoned me," said Yoko-bue when word of this reached her, "but to cast aside secular life altogether—how terrible! If he were planning to withdraw from the world, he at least might have told me. I will go there and show him how I resent it, no matter how cold he may be, hard as it may be for him to bear!"

One evening, therefore, she left the capital and set off uncertainly toward Saga. It was around the tenth day of the Second Month, and from somewhere the spring breeze blowing through the village of Umezu wafted the nostalgic scent of plum blossoms, while over the Ōi River the moon shone hazy and half-veiled in mist. "And whose fault is it," she thought to herself, "that I must suffer these pangs of longing!"

She had inquired about the location of the Ōjō-in but was uncertain which retreat to call at, hesitating here, pausing a moment there, perplexed as to how best to proceed. Then from a tumbledown monk's hut, she heard someone intoning the *nenbutsu* and reciting a sutra. She was sure it was Tokiyori's voice. "I have come this far," she thought. "Even though he has taken the tonsure, if I could see him just once more!" She sent the maid who had accompanied her to make inquiries.

Tokiyori's heart was in turmoil as he peered out through a gap in the sliding panel. How pitiful that she had gone to such pains to find him! Firm as he was in his dedication to the religious life, it seemed as though he might weaken. But in the end he sent a fellow monk to the door with this message: "There is no such person here. You must have the wrong place!" Yokobue was sent away without a glimpse of him. Bitter and heartless as she found this, she had no choice but to make her way back to the capital fighting back her tears.

"In a quiet and secluded spot like this I can devote myself to *nenbutsu* practice without interruption," said Tokiyori to the monk with whom he shared his lodging. "But I parted from a woman, though I still loved her, and now she has discovered my whereabouts. I had strength of mind enough to send her away once, but if she should come again, I'm afraid my resolve will falter. I had better be on my way." Thus he left Saga and went to Mount Kōya, where he took up residence in the Shōjōshin-in.

Later, when word came to him that Yokobue had entered religious life as well, Tokiyori, now known as Priest Takiguchi, sent her this poem:

Till you shaved your head, you hated me.
Now I rejoice you're launched on the path of Truth, firm as a
    catalpa bow.

Yokobue replied with this poem:

I shaved my head, but what was there to hate?
There was no blunting your keen resolve, firm as a catalpa bow.

Yokobue lived at the Hokke-ji nunnery in Nara. But perhaps because of the burden her memories imposed on her, she died not

long afterward. When Priest Takiguchi received word of this, he devoted himself with even greater zeal to his religious duties. His father forgave him for his act of disobedience; all those who knew him greatly trusted and respected him; and he came to be known as the saint of Kōya.

This was the man on whom Koremori now called at Mount Kōya. When Koremori had known him in the past in the capital, he had been dressed in an unfigured hunting robe and tall black hat, his clothing neatly arrayed, his sidelocks smoothed: a young man in the prime of life. But now that he had renounced the world, though not yet thirty, he had the lean, wizened look of a monk of advanced years and was attired in a deep-dyed black robe and surplice of the same color. Koremori could only envy someone whose heart was so fervently dedicated to the path of religion. Had he been in the bamboo grove where the Seven Sages of the Jin dynasty resided or on Mount

Yokobue (*right*) seeks
out Tokiyori at the
Ōjō-in retreat in Saga
but is turned away.
Tokiyori (*left*) goes to
Mount Kōya, where
he practices the
Buddhist way.

Shang, the retreat of the four white-haired recluses of the Han, he
could not have been more impressed.

Koremori Becomes a Monk (10:10)

"I am like the bird in the Himalayas who shivers at night, swearing
it will build a nest the next day, but forgets its resolve when morning
comes!" declared Koremori sadly, his tears falling. "I keep put-
ting off from day to day what I have in mind to do." His face tanned
by the salt sea winds, his body worn with care and anxiety, he hardly
seemed the same person he had been in former days, yet even so he
stood out above others.

    That night when he returned to the retreat where Priest Takiguchi
lived, he spent the whole night talking with the priest of old times.

Observing the holy man's activities and way of life, he could see that he was deeply immersed in the search for enlightenment, seeking through his devotions to polish the jewel of true understanding; at intervals in the night and dawn sounding the bell that accompanied his invocations, he labored to wake himself from this dream realm of birth and death. If I too should become a monk, thought Koremori, this is how I would want to be! When dawn came, he made his way to the Venerable Chikaku, a holy man residing in the Tōzen-in, and expressed a desire to become a monk.

He summoned Yosōbyōe Shigekage and Ishidōmaru, two of the men who had accompanied him from Yashima. "Unknown to others, I long to see my loved ones to a degree that others can hardly be aware of," he said, "but the world is small and I am not free to move about as I might wish. My own case is hopeless. But there are many others these days who are prospering. Whatever the circumstances you face, you will surely be able to get along somehow. Once you have seen the end of me, you must hurry back to the capital and look after your own livelihood. Take good care of your wives and children, and on occasion sometimes pray for my well-being in the life hereafter!"

The two men listened in tearful silence and for a time were unable to reply. Finally Shigekage, wiping back his tears, spoke up. "At the time of the Heiji insurrections my father, Kageyasu, was in the service of his lordship, your deceased father Shigemori. In the fighting around the Nijō Horikawa intersection, he clashed with the forces of Kamadabyōe and was struck a mortal blow by Akugenda. I, too, am capable of such service!

"At the time of my father's death I was only two, so I have no memory of the event. I lost my mother when I was seven, and after that there was no one to pity or look after me. But your late father said, 'This is the son of the man who gave his life for me!' and he took me under his care. When I was nine and you had your coming-of-age ceremony, I also was allowed to bind up my hair in similar fashion. At that time your father said, 'The name *Mori* is traditional in our family, and so I will give it to this son of mine and call him Koremori. And the name *Shige* I will give to this boy Matsuō.' That was how I came to be given the name Shigekage. And the reason I had been called Matsuō before that was because on the fiftieth day after I was born, my father took me in his arms and showed me to his lordship. Your father said, 'Since this house we live in is known as the Komatsu mansion, we will take his name from that.' And that is how I came to be called Matsuō. Thanks to my father's noble death, I was able to enjoy all these marks of favor. And I was also treated with unusual kindness by your father's retainers.

"When his lordship, your father, was on his deathbed, he had set aside all thought of worldly affairs and spoke of them no longer. But he called me to his side and said, 'Ah, poor boy! You have always looked on me as a memento of your father, and I have looked on you as a memento of him, my loyal retainer Kageyasu. At the next round of promotions I had hoped to see you raised to the rank of captain of the imperial guard so that you could be called by the same title that your father was. All those hopes are vain now. But you must never be disloyal to my son Koremori!'

"Did you think that if you found yourself in difficult circumstances, I would desert you and run away? If that was your thought, then it reflects deep dishonor on me! You speak of those many persons who prosper in the world today. But nowadays it is only the retainers of the Genji who do so. After you have become a god or a buddha or whatever you are destined to become, even though I might enjoy some degree of worldly happiness, could it go on for a thousand years? Although I might live for ten thousand years, would it not come to an end eventually? The circumstances all point to it—what better time than now to enter the religious life!" Then with his own hands he cut off his topknot and, weeping as he did so, asked Priest Takiguchi to shave his head.

Seeing this, Ishidōmaru cut off his hair at the clasp, and he too had his head shaved by Priest Takiguchi. He had been in Koremori's service from the age of eight and had enjoyed a degree of favor equal to that of Shigekage.

Seeing how these others had taken the lead in entering religious life, Koremori grew more downcast than ever. Aware that he could postpone the step no longer, however, he recited the passage that reads: "While you transmigrate within the Threefold World,[4] the bonds of familial affection can never be broken. Cast aside affection,

4. The Threefold World is the world of unenlightened beings. In turn, it is subdivided into the world of desire (whose inhabitants have appetites and desires), the world of form (whose inhabitants have neither appetites nor desires), and the world of formlessness (whose inhabitants have no physical forms).

enter the Absolute, and there gain the true fruits of affection." Chanting it over three times, he at last allowed his head to be shaved.

"How sad!" he said. "Before I shaved my head, if only I could have seen my loved ones once more as I did in the past, I would have nothing to regret!" To have said such a thing shows how immersed he still was in blameworthy thoughts! At the time these events took place, both Koremori and Shigekage were twenty-seven years old. Ishidōmaru was eighteen.

Koremori then summoned his retainer Takesato. "You must return at once to Yashima," he told him. "Do not try to go to the capital, for this reason. My wife will eventually find out about the step I have taken. But if she hears an account of it from you, whom she knows to be reliable, I am afraid she will rush to enter religious life herself.

"When you return to Yashima, give the people there this message from me. 'As you have no doubt observed already, the situation in the world today has become in every respect irksome and hateful, and I can only believe that further tribulations lie ahead. Therefore, without informing you beforehand, I have entered religious life. I realize that, following the loss of my brother Kiyotsune in the west and the death of my brother Moromori at Ichi-no-tani, the news that I have taken such an action as this will cause you considerable dismay, and that thought weighs heavily on my mind. The suit of armor known as Karakawa, Chinese Leather, and the sword called Kogarasu, Little Crow, have been handed down in our family from the time of the Taira military commander Sadamori. I am ninth in the line of those who have inherited them. If by some miracle the fortunes of our family should revive, these heirlooms should be handed over to my son Rokudai.'"

"I would like to postpone my trip to Yashima until I have seen how things go with you, my lord," said Takesato.

"If that is the case…" replied Koremori, and he retained Takesato as a member of his party. He also kept Priest Takiguchi with him so that the latter could counsel him in religious matters. Thus the group, dressed as mountain worshipers on a pilgrimage, left Mount Kōya and made their way to Sandō in the same province.

They stopped first at Fujishiro, one of the shrines on the road to Kumano, and then at the succeeding shrines, pausing to offer prayers at each. When they reached the Iwashiro Shrine just north of the beach known as Senri-no-hama, they encountered a party of seven or eight men on horseback dressed in hunting costume.

Koremori and the others of the group, fearful that they were about to be taken captive, gripped the daggers at their waist, prepared to slit open their stomachs if that should be necessary. But although the riders passed close by, they gave no indication of any hostile intent but instead hurriedly dismounted from their horses and bowed in a deeply respectful manner before riding on.

"They appear to have recognized me," thought Koremori uneasily. "Who could they be?" He quickened his pace, eager to be gone from the place.

The leader of the party of horsemen was Yuasa Munemitsu, the son of a native of the province named Yuasa Muneshige.

"Who was that?" asked Munemitsu's retainers.

Munemitsu wept as he replied, "Ah, I hesitate even to speak of it! That was none other than Middle Captain Koremori, the eldest son of the Komatsu minister of state, Shigemori! I wonder how he managed to escape from Yashima and make his way here. He has shaved his head and become a monk, and Yosōbyōe and Ishidōmaru have done likewise and are accompanying him. I would like to have gone closer to pay my respects. But I was afraid it might embarrass him, so I went on my way. What a pitiful sight he is!"

Munemitsu pressed his sleeve to his face as he spoke, shedding tears, and his retainers all did the same.

Koremori Drowns Himself (10:12)

Having completed his pilgrimage to the three sacred mountain sites of Kumano without incident, Koremori went to the seaside shrine known as Hama-no-miya, where he boarded a boat and set out on the boundless reaches of the sea. Far away in the offing was an island called Yamanari-no-shima, and he had the rowers row him there. Landing on the shore, he stripped off a piece of bark from a large pine tree and wrote his name on the trunk in the following manner: "Grandfather: Prime Minister Taira no Ason Kiyomori, religious name Jōkai. Father: Palace Minister and Major Captain of the Left Shigemori, religious name Jōren. Middle Captain of the Third Court Rank Koremori, religious name Jōen, age twenty-seven. Juei third year, Third Month, twenty-eighth day, entered the sea off the shore of Nachi." Having left this inscription, he had the boat rowed once more toward the offing.

He had made up his mind what he intended to do. But now that the time to do it had arrived, he found himself feeling downhearted and forlorn. Since it was the twenty-eighth day of the Third Month, a haze lay over the water as far as the eye could see, lending a melancholy tone to the scene. Even in the most ordinary times, the late spring sky has an air of sadness, and how much sadder it seemed to one who knew that this would be his last day to see it. As he watched a fishing boat far off bobbing and all but sinking among the waves, he could not help dwelling on the ups and downs of his own fortunes. Observing a wild goose leading a line of its companions as they flew, crying to their home in the north, he recalled how the Chinese statesman Su Wu, held captive in a barbarian land to the north, had tied a letter to the foot of a wild goose and so sent news to his loved ones back home. Su Wu's longings could hardly have been greater than his own, he thought.

"What am I doing?" he asked himself. "Will I never be free of these deluded ties and attachments?" He faced west, pressed his palms together, and invoked the name of Amida Buddha. But his mind ran on as before: "My end is at hand, but how can my loved ones in the capital be aware of that? Even now, moment by moment they are waiting for some chance word of me. In the end, of course, they will learn the truth, but what will they think then, how will they lament when they know I am no longer of this world?"

He ceased his invocations, lowered his hands, and turned to the holy man, Priest Takiguchi. "What pathetic things we are—better if we had no wives or children!" he said. "They not only fill us with longings for this world but also make it hard for us to gain enlightenment in the world beyond. Even now, much as I regret it, I keep thinking of them. And they say that it is a great sin to have such thoughts at a time like this! I confess my guilt—I am much to blame."

The priest was deeply moved, but he felt that it would not do if he, too, gave way to weakness at such a moment. And so, holding back his tears, he assumed an air of composure. "It is just as you say," he replied. "When it comes to powerlessness before the ties of love and affection, we all are alike, whether highborn or low. Even though husband and wife may share a pillow for no more than a single night, the bonds of karma that link them reach back five hundred lifetimes in the past, and vows from a former existence are not easily undone. But all who are born must perish, and all who come together must surely part—such is the law of this fleeting life of ours. The dewdrop on the leaf tip and the dew on the stalk of the plant—one may go quickly, one linger a little longer, yet in the end both alike must fade.

"At the Mount Li Palace in China, Emperor Xuanzong and his consort Yang Guifei swore by the stars of the autumn evening to be true forever, but their vows brought them only pain and heartache. At the Palace of Sweet Springs, Emperor Wu went on yearning for his beloved, the deceased Lady Li, but his yearnings could not endure forever. Even the immortals Red Pine and Plum Fortune had to face the hateful truth of eventual demise. Even bodhisattvas who have fulfilled the ten stages of practice and are on the verge of attaining buddhahood must still bow to the law of life and death. Though you may taste the joys of longevity, you can never escape this sorrow. Though you live to be a hundred, in the end this same grief will await you.

"The Devil of the Sixth Heaven, that enemy of the Buddhist faith who rules over all the six heavens of the world of desire, hates to see any living being in his domain escape from the law of birth and death. So he assumes the guise of a wife or a husband in order to hinder such beings from gaining release. But the Buddhas of the three existences of past, present, and future regard all living beings as their own children, and so they urge them to seek the Pure Land of Perfect Bliss, from which there is no regressing. Therefore, from endless ages in the past to the present they have given stern warning that wives and children can hinder salvation by binding someone to repeated transmigration in the realm of birth and death. So you must not weaken in your resolve at this point.

"An ancestor of the Genji clan, Yoriyoshi of Iyo, having received the imperial command, proceeded to the region of Ōshū in the north to put down the rebellion headed by Sadatō and Munetō. Over a period of twelve years he cut off the heads of some sixteen thousand persons, and how many thousands or tens of thousands of beasts of the mountains and fish of the streams he killed is beyond calculation. Yet it is reported that when he lay on his deathbed, because he devoted all his thoughts to the quest for enlightenment, he was able to fulfill his hopes for rebirth in the Pure Land.

"The merit that accrues from the act of becoming a monk is so vast that it cancels out all the sins from your previous existences. This is the point to remember. We are told that even though you may build a tower made of the Seven Treasures[5] so high that it reaches to the Heaven of the Thirty-three Gods,[6] the merit you win cannot equal that gained by becoming a monk for one day only. We are told that even though you give alms to a hundred arhats[7] for a hundred or a thousand years, again the merit cannot equal that gained by becoming a monk for a single day. Deeply immersed in sin as Yoriyoshi was, because his mind was firm in faith, he was able to be reborn in the Pure Land. And your own sins are surely nothing compared with his, so why should you not be able to do likewise?

"Furthermore, the deity of this Kumano Shrine is an avatar of the Thus Come One Amida Buddha. He has taken forty-eight vows, beginning with the vow that 'there shall no longer be Three Evil Paths of Existence'[8] and ending with the vow that 'they shall gain the three types of clear cognition.' Each of these forty-eight vows is intended to bring salvation to living beings. The eighteenth vow in particular states: 'After I attain Buddhahood, if living beings in the lands in the ten directions, most sincere in heart, trusting in my vows, should wish to be reborn in my country and should call on my name ten times, then if they cannot do so, may I not gain true enlightenment!' So we have only to call on his name once or ten times. We must have complete faith and never for a moment entertain the least doubt!

"If now, summoning up a truly earnest desire for salvation, you recite the *nenbutsu* ten times or even once, then Amida will reduce his body, indescribably huge in its dimensions, to sixteen feet in height and, with the bodhisattvas Kannon and Seishi and a number-less host of saintly beings and bodhisattvas in temporary manifesta-tions surrounding him a hundredfold or a thousandfold, all playing music and singing songs, will issue forth from the eastern gate of the Land of Bliss and will come to greet you. Then, even though it may seem that your bodily form has sunk to the depths of the blue

5.   The Seven Treasures are gold, silver, lapis lazuli, crystal, agate, ruby, and cornelian.
6.   The Heaven of the Thirty-three Gods is located on top of Mount Sumeru and is considered to be the second heaven of the world of desire.
7.   An arhat is a being who has achieved Buddhist enlightenment.
8.   The Three Evil Paths of Existence are hell, the world of hungry ghosts, and the world of animals.

sea, in fact you will rise up on purple clouds. And once you have attained the emancipation of Buddhahood and won enlightenment, you may return to your old home in this transient world of ours and lead your wife and children to salvation. For, like Amida himself, you can 'return to the world of defilement to save human and heavenly beings.'[9] You must have no doubts!"

With these words of encouragement, he sounded his bell. Realizing now what a good friend and guide he had in the priest, Koremori immediately cast off all his doubts and delusions. Facing west and pressing his palms together, he performed a hundred recitations of the *nenbutsu* in a loud voice, and as he pronounced the last "Hail!" he cast himself into the sea.

Likewise, Yosōbyōe and Ishidōmaru, calling on the sacred name of Amida, one after the other threw themselves into the water.

News of Koremori's end reaches the Taira. Suffering further defeats, the Taira escape to the sea.

9.   This is a quotation from the *Hōjisan*, a Tang-period Buddhist text.

BOOK ELEVEN

ANTOKU: emperor and son of Emperor Takakura and Kenreimon'in.

GoShirakawa: retired emperor and head of the imperial clan.

KAGETOKI (Kajiwara): deputy commander of Minamoto forces and rival of Yoshitsune.

KENREIMON'IN (Taira): daughter of Kiyomori and Nun of the Second Rank.

MORITSUGI (Taira): warrior serving Munemori.

MUNEMORI (Taira): son of Kiyomori, Taira clan head, and leader of the Taira forces at Yashima.

NORITSUNE (Taira): nephew of Kiyomori and leading Taira commander.

NUN OF THE SECOND RANK (Taira): widow of Kiyomori and grandmother of Emperor Antoku.

YOSHIMORI (Minamoto): warrior serving Yoshitsune.

YOSHITSUNE (Minamoto): younger half brother of Yoritomo and leader of the Genji forces at Yashima and Dan-no-ura.

After landing with a small force on the island of Shikoku, Yoshitsune leads his Genji troops to the rear of the Taira camp at Yashima, where the Taira have set up their headquarters. With a small force, he manages to bluff the Taira, led by Munemori, into retreating to their boats.

The Death of Tsuginobu (11:3)

That day Yoshitsune wore a red brocade battle robe and a suit of armor shaded deep purple at the lower edge. He carried a sword with

gilt-bronze fittings and arrows decorated with black and white feathers. Gripping the middle of his rattan-wrapped bow, he glared at the
enemy boats and in a loud voice called out his name: "Minamoto
no Yoshitsune, envoy of the retired emperor, fifth-rank lieutenant of
the imperial police!" He was followed by Nobutsuna of Izu, Ietada
of Musashi, Chikanori of Musashi, and Yoshimori of Ise. Next
came Sanetomo, his son Motokiyo, Tsuginobu of Ōshū, his brother
Tadanobu, Genzō of Eda, Kumai Tarō, and Musashibō Benkei, each
galloping forward to announce his identity.

"Shoot them down!" cried the Heike men, whereupon some of
the boats discharged powerful long-range arrows, and others showered down volleys of lighter ones. The Genji warriors surged ahead,
shooting arrows now to the left, now to the right, shouting and hal-
looing as they pressed forward or rested their horses in the lee of the
beached boats.

Sanetomo, one of the Genji leaders and a seasoned warrior,
did not join in the fray but instead forced his way into the makeshift imperial palace and, setting fire to it here and there, instantly
reduced it to ashes.

The Heike leader, Munemori, summoning his samurai attendants, asked, "How large are the Genji forces today?"

"At the moment they number only about seventy or eighty
mounted men," the attendants replied.

"This is absurd! With that small a force, we could have picked
them off one hair at a time and still had no trouble overwhelming
them. But instead of attacking, we scrambled to board the boats and
so gave them a chance to burn the palace. How disgraceful! Where is
Noritsune? We must beach the boats and engage them at once!"

"As you command," replied Noritsune, and setting out in one
of the smaller boats along with Moritsugi, he made his way to the
beach in front of the burned-out main gate of the camp, where he
drew up his forces in battle formation. The more than eighty men
under Yoshitsune's command meanwhile advanced to the point
where they were within range of the enemy's arrows, and there they
halted.

Speaking from the deck of one of the boats, Moritsugi shouted to
the Genji forces, "We heard you calling out your names, but with so
much water between us we couldn't make out the words distinctly.
Who did you say was the commander of the Genji forces today?"

Spurring his horse forward, Yoshimori of Ise replied, "What need is there to repeat it? Yoshitsune, younger brother of the lord of Kamakura and tenth-generation descendant of Emperor Seiwa!"

"Ah, now I remember," said Moritsugi. "The orphan of that man who was killed some years ago in the Heiji fighting. He was an acolyte at the Kurama-ji temple and later served as flunky to a traveling merchant. The little fellow who used to carry goods back and forth to the Ōshū region!"

"Watch how you let your tongue run on when you speak about my master!" said Yoshimori. "You're the ones who were trounced in the fighting at Tonamiyama and barely escaped with your lives, are you not? And then, after wandering around in the Hokuriku area, you came whimpering and begging your way back to the capital!"

"Why would we have to beg?" replied Moritsugi. "Thanks to our lord's largesse, we had all we needed and more! But I'm told that you've been robbing people holed up around Mount Suzuka in Ise to get by and feed your families, living the life of bandits so you can feed yourselves and your wives and children!"

At this Ietada spoke up from the Genji side: "Enough of this useless slander, gentlemen! Hurling groundless insults back and forth will never decide the matter. But last spring at Ichi-no-tani I believe you saw what our men, the young lords of Musashi and Sagami, could do in battle, did you not?"

Before he had finished speaking, his younger brother Chikanori, who was at his side, selected an arrow of unusual length and, fitting it in place, drew his bow far back and let it fly. The arrow struck Moritsugi in the chest, passing all the way through the breastplate of his armor, and this put an end to the battle of words.

"Battling from a boat has its own requirements," declared Noritsune. He had not put on a long battle robe but was wearing only a short-sleeved jacket with a rolled Chinese design and a suit of finely laced armor. At his waist he wore an enormous sword; on his back was a quiver holding twenty-four arrows fledged with black hawk feathers; and he grasped a rattan-bound bow. Once he had been the strongest bowman and the fiercest fighter in the capital, and no one could come within range of his arrows without being felled. And today he had determined to shoot down none other than Yoshitsune himself.

But the Genji warriors anticipated his intentions. Tsuginobu, his younger brother Tadanobu, Yoshimori, Hirotsuna, Genzō, Kumai Tarō,

Musashibō Benkei, and the others, each a match for a thousand ordinary warriors, pressed forward on their horses, jostling with one another for first place and forming a barrier to meet Noritsune's arrows.

"You worthless fellows, get out of the way of my arrows!" Noritsune shouted helplessly. Again and again he fitted arrows to his bow and sent them flying, and in an instant ten or more armored warriors were felled. Among them was Tsuginobu of Ōshū, who was pierced by an arrow that entered his left shoulder and came out on his right side, and he tumbled headlong from his horse.

A young boy in Noritsune's service named Kikuō was famous for his strength and daring. Wearing a greenish yellow stomach guard and a three-plate helmet, he drew from its sheath a wooden-handle halberd and rushed forward in hopes of cutting off Tsuginobu's head. But Tsuginobu's brother Tadanobu, determined to thwart him, drew his bow all the way back and aimed an arrow. It struck the back joint of the boy's stomach guard and shot through him, sending him sprawling on all fours.

Observing what had happened, Noritsune leaped from his boat and, grasping his bow in his left hand, used his right to seize Kikuō and drag him into the boat. Thus he prevented the Genji men from taking the boy's head, although the boy died of his wound. He had originally been a page in the household of Noritsune's older brother Michimori, but after the latter's death, he had been taken into Noritsune's service. He was only eighteen at the time of his death. Noritsune was so grief stricken at what had happened that he took no further part in the day's battle.

Meanwhile Yoshitsune, giving orders for the stricken Tsuginobu to be carried to the rear, got off his horse and, taking Tsuginobu's hand, asked, "How are you feeling?"

Speaking in a faint and breathless voice, Tsuginobu replied, "This is the end for me."

"Is there anything more you want to say?" asked Yoshitsune.

"I have nothing more to say," was the reply. "I'm sorry only that I must die before I have seen my lord gain his rightful place in the world, that's all. Any man who takes up bow and arrow knows that one day he may die by the arrows of his enemy. But in future ages, when they talk about these wars between the Genji and the Heike, if they say that Tsuginobu of Ōshū fell on the beach at Yashima in Sanuki, giving up his life to save that of his lord, then that is all a warrior could hope for by way of recognition in this life and remembrance in the life hereafter." As he spoke, his voice grew fainter and fainter.

Speaking through his tears, Yoshitsune asked whether any worthy monks were nearby. When one was found, Yoshitsune told him, "This man is now dying of his wounds. See that you spend the day copying out sutra texts for the repose of his soul." Then he took a sturdy, well-fed black horse fitted with a gold-bordered saddle and gave it as payment to the monk. The horse was known as Lord Black of the fifth rank and had been given to Yoshitsune when he was promoted to the post of fifth-rank lieutenant. Yoshitsune had ridden this very horse when he crossed over Hiyodori Pass to attack Ichi-no-tani.

Tsuginobu's brother Tadanobu and the other warriors all looked on in tears, exclaiming, "For a lord like this, a man could give up his life without having the smallest particle of regret!"

Nasu no Yoichi (11:4)

In the provinces of Awa and Sanuki those persons who had stopped siding with the Heike and were awaiting only the arrival of the Genji now began to appear, fourteen or fifteen horsemen here, twenty horsemen there, coming down from the mountains or emerging from caves where they had been hiding, until Yoshitsune in no time found himself with a force of more than three hundred mounted men.

"The day is too far gone," he announced. "There's no hope of a decisive victory today!" He had just begun withdrawing his men when a small boat, beautifully decorated, appeared in the offing, rowing in the direction of the shore. When it had come within a couple of hundred feet of the shore, it turned sideways.

"What is that?" exclaimed the onlookers, for they could now see a woman of eighteen or nineteen, very lovely and refined in bearing, wearing crimson trousers over a five-layer robe of green-lined white. Attached to a pole she held a crimson fan with a golden sun painted on it. Wedging the pole into the siding of the boat, she beckoned toward the shore.

Yoshitsune called Sanemoto to his side and said, "What do you suppose is the meaning of that?"

"I think she wants us to shoot at the fan," he replied. "But I sus-
pect they are trying to entice you to move forward where you can get
a better view of the beautiful lady. Then they'll order one of their
expert archers to shoot you down. Even so, we should get someone
to shoot at the fan."

"Do we have anyone on our side capable of hitting it?" asked
Yoshitsune.

"We have many first-rate archers. There's Yoichi Munekata, the son
of Nasu no Tarō Suketaka. Small as he is, he's an expert marksman!"

"How can you tell?"

"If we have a contest shooting birds on the wing, he always manages to down two out of every three he aims at."

"Then send for him!" said Yoshitsune.

Yoichi, a man of around twenty, wore a dark blue battle robe
trimmed with red brocade at the lapels and sleeve edges and a suit of
greenish yellow–laced armor. He carried a sword with a silver cord
ring and a quiver, visible above his head, containing the few black-
spotted white eagle-feather arrows left from the day's shooting. These
were fledged with black and white eagle feathers, and with them he
carried a deer-horn humming arrow with hawk feathers and black
and white eagle feathers. Holding his rattan-bound bow under his
arm and doffing his helmet so that it hung from his shoulder cord,
he made his obeisance before Yoshitsune.

"Now then, Yoichi—hit that red fan square in the middle and
show these Heike what you can do!"

"I'm not sure I can do that," Yoichi replied in a respectful manner.
"And if I should fail, it would reflect badly on our side for a long time
to come. It would be best to summon someone whose skill is certain
to succeed."

Yoshitsune was furious. "All you fellows who have left Kamakura
and come west with me are expected to obey my orders! If you are
going to quibble over every little detail, you can leave my command
at once!"

Thinking it inappropriate to decline any further, Yoichi replied,
"I'm not certain I can make a hit, but since it is my lord's wish, I'll
see what I can do."

Retiring from Yoshitsune's presence, he got on a sturdy black
horse fitted with a tasseled crupper and a saddle decorated with
a sand-dollar design. Readjusting the bow in his hand and taking

up the reins, he advanced toward the edge of the water. The Genji troops kept their eyes fixed on him from the rear, exclaiming, "This lad will make a good showing, you may be sure!" Yoshitsune too watched with confident expectation.

Because the target was too far to be within range, Yoichi advanced some forty feet into the water, but he could see that the fan was still more than two hundred and fifty feet away. It was the eighteenth day of the Second Month of the lunar calendar, around six o'clock in the late afternoon, and a strong north wind was blowing, sending high waves surging up on the beach. The boat was wobbling up and down on the waves, and the fan, not firmly fastened, flapped back and forth. Out in the sea the Heike watched from their boats strung out over the water while the Genji, their horses lined up side by side, looked on from the shore.

Yoichi closed his eyes. "Hail to Bodhisattva Hachiman and to the gods of my homeland of Shimotsuke, the Buddha in his manifestation

A beautiful woman (*right*) in a Heike boat raises a fan as a challenge to the Genji archers. Under orders from Yoshitsune, Nasu no Yoichi (*left*) hits the target with his arrow.

at Nikkō, and the gods of Utsunomiya and the Yuzen Shrine in Nasu. Help me hit the fan in the center, I pray you. If I fail in this attempt, I will break my bow and end my life, never to show my face before anyone again. If you would have me return once more to my native land, may my arrow not miss the mark!" Such was the prayer he offered up in his heart.

When he opened his eyes again, he found that the wind had died down a little and the fan had become a somewhat less difficult target. Yoichi took out the humming arrow, fitted it to his bow and, pulling the bow all the way back, sent it whistling on its way.

Yoichi was small in stature, and the arrow measured only three fingers more than the usual ten handbreadths and three fingers in length, but the bow was powerful and the arrow made a long droning noise that resounded all across the water. Then with a crack it struck the fan about an inch above the rivet, knocking it loose. As the arrow plunged beneath the waves, the fan rose up into the sky. For a moment it fluttered about in the empty air, buffeted this way and that by the spring breeze, and then all at once it plummeted into the sea. In the rays of the setting sun, the red fan face with its golden sun could be seen bobbing and sinking as it drifted over the white waves.[1]

Offshore the Heike drummed on the gunwales of their boats to signal their admiration while on the beach the Genji shouted and pounded on their quivers.

The Lost Bow (11:5)

Perhaps he was carried away with the excitement of the moment: in one of the Heike boats a man of about fifty, wearing armor laced with black leather and carrying a wooden-handle halberd, stood up in a spot near where the fan had been displayed and began to do a dance. Yoshimori of Ise, having advanced on his horse to a position right behind Yoichi, said, "The commander has ordered you to shoot down that man!"

This time Yoichi took one of the plain arrows from his quiver and, fitting it into place, drew the bow back fully. With a thud the arrow struck the man's collarbone and sent him tumbling headfirst into the bottom of the boat. The Heike side looked on in silence while among the Genji, some once more rattled their quivers and shouted, "Good shot!" but others exclaimed, "Heartless!"

This was more than the Heike could endure. Three of their warriors, one bearing a shield, a second with a bow, and a third with a halberd, made their way to the beach and, planting the shield there, beckoned to the enemy and shouted, "Attack us if you can!"

"Some of you young fellows on good horses—attack them and kick them out of the way!" ordered Yoshitsune.

Five horsemen—Shirō, Tōōjichi, and Jūrō of Mionoya in Musashi, Shirō of Kōzuke, and Chūji of Shinano—let out a yell and charged forward in a group. From behind the shield the Heike shot a large arrow with a black lacquer shaft and black feathers. Jūrō was riding at the head of the group, and the arrow struck his horse in the left side near the chest rope, burying the tip of the arrow in the horse's flesh. The horse fell over like a toppled screen.

---

1.   Red was associated with the Heike and white with the Genji.

Jūrō of Mionoya, throwing his right leg over the horse's back, leaped down from the left side and immediately drew his sword. One of the Heike men emerged from behind the shield, waving a halberd in a threatening fashion, whereupon Jūrō, judging that with his small sword he could hardly stand up against such an opponent, began to scramble to safety. The man with the halberd was after him at once, but just when it seemed as though he would cut Jūrō down with the halberd, he suddenly thrust the weapon under his left arm and with his right hand snatched at the neck guard of Jūrō's helmet. He could not quite reach it, but after making three unsuccessful tries, he finally, on the fourth, succeeded in grasping the neck guard. For a time the neck guard held fast, but at last Jūrō managed to wrest himself free, snapping off the neck guard at the top plate, and made his escape. The other four riders in his group, reluctant to risk having their horses shot at, looked on from a distance.

Having taken shelter among his companions' horses, Jūrō breathed a sigh of relief. His attacker did not attempt to pursue him but, leaning on his halberd and brandishing aloft the neck guard he had snatched from Jūrō's helmet, shouted in a loud voice, "You've no doubt heard of me for some time now, and today you see me in person! I'm the one the young fellows of the capital call Akushichibyōe[2] Kagekiyo of Kazusa!" Having thus proclaimed his identity, he left the field.

Somewhat subdued by all this, the Heike decided not to try to attack Kagekiyo but instead ordered some two hundred or so of their men to go to the beach, where they arranged their shields so that they overlapped like a hen's wings and gestured to the Genji forces, shouting, "Come on and get us!"

"How dare they!" said Yoshitsune when he saw them, and he ordered Sanemoto and his son Motokiyo and the Kaneko brothers to act as a vanguard, Tadanobu and Yoshimori of Ōshū to take up positions to the left and right, and Tashiro no Kanja to cover the rear, sending more than eighty mounted men yelling and galloping to meet the challenge.

The Heike, most of whom were not mounted but were on foot, decided they would be no match for men on horseback and retreated, returning to their boats. The shields they had planted on

2.   In names, the prefix "Aku-" often has the meaning of "fierce."

the beach soon were scattered to left and right like so many tally slips.

Encouraged by this success, the Genji warriors pressed their attack, riding into the sea until the water came up to the bellies of their horses. Yoshitsune, too, fought his way deep into the water when one of the Heike boats, using rakes, two or three times managed to catch hold of his neck guard. Yoshitsune's men used their swords and halberds to free the neck guard from entanglement. While this was happening, however, Yoshitsune's bow somehow became snagged by the rakes and was dragged away from him.

Bending down from his horse, Yoshitsune tried again and again to use his whip to regain possession of the bow. "Let it go!" his men urged him, but he persisted until he finally recovered the bow and then, laughing, returned to the others.

His seasoned warriors, wagging their fingers in disapproval, said, "Why are you so reluctant to lose a mere bow? Even if it cost a hundred or a thousand strings of coins, how could it be worth risking your life for?"

"It's not that I mind about the cost of the bow," replied Yoshitsune. "If this bow of mine had been the kind that was so stout that it took two or three men to string it—the kind my uncle Tametomo used— then I would deliberately let them snatch it just so they could say, 'Ah, so this is Yoshitsune's bow!' But this one was puny—just think if it had fallen into the hands of my enemies and they had said, 'Just look—this is the kind of bow used by the great Genji Commander in Chief Yoshitsune!' I couldn't bear the thought of their scornful laughter! That's why I risked my life to get it back." His men all were deeply impressed with this answer.

The sun having set by this time, the Genji forces withdrew and made their camp in the fields and hills between Mure and Takamatsu. They had not slept for three whole days. The first day they had set out by boat from Watanabe and Fukushima, and that night they had been so tossed about by the giant waves that they could get no sleep at all. Yesterday they had battled the enemy at Katsuura in the province of Awa and had spent all night crossing the mountains. Today again they had fought the whole day, and all of them were utterly exhausted. Some used their helmets for pillows; others used their quivers or the sleeves of their armor as pillows, falling at once into a deep and heedless sleep. Only Yoshitsune and Yoshimori of Ise remained awake.

Yoshitsune climbed up to a high point in order to look around and watch for an enemy approach and to try to determine what possible route the enemy might use to attack. Yoshimori took up a waiting position in a hollow so he could shoot the horses in the belly if the enemy attacked from that direction.

The Heike appointed Noritsune, the governor of Noto, to command a force of some five hundred horsemen and to prepare to launch a night attack. But because Moritsugi of Etchū and Emi no Jirō Morikata could not agree on which of them would spearhead the attack, the night passed without an attack. What could the Genji have possibly done if a night attack had been launched?[3] But the fact that an attack was not even attempted shows how low the fortunes of the Heike had sunk.

The Cockfights and the Battle of Dan-no-ura (11:7)

Thus Yoshitsune advanced as far as the Suō region, where he joined forces with his older brother Noriyori, the governor of Mikawa. Meanwhile the Heike had arrived at Hikushima in the province of Nagato. Having landed at Katsuura, or Victory Beach, in Awa, the Genji had conquered their foes at Yashima. When word got out that the Heike had reached Hikushima, or Retreat Island, while the Genji were ensconced at a place called Oitsu, or Pursuit Crossing, in the same province, people wondered at the coincidence.

Tanzō, the superintendent of the Kumano Shrine, unable to decide whether to support the Heike or the Genji side, conducted a ceremony at the New Kumano Shrine in Tanabe at which he offered a performance of sacred music to the manifestation of the Buddha worshiped at the shrine and prayed for guidance. He was advised by the deity to "Follow the white flag!" of the Genji. Still doubtful whether this was the correct course, he selected seven white and seven red fighting cocks and set them to battling each other in front of the deity's shrine. Not one of the red cocks won; all fled in defeat. With this, Tanzō decided to give his full support to the Genji.

3.   A variant has "How could the Genji have withstood the attack?"

He summoned all the men under his command—a total of more than two thousand—and had them board around two hundred boats. In one of the boats he carried with him the god of the Nyaku Ōji Shrine, and above his banner he flew a wooden strip painted with an image of the guardian deity Kongō Dōji. When his boats appeared in Dan-no-ura, where the Genji and Heike forces were assembled, both sides paid reverence to his arrival, but the Heike were sadly disheartened when they saw him lead his forces over to the side of the Genji.

In addition, Michinobu of Iyo Province came rowing into sight with a force of one hundred and fifty war vessels, also adding them to the Genji forces. Thus Yoshitsune, having acquired these various allies, felt confident of his fighting strength. The Genji had more than three thousand boats; the Heike, only few more than a thousand, including a few large, Chinese-type vessels. While the Genji forces were increasing in size, those of the Heike were dwindling.

The Genji and Heike forces decided to meet on the twenty-fifth day, Third Month, of the second year of the Genryaku era [1185] at around six in the morning in the straits between the Moji barrier in the province of Buzen and the Akama barrier in order to exchange the volley of arrows that signaled the commencement of hostilities. But when the day arrived, Yoshitsune and Kajiwara Kagetoki almost ended up battling each other.

"Today it is my turn to lead the attack!" Kajiwara Kagetoki insisted.

"Not so long as I am here!" countered Yoshitsune.

"That is not right! Your place is to act as commander in chief."

"Nonsense! The lord of Kamakura is the commander in chief. I simply have been commissioned to carry out his orders. In rank I am the same as you and the others."

Seeing that he would not be allowed to lead the attack, Kajiwara Kagetoki muttered to himself, "This man is not endowed by nature to be the leader of fighting men!"

Overhearing the remark, Yoshitsune exclaimed, "And you are the biggest blockhead in all Japan!" and reached for the handle of his sword.

"Because I acknowledge loyalty to no one but the lord of Kamakura!" replied Kajiwara Kagetoki, and he too made ready to draw his sword.

When this happened, Kajiwara's eldest son Kagesue, his second son Kagetaka, and his third son Kageie gathered around their father.

Observing Yoshitsune's displeasure, Tadanobu of Ōshū, Yoshimori of Ise, Genpachi Hirotsuna, Eda no Genzō, Kumai Tarō, Musashibō Benkei, and others, each of them a match for a thousand ordinary fighting men, hurried forward, surrounding Kajiwara and preparing to attack him themselves.

At this point Miura no Suke took hold of Yoshitsune while Toi no Jirō hastened to restrain Kajiwara. "When we are right on the verge of a critical encounter, if our own leaders start battling each other, it will only bolster the strength of the Heike!" they said, pressing their palms together in supplication. "And if word of this somehow gets back to Yoritomo, there is bound to be trouble!"

At this point, Yoshitsune regained his composure. Kajiwara could not press the matter further. But from this time on, it is said that Kajiwara grew to hate Yoshitsune, and his slander in the end brought about Yoshitsune's downfall.

The Genji and the Heike boats were positioned on the sea about two miles apart. In the waters around Moji, Akama, and Dan-no-ura, the tidal currents are confused and turbulent. The Genji boats headed into the outgoing tide and hence, despite all their efforts, were constantly carried back. The Heike boats, however, were moving with the tide.

Because the current out at sea was very swift, Kajiwara stayed close to shore and used rakes to drag the Heike boats closer as they passed him. Then he and his sons and their followers—fourteen or fifteen men in all—boarded the boats. Wielding weapons in their hands, they slashed mercilessly from bow to stern, cutting down the occupants. They seized a large amount of booty, and their exploits were the first to be noted in the record of that day's fighting.

By this time the Genji and Heike forces were confronting each other and shouting their battle cry. Above, it must have been heard as far away as the Brahma Heaven;[4] below it doubtless alarmed the dragon king in his palace beneath the sea.

The new middle counselor, Taira no Tomomori, took a position beside the cabin of his boat and called out in a loud voice, "Today is the final battle. Don't even think about falling back. There have been many generals and brave fighters of unparalleled renown in

---

4. The Brahma Heaven is the first and lowest of the four heavens in the world of form, where beings have no desires or appetites. It is the abode of Brahma, the highest god in the Hindu pantheon and a protector of Buddhism.

India and China—and in our land of Japan as well. But when their fate ran out, there was nothing they could do. Honor is the only thing that counts! Don't look weak to the easterners! What better time than now to risk our lives? That's the way I see it!"

Kagetsune of Hida, who was attending Tomomori, spoke up. "All you fighting men, listen to these words that have just been spoken!" he ordered.

Next Akushichibyōe Kagekiyo stepped forward. "These men from the eastern region may boast of their skill at fighting on horseback, but what do they know about naval battles? They'll be as helpless as fish trying to climb a tree! We'll grab them one by one and toss them in the sea!"

Then Moritsugi of Etchū spoke up. "If you're grabbing, then make a grab for the commander in chief, Yoshitsune! They say Yoshitsune's easy to spot because he's short and fair skinned, and his teeth stick out. But they also say that because he keeps changing his battle robe and armor, you might not recognize him right away."

"He may be brave at heart, but what can a skinny little fellow like that do?" said Akushichibyōe. "I'll just tuck him under one arm and fling him into the ocean!"

After issuing the orders just described, the new middle counselor, Tomomori, went to speak to his brother Munemori. "Our fighting men seem to be in excellent spirits today. But I'm afraid that Shigeyoshi of Awa in Shikoku is not fully committed to our cause. Perhaps we should have him beheaded."

"How could we behead him when we have no evidence of his disloyalty? He has been perfectly trustworthy in his service. Have someone call him here!"

In response to this command, Shigeyoshi appeared, wearing an orange battle robe and armor with white leather lacing, and made his obeisance before Munemori.

"How are you feeling, Shigeyoshi? Have you had a change of heart?" said Munemori. "You seem dispirited today. I trust you've ordered your men from Shikoku to do their best in battle. Don't lose your nerve!"

"Why would I lose my nerve!" exclaimed Shigeyoshi, as he stood up to leave. "How I'd like to lop this fellow's head off!" thought Tomomori as Shigeyoshi withdrew, and he gripped the handle of his sword hard enough to break it in two, looking fixedly at Munemori. But because the latter refused to give any sign of agreement, Tomomori was powerless to move.

The Heike arranged their thousand or more boats into three groups. Rowing in the vanguard were some five hundred boats under the command of Hidetō of Yamaga in Kyushu. Next came the second group, around three hundred boats of the Matsura clans. The Heike commanders followed in a third group made up of about two hundred boats.

Hidetō was the finest archer in all Kyushu, and he had selected a force of five hundred men who, though hardly his equal in skill, still qualified as expert marksmen. He ordered them to line up shoulder to shoulder in the bow and stern of each of the boats and to shoot their five hundred arrows all at the same time.

The Genji had more than three thousand boats, which meant that they were considerably superior in number. But their arrows came winging from all directions so that it was difficult to determine just where their skilled archers were positioned. Yoshitsune was in the very forefront of the action, but the Genji were so pelted with arrows that they faltered, their shields and armor offering scarcely any protection at all. The Heike, certain that their side was winning, banged away at the drums that signaled the attack and shouted with glee.

Far-Flying Arrows (11:8)

One of the Genji warriors, Wada Yoshimori, did not board a boat but remained on horseback on the beach. After taking off his helmet and handing it to one of his men, he thrust his feet far forward into his stirrups, fully drew back his bow and began releasing his arrows. So powerful and accurate were his shots that he could hit any target he chose within more than a thousand feet. When he shot an arrow at a particularly distant target, he would gesture to the person he had aimed at, inviting him to shoot it back.

Tomomori had one of Yoshimori's arrows brought to him so that he could examine it. It was thirteen handbreadths and two fingers in length, a plain bamboo arrow fledged with white crane feathers mixed with stork feathers, and a handbreadth from the lashing it was inscribed in lacquer with the name "Wada Kotarō Yoshimori."

Although the Heike were numerous, only a few were capable of shooting such a long distance, for only after some delay did Tomomori succeed in summoning Chikakiyo of Iyo and, handing him the arrow, having him shoot it back to the Genji side. The arrow flew some thousand feet or more from the boat in the sea to the shore, where it lodged in the upper left arm of Miura Tarō, who had stopped more than thirty-five feet behind Yoshimori.

Observing what had happened, Miura's men laughed and said, "Look at that! Yoshimori thought that no one could outshoot him. Now he's angry because he's been shown up!"

Overhearing them, Yoshimori exclaimed, "He won't get away with this!" Getting into a small boat, he had himself rowed out into the very midst of the Heike forces. There, fitting one arrow after another into his bow, he succeeded in killing or wounding several men.

Around the same time, a large arrow made of bamboo came winging from the sea and landed in Yoshitsune's boat. As in the case of Yoshimori, the archer challenged him to return it. When Yoshitsune had someone pull out the arrow and examine it, he found that it was fourteen handbreadths and three fingers in length, the shaft of bamboo fledged with pheasant feathers and inscribed with the name "Chikakiyo of Iyo."

Yoshitsune sent for Gotō Sanetomo. "Do we have anyone on our side who can return this arrow?" he asked.

"Lord Asari no Yoichi of the Kai Genji clan is one of our finest archers."

"Send for him!" ordered Yoshitsune, and soon the man appeared.

"Someone out in the ocean shot this arrow here and dares us to shoot it back. Can you do that for me?"

"May I see the arrow?" said Yoichi, and he tested it with his finger. "The bamboo shaft is rather weak and the arrow is too short. If it's all the same, I'll use one of my own arrows."

So saying, he took an arrow fifteen headbreadths in length, with a lacquered bamboo shaft and black eagle feathers. Gripping it in his large fist, he fitted it into his huge nine-foot bow wrapped with rattan and lacquered, drew the bow far back, and sent it off with a whoosh. It sailed a thousand feet and struck Chikakiyo of Iyo, who was standing in the bow of one of the large Heike boats, square in the chest. He tumbled head over heels to the bottom of the boat—whether dead or alive, no one knew. Asari no Yoichi was a natural-born archer. It was rumored that he could shoot deer on the run from as far away as seven hundred feet without ever missing.

After this the Genji and Heike fell on each other with no thought for their own safety, shouting and yelling wildly. It was impossible to say which side was winning, but because the emperor with his ten kinds of virtue and three imperial regalia was with the Heike, the Genji could not help feeling themselves at a disadvantage. Then something that looked like a white cloud appeared in the sky and hovered there for a moment. It was not a cloud, however, but a white banner, with no one holding it, which fluttered down until the cord dangling from its handle seemed to touch the prow of one of the Genji boats.

Yoshitsune was overjoyed. "This is a sign from the Great Bodhisattva Hachiman!" he declared and, rinsing his hands and mouth with water, he bowed in obeisance. All his warriors followed his example.

In addition, some one or two thousand porpoises appeared, coming from the direction of the Genji boats and swimming toward those of the Heike. Munemori, the Heike commander, observing this, summoned Harenobu, a doctor of divination, and stated, "There are always porpoises hereabouts, but I've never seen so many of them. What meaning do you divine in this?"

"If these porpoises staying near the surface go back in the direction they came from, it means the Genji are doomed. But if they continue in their current direction, then I'm afraid our own forces will be in danger."

He had hardly finished delivering these words when the porpoises dived directly under the Heike boats and disappeared. "This is the end of our world!" he said.

Shigeyoshi of Awa had faithfully served the Heike lords for three years, again and again going to battle in their defense without thought for his own life. But after his son Saemon had been taken prisoner by the Genji forces, perhaps concluding that his efforts were hopeless, he abruptly shifted his allegiance and went over to the Genji side.

The Heike had contrived a scheme whereby they would assign their high-ranking men to the ordinary boats and their men of inferior class and fighting capacity to the large, Chinese-style ships. They assumed that in the battle the Genji would concentrate on the Chinese vessels and that when they did so, the Heike, having made the necessary preparations, would close in for the kill.

Because Shigeyoshi of Awa had gone over to the other side, however, the Genji, now aware of the scheme, paid no heed to the Chinese vessels but instead directed their attack at the boats in which the Heike commanders, disguised as common soldiers, were riding.

"What a blunder!" exclaimed the Heike leader Tomomori. "I should have cut off and thrown away Shigeyoshi's head!" Much as he might pour out his regrets, however, the situation was now past remedy.

So it was that all the fighting men of Shikoku and Kyushu turned against the Heike and threw in their lot with the Genji. Those who up to now had been models of obedience suddenly turned their bows on their own leaders or drew their swords to menace those who had been their commanders. When the Heike made for this or that shore, they found high waves impeding their approach; when they headed for this or that beach, they discovered the arrows of their enemies waiting for them. The long struggle between the Genji and the Heike for mastery of the realm was destined, it seemed, to end on this very day.

The Nun of the
Second Rank (*right*),
holding the child
emperor (Antoku) in
her arms, prepares
to drown in the sea.
Genji soldiers (*left*)
board the boats
carrying Heike
women.

The Drowning of the Former Emperor (11:9)

By this time the Genji warriors had succeeded in boarding the Heike
boats, shooting dead the sailors and helmsmen with their arrows or
cutting them down with their swords. The bodies lay heaped in the
bottom of the boats, and there was no longer anyone to keep the
boats on course.

Taira no Tomomori boarded a small craft and made his way to
the vessel in which the former emperor was riding. "This is what the
world has come to!" he exclaimed. "Have all these unsightly things
thrown into the sea!" Then he began racing from prow to stern,
sweeping, mopping, dusting, and attempting with his own hands to
put the boat into proper order.

"How goes the battle, Lord Tomomori?" asked the emperor's
ladies-in-waiting, pressing him with questions.

"You'll have a chance to see some splendid gentlemen from the eastern region!" he replied with a cackling laugh.

"How can you joke at a time like this!" they protested, their voices joined in a chorus of shrieks and wails.

Observing the situation and evidently having been prepared for some time for such an eventuality, the Nun of the Second Rank, the emperor's grandmother, slipped a two-layer nun's robe over her head and tied her glossed silk trousers high at the waist. She placed the sacred jewel, one of the three imperial regalia, under her arm, thrust the sacred sword in her sash, and took the child emperor in her arms. "I may be a mere woman, but I have no intention of falling into the hands of the enemy! I will accompany my lord. All those of you who are resolved to fulfill your duty by doing likewise, quickly follow me!" So saying, she strode to the side of the boat.

The emperor had barely turned eight but had the bearing of someone much older than that. The beauty of his face and form seemed to radiate all around him. His shimmering black hair fell down the length of his back.

Startled and confused, he asked, "Grandma, where are you going to take me?"

Gazing at his innocent face and struggling to hold back her tears, the nun replied, "Don't you understand? In your previous life you were careful to observe the ten good rules of conduct, and for that reason you were reborn in this life as a ruler of ten thousand chariots. But now evil entanglements have you in their power, and your days of good fortune have come to an end.

"First," she told him tearfully, "you must face east and bid farewell to the goddess of the Grand Shrine at Ise. Then you must turn west and trust in Amida Buddha to come with his hosts to greet you and lead you to his Pure Land. Come now, turn your face to the west and recite the invocation of the Buddha's name. This far-off land of ours is no bigger than a millet seed, a realm of sorrow and adversity. Let us leave it now and go together to a place of rejoicing, the paradise of the Pure Land!"

Dressed in a dove gray robe, his hair now done in boyish loops on either side of his head, the child, his face bathed in tears, pressed his small hands together, knelt down, and bowed first toward the east, taking his leave of the deity of the Ise Shrine. Then he turned toward the west and began chanting the *nenbutsu*, the invocation of Amida's name. The nun then took him in her arms. Comforting him, she said, "There's another capital down there beneath the waves!" So they plunged to the bottom of the thousand-fathom sea.

How pitiful that the spring winds of impermanence should so abruptly scatter the beauty of the blossoms; how heartless that the rough waves of reincarnation should engulf this tender body! Long Life is the name they give to the imperial palace, signaling that one should reside there for years unending; its gates are dubbed Ageless, a term that speaks of a reign forever young. Yet before he had reached the age of ten, this ruler ended as refuse on the ocean floor.

Ten past virtues rewarded with a throne, yet how fleeting was that prize! He who once was a dragon among the clouds now had become a fish in the depths of the sea. Dwelling once on terraces lofty as those of the god Brahma, in palaces like the Joyful Sight Citadel of the god Indra, surrounded by great lords and ministers of state, a throng of kin and clansmen in his following, now in an instant he ended his life beneath this boat, under these billows — sad, sad indeed!

Yoshitsune returns to the capital with the imperial regalia and the Heike prisoners. The praise and awards showered on him arouse the suspicions of Yoritomo, and the situation is exacerbated when Kajiwara Kagetoki slanders Yoshitsune. Meanwhile, Munemori and his son, as well as Shigehira and other leading members of the Taira family, are executed.

BOOK TWELVE

MONGAKU: Buddhist practitioner; incites Yoritomo to move against the Heike.

ROKUDAI (Taira): son of Koremori and sole remaining heir to the main Taira line.

TOKIMASA (Hōjō): father-in-law of Yoritomo.

A large earthquake strikes the capital. Yoshitsune is forced to flee Kyoto when his brother Yoritomo moves against him with an army under the command of Hōjō Tokimasa. While in the capital, Tokimasa seeks and executes all presumptive heirs to the Heike family. He discovers Koremori's son Rokudai, the last surviving male heir of the Taira. Mongaku appeals to Yoritomo, who spares the boy's life on condition that Rokudai agree to take the tonsure.

The Execution of Rokudai (12:9)

And so the years passed, and when Rokudai reached the age of fourteen or fifteen, he became even more handsome in face and form, seeming to cast a brilliance over everything around him. Watching him, his mother declared, "If only things were now as they were in the past, he would be a captain of the imperial guard!" She should not have put it in so many words.

Yoritomo, the lord of Kamakura, never ceased to feel uneasy about Rokudai. Whenever he had occasion to write to his keeper, Mongaku, the holy man of Takao, he would ask, "What is that son of Koremori up to? You once predicted that I would overthrow the enemies of the throne and remove the disgrace suffered by my father. Is he that sort of person?"

Mongaku would reply, "He's nothing, an utter coward! You needn't have the slightest worry on that score!" But Yoritomo was not satisfied with such answers. "If someone were to raise a revolt, Mongaku is the sort who would immediately become his ally. As long as I'm alive, I know of no one who could overthrow our family. But who is to know how my sons and grandsons may fare?"

These were words of sinister import,[1] and when Rokudai's mother heard about them, she exclaimed, "No other course is open—Rokudai must enter the priesthood as soon as possible!"

Accordingly, sometime in the spring of the fifth year of the Bunji era [1189], Rokudai, who was sixteen at the time, took scissors and cut off the beautiful long hair that had hung around his shoulders. Equipping himself with a robe and a pair of trousers dyed in persimmon juice and a traveler's knapsack, he took leave of Mongaku and set out to devote himself to religious practice. His two retainers, Saitōgo and Saitōroku, dressed in similar fashion, accompanied him.

Rokudai went first to Mount Kōya, where he sought out Koremori's mentor in religion, Priest Takiguchi. From him he heard a detailed account of how Koremori had taken the tonsure and of his final moments. Then, as part of his religious practice and in order to view for himself the places where his father had been, he went to the Kumano Shrine. When he reached the small shrine of Hama-no-miya on the seashore, he could gaze across the waters at the island, Yamanari-no-shima, to which his father had gone. Rokudai would have liked to make the trip there himself, but adverse winds and waves prevented him from doing so.

His plans thwarted, he could only look out over the water, wondering just where his father had gone down, wishing that he could ask the white waves rolling in to give him an answer. And as he looked with these feelings around him at the sand on the beach, thinking that his father's bones might be mingled in with it, he found tears wetting his sleeves. Like the sleeves of the women diving for shellfish, they never seemed to be dry for a moment.

---

1.   This has been understood either to hint at Rokudai's later fate or to foreshadow M revolt.

Rokudai spent the night on the beach, repeating the *nenbutsu*, reciting sutras, and drawing images of the Buddha in the sand with his finger. The following day, he summoned an eminent Buddhist priest and asked him to perform memorial services for his father and to see that whatever religious merit might accrue from the activities he himself had performed was directed to his father's well-being in the other world. Then, begging leave of the departed spirit, he made his way back to the capital in tears....

Emperor GoToba, who was reigning at this time, spent much time thinking about his amusements and none at all about affairs of state. All was left to the whim of Lady Kyō-no-tsubone, the mother of his consort, which occasioned endless foreboding and discontent.

In ancient China, because the king of Wu delighted in sword fighting, numerous men in the empire suffered wounds, and because the king of Chu doted on women with slender waists, many of the palace ladies starved themselves to death. The tastes of those in power are inevitably copied by those under them.

People who saw the dangers inherent in the situation and were genuinely concerned could only despair. And then the holy man Mongaku, most troublesome in nature, interfered where he had no business to interfere. Because Emperor Takakura's second son was diligent in his studies and dedicated to correct principles, Mongaku began scheming to somehow have this son made heir to the throne. While Yoritomo remained alive, his efforts came to naught. But when Yoritomo died on the thirteenth day of the first month of Kenkyū 10 [1199], Mongaku immediately made plans for a revolt. These were speedily discovered; the government officials descended on his quarters at Nijō Inokuma in the capital; and he was handed over for questioning. Even though he was over eighty by this time, he was exiled to the island province of Oki.

As Mongaku was leaving the capital, he announced, "An old man like me, who doesn't know whether he'll live from one day to the next—even though it's an imperial command, to banish me to the far-off island of Oki instead of somewhere close to the capital! How I hate that ballplaying young man! Some day he'll end up on that very same Oki Island where I'm being sent!"

It was a fearful thing to have said. Emperor GoToba loved to play mallet ball, which is why Mongaku referred to him in this derogatory manner. Strangely enough, at the time of the Jōkyū rebellion [1221], when the imperial forces attempted to overthrow the Kamakura government, Emperor GoToba, who by this time had retired from the throne, was in fact exiled, and of all the provinces to which he might have been sent, he was banished to this very same island of Oki. It is said that Mongaku's departed spirit caused much mischief there and repeatedly appeared and spoke to the retired emperor.

Meanwhile, Rokudai, known now by the title of third-rank meditation master, continued to live at Takao and devote his time to religious practice. But Yoritomo was forever saying of him, "Considering whose son he is and whose disciple he is, even though he may have a monk's head, who knows what's in his heart!" So he gave orders to the police commissioner Sukekane to arrest Rokudai and have him sent to the Kantō region. On the banks of the Tagoe River, he was beheaded by a certain Yasutsuna, a native of the province of Suruga who had been ordered to do so. People said that the fact that he had been able to remain alive from the age of twelve to over thirty was due entirely to the divine protection of Bodhisattva Kannon of Hase.

Thus, with Rokudai, the Heike line came to an end for all time.

THE INITIATES' BOOK

GoShirakawa: retired emperor, head of the imperial clan, and paternal grandfather of Emperor Antoku.

Kenreimon'in (Taira): daughter of Kiyomori, consort of Emperor Takakura, and mother of the deceased emperor Antoku; taken prisoner at Dan-no-ura.

The Imperial Lady Becomes a Nun (1)

Kenreimon'in took up residence in the Yoshida area, at the foot of the eastern hills, in a small hermitage belonging to a Buddhist monk of Nara named Kyōe. No one had lived there for many years, and the hut had fallen into disrepair. The garden was buried in weeds, and wild ferns sprouted by the eaves. The blinds had rotted away, leaving the sleeping room exposed to view and offering little shelter from the wind or rain. Although blossoms of one kind and another opened in season, no occupant was present to admire them; and although the moonlight streamed in night after night, no one sat up until dawn delighting in it.

In earlier times, Kenreimon'in had rested on a jeweled dais, brocade hangings surrounding her, but now, parted from all those who had meant anything to her, she resided in this shabby, half-decayed retreat. One can only surmise how forlorn her thoughts must have been. She was like a fish stranded on land, a bird that has been torn from its nest. Such was her present life that she recalled with longing those earlier days when her home had been no more than a boat tossing on the waves. Her thoughts, journeying far away over blue-billowed waters, rested once again on the distant clouds of the western sea. In her reed-thatched hut deep in moss, she wept to see the moonlight fill her garden by the eastern hills. Truly, no words can convey her sadness.

On the first day of the Fifth Month in the first year of the Bunji era [1185], Imperial Lady Kenreimon'in took the tonsure and became a nun. The priest who administered the precepts to her was the Reverend Insei of Chōraku-ji. In return she made an offering to him of an informal robe that had belonged to her son, the late emperor Antoku. He had worn the robe until his final days, and it still retained the fragrance of his body. She had brought it all the way with her when she returned to the capital from the western region, regarding it as a last memento of her child, and had supposed that whatever might come, she would never part with it. But since she had nothing else to serve as a gift, she offered it with a profusion of tears, hopeful that at the same time it might help her son attain buddhahood.

The Reverend Insei could find no words with which to acknowledge the offering but, wetting the black sleeves of his clerical robe, made his way from the room in tears. It is said that he had the robe remade into a holy banner to hang in front of the Buddha of Chōraku-ji.

By imperial order when she was fifteen, Kenreimon'in had been appointed to serve in the palace, and when she was sixteen, she advanced to the position of imperial consort, attending at the emperor's side. At dawn she urged him to look to the official business of the court; when evening came she was his sole companion for the night. At the age of twenty-two she bore him a son, who was designated as the heir apparent, and when he ascended the throne she was honored with the palace appellation of Kenreimon'in.

Because she was not only the daughter of the lay priest and prime minister Kiyomori but the mother of the nation's ruler as well, she was held in the highest respect by everyone in the realm. At the time of which we are speaking, she had reached the age of twenty-nine. Her complexion retained the freshness of peach or damson petals; her face had not lost its lotuslike beauty. But hair ornaments of kingfisher feathers were no longer of any use to her, for her hair had been shorn; her whole figure had suffered a change.

Despairing of this fickle world, Kenreimon'in had entered the true path of religion, but this had by no means brought an end to her sighs. While she could still recall how those she loved had sunk beneath the waves, the figure of her son, the late emperor, and her mother, the Nun of the Second Rank, remained to haunt her memory. She wondered why her own dewdrop existence had continued for so long, why she had lived on only to see such painful sights, and her tears flowed without end. Short as the Fifth Month nights were, she found them almost too long to endure, and since sleep was, by the nature of things, denied her, she could not hope to recapture the past even in her dreams. The lamp, its back to the wall, gave only a flicker of dying light, yet all night she lay awake listening to the mournful pelting of rain at the dark window. The Shangyang lady, imprisoned in Shangyang Palace, had endured similarly mournful nights, but her grief could hardly have been greater than Kenreimon'in's.[1]

Perhaps to remind himself of the past, the previous owner of the retreat had planted an orange tree by the eaves, and its blossoms now wafted their poignant fragrance on the breeze, while a cuckoo from the hills, lighting there, sang out two or three notes. Kenreimon'in, remembering an old poem, wrote the words on the lid of her inkstone box:

> Cuckoo, you come singing, tracing the orange tree's scent—
> is it because you yearn for someone now gone?

The ladies-in-waiting who had once attended her, but lacked the strength of character needed to drown themselves on the sea bottom as had the Nun of the Second Rank or the Third-Rank Lady of Echizen, had been taken prisoner by the rough hands of the Genji warriors. Returned now to the capital where they had once lived, young and old alike had become nuns, their aspect wholly changed, their purpose in life utterly vanished. In remote valleys, among rocky cliffs, sites they had never even dreamed of in the past, they passed their days. The houses where they had dwelled before all had disappeared with the smoke of battle; mere traces of them remained, little

1. When Yang Guifei came to monopolize the affections of Emperor Xuanzong, the other ladies who had enjoyed his attentions were forced to retire to seclusion in the Shangyang Palace. The passage alludes to a poem by Bo Juyi on the fate of one such lady.

by little overgrown with grasses of the field. No familiar figures came there anymore. They must have felt as desolate as those men in the Chinese tale who, having spent what they thought was a mere half day in the realm of the immortals, returned to their old home to confront their seventh-generation descendants.

And then, on the ninth day of the Seventh Month, a severe earthquake toppled the tile-capped mud wall and rendered Kenreimon'in's dwelling, already dilapidated, even more ruinous and unsound, so that it was hardly fit for habitation. Worse off than the lady of Shangyang Palace, Kenreimon'in had no green-robed guard to stand at her gate. The hedges, now left untended, were laden with more dew than the lush meadow grasses, and insects, making themselves at home there, had already begun crying out their doleful chorus of complaints. As the fall nights grew longer, Kenreimon'in found herself more wakeful than ever, the hours passing with intolerable slowness. To the endless memories that haunted her were now added the sorrows of the autumn season, until it was almost more than she could bear. Since her whole world had undergone such drastic change, no one was left who might offer her so much as a passing word of consolation, no one to whom she might look for support.

The Move to Ōhara (2)

Although such was the case, the wives of the Reizei senior counselor, Takafusa, and of Lord Nobutaka, Kenreimon'in's younger sisters, while shunning public notice, managed to call on her in private. "In the old days I would never have dreamed that I might sometime be beholden to them for support!" exclaimed the imperial lady, moved to tears by their visit, and all the ladies in attendance shed tears as well.

The place where Kenreimon'in was living was not far from the capital, and the bustling road leading past it was full of prying eyes. She could not help feeling that fragile as her existence might be, mere dew before the wind, she might better live it out in some more remote mountain setting where distressing news of worldly affairs was less likely to reach her. She had been unable to find a suitable location, however, when a certain lady who had called on her mentioned that the Buddhist retreat known as Jakkō-in in the mountains of Ōhara was a very quiet spot.

A mountain village may be lonely, she thought to herself, recalling an old poem on the subject, but it is a better place to dwell than among the world's troubles and sorrows. Having thus determined to move, she found that her sister, the wife of Lord Takafusa, could probably arrange for a palanquin and other necessities. Accordingly, in the first year of the Bunji era, as the Ninth Month was drawing to a close, she set off for the Jakkō-in in Ōhara.

As Kenreimon'in passed along the road, observing the hues of the autumn leaves on the trees all around her, she soon found the day coming to a close, perhaps all the sooner because she was entering the shade of the mountains. The tolling of the evening bell from a temple in the fields sounded its somber note, and dew from the grasses along the way made her sleeves, already damp with tears, wetter than ever. A stormy wind began to blow, tumbling the leaves from the trees; the sky clouded over; and autumn showers began to fall. She could just catch the faint sad belling of a deer, and the half-audible lamentations of the insects. Everything contrived to fill her with a sense of desolation difficult to describe in words. Even in those earlier days, when her life had been a precarious journey from one cove or one island to another, she reflected sadly, she had never had such a feeling of hopelessness.

The retreat was in a lonely spot of moss-covered crags, the sort of place, she felt, where she could live out her days. As she looked about her, she noted that the bush clover in the dew-filled garden had been stripped of its leaves by frost, that the chrysanthemums by the hedge, past their prime, were faded and dry—all reflecting, it seemed, her own condition. Making her way to where the statue of the Buddha was enshrined, she said a prayer: "May the spirit of the late emperor attain perfect enlightenment; may he quickly gain the wisdom of the buddhas!" But even as she did so, the image of her dead son seemed to appear before her, and she wondered in what future existence she might be able to forget him.

Next to the Jakkō-in she had a small building erected, ten feet square in size, with one room to sleep in and the other to house the image of the Buddha. Morning and evening, day and night, she performed her devotions in front of the image, ceaselessly intoning the Buddha's name over the long hours. In this way, always diligent, she passed the months and days.

On the fifteenth day of the Tenth Month, as evening was approaching, Kenreimon'in heard the sound of footsteps on the dried oak leaves that littered the garden. "Who could be coming to call at a place so far removed from the world as this?" she said, addressing her woman companion. "Go see who it is. If it is someone I should not see, I must hurry to take cover!" But when the woman went to look, she found that it was only a stag that had happened to pass by.

"Who was it?" asked Kenreimon'in, to which her companion, Lady Dainagon no Suke, struggling to hold back her tears, replied with this poem:

> Who would tread a path to this rocky lair?
> It was a deer whose passing rustled the leaves of the oak.

Struck by the pathos of the situation, Kenreimon'in carefully inscribed the poem on the small sliding panel by her window.

During her drab and uneventful life, bitter as it was, she found many things that provided food for thought. The trees ranged before the eaves of her retreat suggested to her the seven rows of jewel-laden trees that are said to grow in the Western Paradise, and the water pooled in a crevice in the rocks brought to mind the wonderful water of eight blessings to be found there. Spring blossoms, so easily scattered with the breeze, taught her a lesson in impermanence; the autumn moon, so quickly hidden by its companion clouds, spoke of the transience of life. Those court ladies in the Zhaoyang Hall in China who admired the blossoms at dawn soon saw their petals blown away by the wind; those in the Changqiu Palace who gazed at the evening moon had its brightness stolen from them by clouds. Once in the past, this lady too had lived in similar splendor, reclining on brocade bedclothes in chambers of gold and jade, and now in a hut of mere brushwood and woven vines—even strangers must weep for her.

The Retired Emperor Visits Ōhara (3)

Things went along like this until the spring of the second year of the Bunji era [1186], when the retired emperor, GoShirakawa, decided that he would like to visit Kenreimon'in in her secluded retreat in Ōhara. During the Second and Third Months, the last of the winter cold lingered, and the winds continued to bluster. The snow on the mountain peaks had not yet melted, and the icicles remained frozen in the valleys. The spring months had given way to summer and the festival of the Kamo Shrine was already over when the retired emperor, setting out before dawn, began the journey to the mountain recesses of Ōhara.

Although the progress was unofficial, the retired emperor was accompanied by six ministers of state, among them Fujiwara no Sanesada, Fujiwara no Kanemasa, and Minamoto no Michichika, as well as eight high-ranking courtiers and a small number of armed men from the imperial guard. The party proceeded by way of the village of Kurama, stopping along the route so that the retired emperor might see Fudaraku-ji, the temple founded by Kiyohara no Fukayabu,[2] and the site where Empress Dowager Ono[3] had resided after she retired from court life and became a nun. From there he continued the journey by palanquin.

The white clouds hovering over the distant mountains seemed like mementos of the cherry blossoms that had earlier bloomed there and scattered, and the green leaves that had replaced them in the treetops spoke regretfully of the spring now gone. Since it was already past the twentieth day of the Fourth Month by the lunar calendar, the party found themselves pushing through lush summer grasses. And since this was the first time that the retired emperor had made the journey, he was not familiar with any of the places they passed. Encountering not a soul along the way, how bleak it all must have seemed to him.

At the foot of the western hills stood a little hall, the Jakkō-in, or Cloister of Tranquil Light. The ornamental pond in front of it and the groves of trees told of the long history surrounding it. It perhaps was the sort of place the poet had in mind when he wrote

Roof tiles broken, the odor of mist forever lingers there;
doors fallen off, the moon shines in like a constantly lighted lamp.

---

2. Kiyohara no Fukayabu was a tenth-century courtier and poet who was later designated as one of the thirty-six sages of poetry.
3. The empress was the wife of Emperor GoReizei (r. 1045–1068).

The garden overflowed with new foliage; green strands from the willows hung down in a tangle; and the duckweed on the surface of the pond, undulating with the ripples, could have been mistaken for brocade stretched out to dry. Wisteria clinging to the pine on the island in the pond descended in cascades of purple; the last late cherry flowers remaining among the newly opened green leaves appeared more to be prized than the first blossoms of the season. Kerria roses flowered in profusion on the banks of the pond, and from a rift in the many-layered clouds sounded the note of a cuckoo, as if to herald the ruler's arrival.

Surveying the scene, the retired emperor recited this poem:

> Cherries on the bank have strewn the pond with petals —
> wave-borne blossoms now are in their glory.

Even the sound of the water as it dripped from a cleft in the age-old rocks seemed to mark this as a setting of rare charm. The fence of green vines and creepers, the blue hills beyond, darkened as though with an eyebrow pencil, surpassed anything that could be captured in a painting.

When the retired emperor examined Kenreimon'in's little dwelling, he noted the ivy and morning glories twined around the eaves and the daylilies mixed in among the ferns, and they reminded him of Yan Yuan, the impoverished disciple of Confucius who lived in a grass-grown alley and whose dipper and rice bowl were so often empty, and Yuan Xian, another disciple, his pathway clogged with pigweed and his door soaked with rain. In Kenreimon'in's retreat the autumn showers, the frost, and the falling dew seeped in through cracks in the cedar shingles, vying with rays of moonlight, since there was little to keep any of them out. With hills behind, barren fields in front, the wind rustling through the scant bamboo grass that grew there, its knotted posts of bamboo suggested the knotty trials and grief constantly borne by one living away from the world; and its gaping fence of stalks hinted at how far removed the spot was from all news of the capital. Few sounds reached there other than the cries of monkeys springing from limb to limb in hilltop trees or the echo of a lowly woodcutter's ax; aside from the prying tendrils of creepers clinging to the spindle tree or the strands of green ivy, few sought entrance there.

"Is anyone in? Is anyone in?" called the retired emperor, but no one responded. Finally, after some time, an elderly nun, bent with age, appeared.

"Where is the imperial lady?" asked the retired emperor.

"She has gone to the hilltop to pick flowers," was the answer.

"Doesn't she have someone who can do such things for her?" he asked. "This is too pitiable, even for someone who has renounced the world!"

"The good karmic effects resulting from her observance of the Five Precepts and the Ten Virtuous Acts in a previous existence have ended," the old nun explained, "and so she has been reduced to the state in which you see her. But when one has renounced the world to pursue religious practice, why recoil from such hardships? As the Sutra on Cause and Effect tells us, 'If you would know past causes, look to present effects; if you would know future effects, observe present causes.' When Your Majesty understands the relationship between cause and effect in the past and future, you will see that there is no occasion for lamentation. At the age of nineteen the crown prince Siddhartha left the city of Gaya and went to the foot of Mount Dadaloka. There, fashioning a garment of tree leaves to cover his nakedness, he climbed the peaks to gather firewood, descended into the valleys to draw water, and through the merit accruing from these difficult and painful practices he was able in the end to gain complete and perfect enlightenment."

Looking at the nun more closely, the retired emperor could see that she was dressed in a sort of patched robe in which bits of silk and plain cloth had been randomly sewn together. Wondering that such a speech should emanate from a person dressed like this, he asked, "Who are you?"

Breaking down in sobs, the nun was at first unable to reply. Finally, mastering her tears, she replied, "I cannot answer without feelings of great embarrassment! I am the daughter of the late lesser counselor and lay priest Fujiwara no Shinsei. I was known by the name Awa-no-naishi. My mother was the Kii Lady of the Second Rank. At one time you were kind enough to treat me with great favor. If now you no longer recognize me, then, old and decrepit as I am, what good would there be in trying to remind you..." She hid her face in her sleeve, helpless to control her emotions, a sight too pitiable to behold.

"Are you really Awa-no-naishi?" the retired emperor exclaimed, tears welling up in his eyes. "Indeed, I did not recognize you. This all seems like a dream!"

The lords and courtiers accompanying him remarked to one another, "We thought she was a very unusual nun, and now it appears we had good reason to do so."

Turning his gaze this way and that, the retired emperor could see that the many different plants in the garden were heavy with dew, their stalks bending down toward the hedges. Water brimmed in the paddy fields beyond, leaving hardly enough space for a snipe to alight.

Entering the hut, the retired emperor slid open the paper panel and walked in. In one room were enshrined the three venerable ones who come to greet those who are on their deathbed, the Buddha Amida and his attendants and the bodhisattvas Kannon and Seishi. A five-color cord was attached to the hand of the Buddha, the central figure.[4] To the left of the images hung a painting of the bodhisattva Fugen, while on the right were paintings of the Chinese priest Shandao and of Kenreimon'in's son, the late emperor. The eight scrolls of the Lotus Sutra and the nine chapters of Shandao's writings on the Pure Land also were nearby. The rich fragrance of orchid and musk that in earlier days had surrounded the imperial lady had vanished, giving way now to the scented smoke of altar incense. That ten-foot-square chamber of the lay believer Vimalakirti, which nevertheless, we are told, could accommodate thirty-two thousand seats set out for the buddhas of the ten directions when he invited them to call, must have been a room just like this. Here and there on the sliding panels were key passages from the Buddhist scriptures, written out on colored paper and pasted there. Among them were the lines by the Buddhist prelate Ōe no Sadamoto that he wrote shortly before his death at Mount Qingliang in China:

Pipes and songs far off I hear from a lone cloud—
in the setting sun the sacred hosts coming to greet me!

A little to one side was a poem that appeared to be by the imperial lady herself:

Did I ever think that, dwelling deep in these mountains,
I would view from far off the moon that shone on the palace?

---

4.   A dying person took hold of the cord attached to Amida's hand to ensure that he or she would be reborn in the Pure Land, or Western Paradise.

Looking in the other direction, the retired emperor saw what appeared to be a sleeping apartment, with a hempen robe, paper bedclothes, and other articles hanging from a bamboo pole. The adornments of silks, gauzes, brocades, and embroideries, the finest to be found in all Japan or China, that the imperial lady had once known in such abundance, were now no more than a dream. Having had glimpses of her in former times, the courtiers and high ministers seemed to see her still as she was then, and their tears rained down.

Soon two nuns dressed in robes of deep black were to be seen cautiously making their way down the steep rocky trail that led from the hilltop.

"Who is that?" the retired emperor inquired, whereupon the old nun, repressing her tears, replied, "The one with the flower basket on her arm, carrying branches of wild azalea, is the imperial lady. The one carrying brushwood and bunches of edible ferns is the daughter

Retired Emperor GoShirakawa (*right*) visits Ken'reimonin at the Jakkō-in at Ōhara. GoShirakawa (*left*) watches Ken'reimonin come down the mountain with flowers that she has gathered.

of Junior Counselor Korezane. She became the adopted daughter of Senior Counselor Lord Kunitsuna and afterward was the wet nurse to the late emperor, going by the name Dainagon no Suke." Her voice trailed off in tears. The retired emperor, too, moved by the scene, could not keep from weeping.

Taking note of the situation, Kenreimon'in thought to herself, "I have abandoned all concern for worldly affairs, yet I would hate to have them see me dressed like this. If only there were someplace I could hide!" But such hopes were vain. Evening after evening she wet her sleeves as she dipped water for the Buddha's altar, and each dawn when she rose the dew on the mountain path further damp-ened her sleeves, so that they were seldom wrung dry. Added to these now were her tears. She could not return to the hilltop, nor could she enter her own rooms unseen. She stood in blank indecision until the old nun, Awa-no-naishi, went to her and took the flower basket from her arm.

The Six Paths of Existence (4)

"A nun must look as you do—why should it seem such a hardship?" said Awa-no-naishi. "You must receive His Majesty so that he may begin his journey back." Kenreimon'in accordingly returned to her hut.

"In front of the window where I recite a single invocation of the Buddha's name, I look for the rays of light that proclaim his advent. By my brushwood door with ten invocations I await the host of holy ones coming to escort me. But how strange and beyond all thought is this visit from Your Majesty!" She wept as she greeted him.

The retired emperor surveyed her form and attire. "Even those beings in the abode of No-Thought, though they live for eighty thousand kalpas," he said, "must suffer the sadness of inevitable extinction. Even those in the Sixth Heaven[5] of the realm of form cannot escape the pain of the Five Marks of Decay.[6] The delights of longevity enjoyed by the god Indra in his Joyful Sight Citadel or the soaring pavilions of the god Brahma in the midst of the Meditation Heavens are no more than dreamlike boons, phantom pleasures of the moment.[7] All are bound to the wheel of unending change and transmigration, like cartwheels turning. The sadness of the Five Marks of Decay suffered by these heavenly beings must be borne, it seems, by us humans as well!" And then he added, "Who comes to visit you here? You must brood much on the events of the past."

"I do not receive visits from anyone," Kenreimon'in responded, "although I have some tidings now and then from my sisters, the wives of Takafusa and Nobutaka. In the past I would never, for a moment, have supposed that I would one day look to them for support." She wept as she said this, and the women attending her likewise wet their sleeves with tears.

Restraining her tears, Kenreimon'in spoke once more. "My current existence is no more than a passing tribulation, and when I think that it may lead to wisdom in the world to come, I look on it as joyful. I have made haste to join the latter-day disciples of Shakyamuni

5. The Sixth Heaven is the highest realm in the world of desire and is inhabited by gods.
6. The Five Marks of Decay are when human beings' clothes become dirty, their hair flowers fade, their bodies smell, they sweat, and they no longer enjoy their original status.
7. Brahma and Indra are two of the main gods of Hindu mythology. They were incorporated into Buddhist cosmology as protectors of Buddhism, although their heavens are located in the Six Paths of Existence.

and reverently entrusted myself to Amida's original vow of salvation so that I may escape the bitterness of the five obstacles and three submissions imposed on a woman.[8] Three times daily and nightly I labor to purify the six senses, hopeful that I may immediately win rebirth in one of the nine grades of the Pure Land. My only prayer is that all we members of the Taira clan may gain enlightenment, always trusting that the three venerable ones will come to greet us. The face of my son, the late emperor, I will never forget, whatever world may come. I try to forget but I can never do so; I try to endure the pain but it is unendurable. There is no bond more compelling than that between parent and child. Day and night I make it my duty to pray for his salvation. And this endeavor has been like a good friend leading me into the path of the Buddha."

The retired emperor offered an answer. "Although I have been born in these far-off islands no bigger than scattered millet seeds, because I reverently observed in a past existence the Ten Good Acts of Conduct, I have been privileged in this one to become a ruler of ten thousand chariots. Everything I could wish for has been granted to me; my heart has been denied nothing. And most particularly, because I was fortunate enough to be born in an age when the Buddhist teachings are propagated, I have set my heart on practicing the Buddha's way and do not doubt that in the time to come I will be reborn in a far better place. We should have learned by now, I suppose, not to question the miseries of human existence. And yet, seeing you like this seems too pitiful a sight!"

The imperial lady began to speak once more. "I was the daughter of the Taira prime minister and the mother of the nation's ruler— anything in the entire realm and the four seas surrounding it was mine for the asking. Beginning with the rites that mark the advent of spring, through the seasonal changes of clothing, to the recitation of Buddha names that brings the year to a close, I was waited on by all the high ministers and courtiers, from the regent on down. There were none of the hundred officials who did not look up to me with awe, as though I dwelled on the clouds of the Six Heavens of the realm of desire or the four Meditation Heavens, with the eighty thou-

---

8. According to Buddhist belief, a woman may not become (at least directly) a Brahma, an Indra, a devil king, a wheel-turning king, or a buddha. She is expected to submit to and obey her father in childhood, her husband in maturity, and her son in old age when she is widowed.

sand heavenly beings encircling me. I lived in the Seiryō or Shishin-den palaces, curtained by jeweled hangings, in spring spending the days with my eyes fixed on the cherries of the Southern Pavilion; enduring the oppressive heat of summer's three months through the comfort of fountain waters; never left without companions to watch the cloud-borne autumn moon; on winter nights when the snow lay cold, I was swathed in layers of bed clothing. I wanted to learn the arts of prolonging life and evading old age, even if it meant seek-ing the herbs of immortality from the island of Penglai, for my sole wish was to live on and on. Day and night I thought of nothing but pleasure, believing that the happy fortune enjoyed by the heavenly beings could not surpass this life of mine.

"And then, in early autumn of the Juei era [1183], because of threats from Kiso no Yoshinaka or some such person, all the mem-bers of our Taira clan saw the capital that had been our home grow as distant as the clouds themselves, and looked back as our former dwellings in Fukuhara were reduced to fire-blackened fields. We made our way by water from Suma to Akashi, places that in the past were mere names to us, grieving over our lot. By day we plied the boundless waves, moistening our sleeves with spray; at night we cried until dawn with the plovers on sandy points along the shore. Moving from bay to bay, island to island, we saw scenery pleasant enough but could never forget our old home. With no place to take refuge, we knew the misery of the Five Marks of Decay and the prospect of certain extinction.

"Separation from loved ones, meeting with suffering, encounter with all that is hateful—in my life as a human being, I have expe-rienced all of these. The Four Sufferings,[9] the Eight Sufferings[10]— not one of them have I been spared! And then, in a place called Dazaifu in the province of Chikuzen, we were driven away by some Koreyoshi person who refused us lodging in Kyushu—a broad land of mountains and plains but with nowhere that we could take shel-ter. Once more, autumn drew to a close, but the moon, which we

9. The Four Sufferings are the suffering of birth, the suffering of old age, the suffering of sick-ness, and the suffering of death.
10. The Eight Sufferings are the suffering of birth, the suffering of old age, the suffering of sickness, the suffering of death, the suffering of separation from loved ones, the suffering of being with those one hates, the suffering of frustrated desires, and the suffering of attach-ment to self.

used to watch from the heights of the nine-tier palace, this year we watched from salt-sea paths eightfold in their remoteness.

"So the days and nights passed until in the Tenth Month, the Godless Month, the middle captain, Kiyotsune, declared, 'The capital has fallen to the Genji; we have been hounded out of Chinzei by Koreyoshi—we're like fish caught in a net! Where can we find safety? What hope have I of living out my life?' And with these words he drowned himself in the sea, the beginning of our first sorrows.

"We passed our days on the waves, our nights in the boats. No articles of tribute came in as they had in the past, no one gave us any supplies or provisions. Even on the rare occasion when we had food, we had no water with which to eat it. We were afloat on the vast ocean, but its waters, being salty, were undrinkable. Thus I came to know the sufferings of those who inhabit the realm of hungry spirits.

"After that, we won victory in certain encounters such as those at Muroyama and Mizushima, and our people's countenances began to be somewhat more cheerful. But then came Ichi-no-tani, when we lost so many of our clansmen. Thereafter, instead of informal robes and court dress, our men put on helmets, buckled on armor, and from morning until night we heard only the din and cry of battle. Then I knew that the assaults of the asura demons, their clashes with the god Indra, must present just such a spectacle as this.

"After the defeat at Ichi-no-tani, young men perished before their fathers, wives were torn from husbands. When we spied a boat in the sea, we trembled lest it be an enemy craft; when we glimpsed herons roosting in distant pine trees, our hearts stopped, for we mistook them for the white banners of the Genji. Then came the naval battle in the straits between the Moji and Akama barriers, and it seemed as though that day must be our last.

"My mother, the Nun of the Second Rank, said to me, 'At such a time as this a man has little more than one chance in ten thousand of surviving. And even though some distant relative might survive the day alive, he would not be the kind who could offer prayers for our well-being in the life hereafter. But it has been the custom from times past to spare the women in such a conflict. If you should manage to live out the day, you must pray that your son, the emperor, may find salvation in the life to come, and help the rest of us with your prayers as well!' Over and over she urged this on me, and I listened as though in a dream.

"But then the wind began to blow and thick clouds blanketed the sky. Our warriors' hearts failed them, for it seemed that whatever fortune we had enjoyed with Heaven had now run out and that human efforts were no longer of any help.

"When the Nun of the Second Rank saw how things stood, she lifted the emperor in her arms and hastened to the side of the boat. Startled and confused, the child said, 'Grandma, where are you going to take me?'

"'Don't you understand?' she said, gazing at his innocent face and struggling to hold back her tears. 'In your previous life you were careful to observe the Ten Good Rules of Conduct, and for that reason you were reborn in this life as a ruler of ten thousand chariots. But now evil entanglements have you in their power, and your days of good fortune have come to an end. First, you must face east and bid farewell to the goddess of the Grand Shrine at Ise. Then you must turn west and trust in Amida Buddha to come with his hosts to greet you and lead you to his Pure Land. Turn your face to the west now, and recite the invocation of the Buddha's name. This far-off land of ours is no bigger than a millet seed, a realm of sorrow and adversity. Let us leave it now and go together to a place of rejoicing, the Paradise of the Pure Land!'

"The child was dressed in a dove gray robe, his hair done in boyish loops on either side of his head. His face bathed in tears, he pressed his small hands together, knelt down, and bowed first toward the east, taking his leave of the deity of the Ise Shrine. Then he turned toward the west and began chanting the invocation of Amida's name. And when I saw the nun, with the boy in her arms, at last sink beneath the sea, my eyes grew dim and my wits seemed to leave me. I try to forget that moment, but I can never do so. I try to endure the pain, but it is more than I can endure. The wails of the wrongdoers who suffer in the depths of the Hell of Shrieks and the Hell of Great Shrieks could not be more heartrending, I believe, than the screams and cries of those of us who lived to witness these events!

"After that, I was taken prisoner by the Genji warriors and set out on the journey back to the capital. When we had put in at the bay of Akashi in the province of Harima, I happened to doze off, and in my dream found myself in a place far surpassing in beauty the imperial palace I had known in earlier times. My son, the late emperor, was there, and all the high ministers and courtiers of the Taira clan were waiting on him with the most solemn ceremony. Never since leaving the capital had I beheld such magnificent surroundings, and I said to the people, 'What place is this?'

"Someone who appeared to be my mother, the Nun of the Second Rank, replied, 'This is the palace of the dragon king.'

"'What a wonderful place!' I exclaimed. 'And do those who live here not suffer?'

"'Our lot is described in the sutras on dragons and beasts. You must pray in all earnestness for our salvation in the world to come!'

"As soon as she had spoken these words, I awoke from my dream. Since then I have been more diligent than ever in reciting sutras and invoking the Buddha's name, hopeful that thereby I may help them attain salvation. And so you see, in this manner I have experienced all six paths of existence."

When she had finished speaking, the retired emperor said, "The Tripitaka master, Xuanzang, in China is reported to have seen the six paths of existence before he attained enlightenment, and in our own country the Venerable Nichizō, we are told, was able to see them through the power of the deity Zaō Gongen. But that you have seen them before your very eyes is miraculous indeed!"

He wept as he spoke these words, and the lords and courtiers attending him all wet their sleeves with tears. Kenreimon'in, too, broke down in tears, as did her women companions.

The Death of the Imperial Lady (5)

While they were speaking, the bell of the Jakkō-in sounded, signaling the close of the day, and the sun sank beyond the western hills. The retired emperor, reluctant though he was to leave, wiped away his tears and prepared to begin the journey back.

All her memories of the past brought back to her once more, Kenreimon'in could scarcely stem the flood of tears with her sleeve. She stood watching as the imperial entourage set out for the capital, watching until it was far in the distance. Then she turned to the image of the Buddha and, speaking through her tears, uttered this prayer: "May the spirit of the late emperor and the souls of all my clanspeople who perished attain complete and

perfect enlightenment; may they quickly gain the wisdom of the Buddhas!"

In the past she had faced eastward with this petition: "Great Deity of the Grand Shrine of Ise and Great Bodhisattva Hachiman, may the Son of Heaven be blessed with most wonderful longevity, may he live a thousand autumns, ten thousand years!" But now she changed direction and, facing west with palms pressed together, in sorrow spoke these words: "May the souls of all those who have perished find their way to Amida's Pure Land!"

On the sliding panel of her sleeping room she had inscribed the following poems:

When did my heart learn such ways?
Of late I think so longingly of palace companions I once knew!

The past, too, has vanished like a dream—
my days by this brushwood door cannot be long in number!

Ken'reimonin (*right*), together with the nuns Dainagon-no-suke and Awa-no-naishi, pray to the Buddha. Ken'reimonin (*left*) is welcomed to the Pure Land by Amida Buddha and two bodhisattvas riding on a lavender cloud.

The following poem is reported to have been inscribed on a pillar of Kenreimon'in's retreat by Minister of the Left Sanesada, one of the officials who accompanied the retired emperor on his visit:

You who in past times were likened to the moon—
    dwelling now deep in these faraway mountains, a light no longer
        shining—.

Once, when Kenreimon'in was bathed in tears, overwhelmed by memories of the past and thoughts of the future, she heard the cry of a mountain cuckoo and wrote this poem:

Come then, cuckoo, let us compare tears—
    I too do nothing but cry out in a world of pain

The Taira warriors who survived the Dan-no-ura hostilities and were taken prisoner were paraded through the main streets of the capital and then either beheaded or sent into exile far from their wives and children. With the exception of Taira no Yorimori, not one escaped execution or was permitted to remain in the capital.

With regard to the forty or more Taira wives, no special punitive measures were taken—they were left to join their relatives or to seek aid from persons they had known in the past. But even those fortunate enough to find themselves seated within sumptuous hangings were not spared the winds of uncertainty, and those who ended in humble brushwood dwellings could not live free of dust and turmoil. Husbands and wives who had slept pillow to pillow now found themselves at the far ends of the sky. Parents and children who had nourished each other no longer even knew each other's whereabouts. Although their loving thoughts never for a moment ceased, lament as they might, they had somehow to endure these things.

And all of this came about because the lay priest and prime minister Taira no Kiyomori, holding the entire realm within the four seas in the palm of his hand, showed no respect for the ruler above or the slightest concern for the masses of common people below. He dealt out sentences of death or exile in any fashion that suited him, took no heed of how the world or those in it might view his actions—and this is what happened! There can be no room for doubt—it was the evil deeds of the father, the patriarch, that caused the heirs and offspring to suffer this retribution!

After some time had gone by, Kenreimon'in fell ill. Grasping the five-color cord attached to the hand of Amida Buddha, the central figure in the sacred triad, she repeatedly invoked his name: "Hail to the Thus Come One Amida, lord of teachings of the Western Paradise— may you guide me there without fail!" The nuns Dainagon-no-suke and Awa-no-naishi attended her on her left and right, their voices raised in unrestrained weeping, for they sensed in their grief that her end was now at hand. As the sound of the dying woman's recitations grew fainter and fainter, a purple cloud appeared from the west, the room became filled with a strange fragrance, and the strains of music could be heard in the sky. Human life has its limits, and that of the imperial lady ended in the middle days of the Second Month in the second year of the Kenkyū era [1191].

Her two female attendants, who from the time she became imperial consort had never once been parted from her, were beside themselves with grief at her passing, helpless though they were to avert it.

The support on which they had depended from times past had now been snatched from them, and they were left destitute, yet even in that pitiable state they managed to hold memorial services each year on the anniversary of her death. And in due time they, too, we are told, imitating the example of the dragon king's daughter in her attainment of enlightenment and following in the footsteps of Queen Vaidehi, fulfilled their long-cherished hopes for rebirth in the Pure Land.

GLOSSARY OF CHARACTERS

The characters in *The Tales of the Heike* are usually listed under their personal (given) names, with cross-references provided where necessary. Emperors appear under their posthumous names used in the text (for example, Antoku). Abbreviated book and section references (for example, 1:1) in boldface type indicate the passages in which the historical figures appear in this translation, and those in lightface type signal events in other portions of the narrative. Variant texts of the *Heike monogatari* other than the Kakuichi version translated here and key episodes in later prose and dramatic genres are cited as well.

AKUGENDA: *see* Yoshihira.

AKUSHICHIBYŌE: *see* Kagekiyo.

ANTOKU, EMPEROR (1178–1185, r. 1180–1185): son of Emperor Takakura and Kenreimon'in (Tokuko). Taken by the Taira as they flee from the capital, he drowns at Dan-no-ura. He is also known as "the nation's ruler," "the late emperor," "the emperor," and "my son, the late emperor" [**1:5, 7:16, 7:20, 11:9, Initiates 1, 2, 4, 5**; 3:3, 4:1, 5:1, 7:9, 8:1, 8:3, 11:1].

ARIKUNI: Musashi no Saburōzaemon Arikuni, Taira samurai commander at the battle of Uji. He dies in the campaign against Yoshinaka [**4:11**; 7:4, 7:7].

ARIMORI (d. 1185): son of Taira no Shigemori. He takes his own life at Dan-no-ura [**11:10**; 6:10, 7:14, 7:19, 9:8, 10:1, 10:14].

ARIŌ: boy in Bishop Shunkan's service. He travels to his master's place of exile, witnessing his death. After cremating his master's body, he takes religious orders [**3:8, 3:9**].

ASARI: *see* Yoichi (1).

ATSUMORI (1169–1184): son of Taira no Tsunemori and nephew of Kiyomori. He dies at the hands of Naozane at Ichi-no-tani. Atsumori's death inspired many later works, including a work for the *kōwaka-mai* performance tradition, the nō plays *Atsumori* and *Ikuta Atsumori*, and Muromachi prose tales about the appearance of Atsumori's ghost to his son (*Ko Atsumori*) [9:16; 7:19].

AWA-NO-NAISHI: daughter of Fujiwara no Shinsei (or, according to other texts, his granddaughter). One of Kenreimon'in's companions in the Jakkō-in refuge, she is referred to as "an elderly nun" [Initiates 3–5].

BENKEI: Musashibō Benkei (d. 1189), warrior monk serving under Yoshitsune. Although Benkei has only a small role in the Kakuichi version, he plays an important part in the history of the Yoshitsune legend. Benkei is a central figure in *The Tale of Yoshitsune* (*Gikeiki*) and in shorter medieval prose tales like *The Tale of Benkei* (*Benkei monogatari*). He also appears in many nō and kabuki plays (*Hashi Benkei, Funa Benkei, Ataka,* and *Kanjinchō*) [9:9, 11:3, 11:7; 9:7, 12:4].

BEPPU NO KOTARŌ: young warrior in Yoshitsune's entourage [9:9; 9:7].

CHANCELLOR: *see* Kiyomori.

CHIKAKIYO: Taira archer from Iyo Province at the battle of Dan-no-ura [11:8].

CHIKAKU: monk at Mount Kōya. He is consulted by Koremori when he takes holy orders [10:10].

CHIKAMASA: Fujiwara Chikamasa (1145–1210), sent by Regent Motomichi with a message for the Nara monks [5:14; 11:11].

CHIKANORI: [Kaneko no Yoichi] Chikanori of Musashi Province, serving under Yoshitsune [11:3; 9:7, 11:1].

CHIKAYOSHI: Saiin [no Jikan] Chikayoshi (1133–1208), official serving under Yoritomo [10:7; 8:5, 10:14].

CHŪJI OF SHINANO: [Kiso no] Chūji, serving under Yoshitsune [11:5].

COMMANDER: *see* Yoshitsune.

DAINAGON NO SUKE, LADY: daughter of Major Counselor Kunitsuna, wife of Taira no Shigehira, and wet nurse to Emperor Antoku. Captured at Dan-no-ura, she accompanies Kenreimon'in to the Jakkō-in refuge [Initiates 2, 3, 5; 10:2, 10:4, 10:6, 11:10, 11:11, 11:19].

EMPEROR: many of the references to "the emperor" or "the late emperor" are to Antoku. Other emperors and retired emperors mentioned by name are GoShirakawa, GoToba, Kanmu, Seiwa, Shōmu, Takakura, and Toba.

EMPRESS: *see* Kenreimon'in.

ENJITSU: Buddhist priest who buries Kiyomori's remains [6:7].

FUHITO: Fujiwara no Fuhito (659–720), Lord Tankai, son of Kamatari. A leading political figure of his day, he was the founder of the Kōfuku-ji temple [5:14; 1:11, 7:9].

FUKAYABU: Kiyohara no Fukayabu, tenth-century courtier and poet [Initiates 3].

FUKAZU: Taira warrior at the battle of Uji [4:11].

GENTA: Tsuzuku no Genta, warrior on Prince Mochihito's side at the battle of Uji [4:11; 4:10].

GENZŌ OF EDA: Eda no Genzō, warrior serving under Yoshitsune [11:3; 9:7, 11:7, 11:13, 12:4].

GINYO: younger sister of Giō. She is a *shirabyōshi* dancer [1:6].

GIŌ: daughter of Toji. She is a *shirabyōshi* dancer favored by Kiyomori [1:6].

GISHIN (also read YOSHICHIKA): leader of a rebellion in western Japan in 1100 [1:1; 5:5, 5:11, 6:6].

GOSHIRAKAWA, EMPEROR (1127–1192, r. 1155–1158): fourth son of Emperor Toba and retired emperor from 1169 until his death. His sons include Emperor Takakura and Prince Takakura (Mochihito), and Emperors Antoku and GoToba were his grandsons [1:6, 2:6, 2:7, 3:1, 5:19, 6:7, 7:16, 7:20, 10:5, 12:9, Initiates 3, 4; 1:5, 1:7, 1:9, 1:11–14, 2:1, 2:3, 2:10, 2:12, 2:16, 3:3, 3:15, 3:19, 4:1–4, 4:6, 4:8, 5:1, 5:10, 5:11, 6:1, 6:4, 6:5, 6:7, 6:10, 6:12, 7:13, 8:1, 8:2, 8:5, 8:10, 8:11, 9:1, 9:5, 9:17, 10:1, 10:13, 11:13, 12:1].

GOTOBA, EMPEROR (1180–1239, r. 1183/1185–1198): fourth son of Emperor Takakura and retired emperor until 1221, when he is exiled to the island of Oki. He is chosen to succeed his brother Antoku, whom the Taira have taken with them on their flight from the capital [12:9; 8:1, 8:10, 10:14; 11:13, 11:14].

HABUKU: warrior on Prince Mochihito's side at the battle of Uji [4:11; 1:15, 4:10].

HARENOBU: doctor of divination [11:8].

HEYAKO NO SHIRŌ: Taira warrior at the battle of Uji [4:11].

HIDEKUNI: Kawachi no Hangan Hidekuni, Heike samurai commander [4:11; 7:2, 7:6].

HIDETŌ OF YAMAGA: Yamaga no Hyōdōji Hidetō, Heike commander of the vanguard boats at the battle of Dan-no-ura and the "finest archer in all of Kyushu" [11:7; 8:4].

HIGUCHI JIRŌ: *see* Kanemitsu.

HIROMI: Councillor Tachibana no Hiromi (837–890), author of the poem in Chinese (*Wakan rōeishū*, no. 693) recalled by Shigehira [10:7; 6:10].

HIROTSUNA (1): Genpachi Hirotsuna, Genji warrior serving under Yoshitsune [11:3, 11:7; 9:7, 11:11].

HIROTSUNA (2): Sanuki no Hirotsuna, Heike warrior at the battle of Uji [4:11; 9:7].

HOKKYŌ (DHARMA BRIDGE): Buddhist priest from Onaka in Kumano Province [9:15].

HŌNEN (1132–1212): "Priest Hōnen of Kurodani" on Mount Hiei, one of the founders of Pure Land Buddhism in Japan. He administers Buddhist precepts to Shigehira [10:5].

HOSSHŌ-JI ADMINISTRATOR: see Shunkan.

HOTOKE: *shirabyōshi* dancer from Kaga Province, whose name means "Buddha." She is the subject of the nō play *Hotoke no hara* [1:6].

HŌZŌ: high-ranking tenth-century Tōdai-ji priest who was said to have visited hell (*Genkyōshaku*, book 4) [6:7].

ICHIRAI: warrior monk on Prince Mochihito's side at the battle of Uji [4:11; 4:10].

ICHIJŌ OF KAI: see Tadayori.

IESADA: Sahyōe-no-jō Iesada, retainer of Taira no Tadamori [1:2].

IETADA OF MUSASHI: Kaneko no Jūrō Ietada, one of the "Kaneko brothers," warriors serving under Yoshitsune [11:3; 9:7, 11:1].

IKE NUN: second wife of Taira no Tadamori, stepmother of Kiyomori, and mother of Yorimori. Her name (Ike no zenni) comes from the Ike home, Ike-dono (Pond Mansion), at Rokuhara. After the Heiji rebellion (1159), she asks that the thirteen-year-old Yoritomo be exiled rather than executed [5:10, 7:19, 10:13, 11:18].

IMAI: see Kanehira.

IMPERIAL CONSORT, IMPERIAL LADY: see Kenreimon'in.

INSEI: Reverend Insei (or, in some texts, Inzei), Chōraku-ji priest who administers Buddhist precepts to Kenreimon'in [**Initiates** 1].

ISHIDŌMARU: boy who accompanies Koremori, drowning with him [10:8, 10:9, 10:12].

JŪMYŌ MEISHŪ: warrior monk on Prince Mochihito's side at the battle of Uji [4:11; 4:10, 4:16].

JŪRŌ OF MIONOYA: warrior serving under Yoshitsune [11:5].

KAGEIE (1): third son of Kajiwara Kagetoki and Genji warrior [11:3; 9:7, 9:11, 11:7].

KAGEIE (2): governor of Hida Province and Taira samurai commander [4:11; 2:3, 4:12, 7:9].

KAGEKIYO: Akushichibyōe Kagekiyo of Kazusa Province, Heike warrior. He continues to fight against the Genji after the battle of Dan-no-ura. Some variants of *The Tales of the Heike* describe how he is captured as he tries to assassinate Yoritomo at Nara. He also is the subject of nō drama (*Kagekiyo*) and other genres [4:11, 11:5, 11:7; 7:2, 8:9, 9:10, 10:14, 11:11, 12:9].

KAGESUE: eldest son of Kajiwara Kagetoki and Genji warrior [9:15, 11:7; 9:1–3, 9:7, 9:11].

KAGETAKA (1): second son of Kajiwara Kagetoki and Genji warrior [11:3; 9:7, 9:11].

KAGETAKA (2): son of Kageie, the governor of Hida Province, and Taira warrior. He dies in the northern campaign against Yoshinaka [4:11; 7:2, 7:6].

KAGETOKI: Kajiwara [no] Kagetoki (d. 1200), Genji commander. His dislike of Yoshitsune leads him to speak slanderously of him to Yoritomo [11:7; 4:5, 9:7, 9:11, 9:16, 10:6, 10:7, 11:1, 11:6, 11:17, 12:4, 12:9].

KAGETSUNE OF HIDA: dies at the battle of Dan-no-ura trying to rescue his foster brother Taira no Munemori [11:7; 10:14, 11:10].

KAJIWARA: *see* Kagesue; Kagetoki.

KAMADABYŌ: Kamadabyō Masakiyo (1132–1160), retainer of Minamoto no Yoshitomo in the Heiji rebellion (1159). He later is assassinated [10:10; 12:2].

KANEHIRA: Imai [no] Kanehira (d. 1184), foster brother of Kiso no Yoshinaka and brother of Higuchi no Jirō Kanemitsu and, possibly, of Tomoe. Depicted as both a loyal retainer of Yoshinaka and a wise adviser who tries to restrain some of his master's excesses after his forces occupy the capital (book eight), he remains with Yoshinaka to the end, taking his own life after Yoshinaka dies. He is the subject of the nō play *Kanehira* [9:4; 7:1, 7:4, 7:7, 8:6, 8:8, 8:10, 9:1].

KANEKO BROTHERS: Ietada and Chikanori, serving under Yoshitsune [11:5; 9:7, 11:1, 11:3].

KANEMASA: Fujiwara no Kanemasa (1144–1200), accompanies Emperor GoShirakawa to Ōhara. Married to one of Kiyomori's daughters, he rises to the position of minister of the left [**Initiates 3**; 1:5, 1:12, 2:8].

KANEMITSU: Higuchi no Jirō Kanemitsu, elder brother of Imai no Kanehira and leading retainer of Kiso no Yoshinaka. He is executed after their deaths [**7:8**; 7:4, 7:7, 8:9, 8:10, 9:5].

KANEYASU: Senoo Kaneyasu, chief of police of Yamato Province. Sent as a messenger to the Nara monks, he is Kiyomori's right-hand man in this narrative as well as in those dealing with the earlier Hōgen and Heiji rebellions (1156, 1159) [**5:14**; 2:4, 2:9, 3:12, 7:6, 8:8].

KANMU, EMPEROR (737–806, r. 737–806): sovereign from whom Kiyomori's branch of the Taira family descended [1:1, 1:2; 5:1, 7:12].

KEISHŪ: Reverend Master Keishū of the Jōen Cloister (Mii-dera) [4:11; 4:9, 4:10].

KENREIMON'IN: Tokuko (1155?–1213?), daughter of Taira no Kiyomori and Tokiko (Nun of the Second Rank); sister of Munemori, Tomomori, and Shigehira; and, from 1171, consort of Emperor Takakura, with whom she has four sons. Her first son becomes Emperor Antoku, and her fourth son becomes Emperor GoToba. She is also known as the "imperial consort," "imperial lady," and "empress." She takes religious precepts after the Heike's defeat in 1185 at the battle of Dan-no-ura and dies as a recluse in Ōhara. Several documents state that she died at the age of fifty-eight or fifty-nine in 1213, but other sources say the date could be as early as 1191 or as late as 1224. Unlike early versions of the Heike narrative that close with the death of Rokudai, the Kakuichi version ends with "The Initiates'

Book" (Kanjō no maki), describing Kenreimon'in's fate. She also is the subject of the nō play *The Imperial Visit to Ohara* (*Ohara gokō*) [1:5, 3:1, 3:2, 5:14, 11:9, Initiates 1–5; 3:3, 4:2, 5:1, 6:2, 6:12, 7:13, 7:19, 11:1, 11:2, 11:10, 11:11, 12:3].

KIKUŌ: young boy in Noritsune's service. He is killed at the battle of Yashima [11:3].

KIRIU NO ROKURŌ: Heike warrior at the battle of Uji [4:11].

KISO, LORD KISO: *see* Yoshinaka.

KIYOMORI (1118–1181): descendant of Emperor Kanmu; eldest son of Taira no Tadamori; brother of Tsunemori, Norimori, Yorimori, and Tadanori; and father of Shigemori with his first wife and of Munemori and more than a dozen other children with his second wife, Tokiko (Nun of the Second Rank). He is also known as "the Taira Chancellor." According to an anecdote in section 6:10, Kiyomori's real father was Emperor Shirakawa, who had Tadamori adopt him. Kiyomori succeeds Tadamori as head of the Taira clan in 1153. The Hōgen and Heiji rebellions (1156, 1159) give Kiyomori an opportunity to eliminate political and military rivals. Over the next twenty years, he wields great political power. Kiyomori rises swiftly up the court hierarchy, becoming prime minister (*daijō daijin*) and junior first rank in 1167. He takes Buddhist orders and the religious name Jōkai after an illness in 1168 and becomes the father-in-law of the reigning emperor after his daughter Tokuko (Kenreimon'in) becomes the empress of Takakura in 1171 [1:1–6, 2:6, 2:7, 3:1, 3:2, 5:14, 6:7, 7:20, 10:5, 10:12, 12:9, Initiates 1, 5; 2:1, 2:3–5, 2:9–12, 2:16, 3:3–5, 3:11, 3:15–19, 4:1–9, 4:13, 4:16, 5:1, 5:3, 5:4, 5:12, 5:13, 6:4–6, 6:8–10, 7:5, 8:4, 8:11, 9:7, 10:2, 10:4, 10:14, 12:2–4].

KIYOMUNE (1171–1185): grandson of Taira no Kiyomori and son of Munemori. Captured at the battle of Dan-no-ura, he is brought as a prisoner to Kamakura and is executed [4:14, 7:12, 7:19, 9:17, 11:10, 11:11, 11:13, 11:16, 11:18].

KIYONORI: Takechi Kiyonori of Iyo Province, Taira defender at the battle of Ichi-no-tani [9:12].

KIYOTSUNE: Middle Captain Kiyotsune (1163–1183), grandson of Taira no Kiyomori and son of Shigemori. He takes his own life after the Heike are driven from Kyushu. Kiyotsune is the subject of the nō play *Kiyotsune* [10:10, Initiates 4; 6:10, 7:14, 7:19, 8:4, 10:13].

KOJIRŌ: *see* Naoie.

KOREMORI (1157–1184?): grandson of Taira no Kiyomori, eldest son of Shigemori, and father of Rokudai. He is unsuccessful as a leader in battles against Yoritomo (Fuji River, 1180) and Yoshinaka (Mount Tonamiyama, 1183). When the Heike flee from the capital, Koremori leaves his wife and children behind. He does not participate in the battle of Ichi-no-tani and abandons the rest of his clan during the campaign in Shikoku. Crossing to Kii Province, he takes religious orders and makes a pilgrimage to Kumano and Nachi, where he drowns himself [1:5, 10:8, 10:10, 10:12, 12:9; 1:16, 2:4, 2:11, 3:3, 3:11, 3:12, 5:11, 5:12, 7:2–4, 7:6, 7:12, 7:14, 7:19, 7:20, 9:7, 10:1, 10:9, 10:12–14, 12:7, 12:8].

KOREYOSHI: Okata no Saburō Koreyoshi of Bungo Province in Kyushu. In 1183 Koreyoshi allies himself with the Genji and drives the Heike from Kyushu, where they had sought safe haven [Initiates 4; 6:6, 8:3, 8:4, 9:4, 11:16, 12:5].

KOZAISHŌ: Third-Rank Lady of Echizen and wife of Taira no Michimori, governor of Echizen Province. On the eve of the battle of Ichi-no-tani, Michimori brings Kozaishō to the camp to say good-bye but sends her back to the Heike ships offshore when his brother Noritsune disapproves. Michimori was overjoyed to hear that Kozaishō is pregnant. After Kozaishō learns that her husband has been killed, she cannot bear to go on living and drowns herself. The section ends with an account of how, with the help of Empress Kenreimon'in, Michimori married Kozaishō. More details are revealed in the diary of another lady in the empress's service (*The Poetic Memoirs of Lady Daibu*) [9:9, Initiates 1; 9:19].

KUMAGAE: *see* Naozane.

KUMAI TARŌ: retainer of Minamoto no Yoshitsune [11:3, 11:7; 9:7, 11:13, 12:4].

KUMAŌ: *see* Yoshihisa.

KUNITAKA: Kondō Kunitaka, given charge of Mongaku in exile [5:10].

KUNITSUNA (1122–1181): [Gojō] major counselor, member of the northern branch of the Fujiwara, and father of Lady Dainagon-no-suke. Elsewhere in the Kakuichi version, Kunitsuna is remembered chiefly for his ostentatious displays of his wealth [7:20, Initiates 3; 3:3, 3:4, 4:2, 5:1, 6:10, 11:19].

LORD NOTO: *see* Noritsune.

LORD OF KAMAKURA: *see* Yoritomo.

MASAKADO: Taira no Masakado (d. 940), rebel who laid claim to eight provinces in eastern Japan as a "Taira prince of the blood" before being crushed by imperial forces. A lengthy narrative concerning his rebellion survives in an early text, *The Account of Masakado (Shōmonki)* [1:1; 1:11, 4:12, 5:5, 5:11, 5:12, 6:12, 7:9, 9:7, 10:4].

MICHICHIKA: Minamoto no Michichika (1149–1202), high-ranking courtier who accompanies Emperor GoShirakawa to Ōhara. Michichika also accompanies Emperor Takakura to the Itsukushima Shrine. His account of the pilgrimage, which survives, is the main source of the account in section 4:1. Michichika was an important figure in court politics after the war, a favorite of Emperor GoToba. Thirty-two of his poems are included in imperial anthologies [Initiates 3; 3:4, 5:1].

MICHIMORI (d. 1184): son of Taira no Norimori, nephew of Kiyomori, and governor of Echizen Province. He is one of the commanders in the attack on the Nara temples and in the Hokuriku campaign against Yoshinaka. At the battle of Ichi-no-tani, he and his brother Noritsune are assigned to guard the Hiyodori Pass region. Michimori is killed in the fighting, and his wife, the Third-Rank Lady of Echizen (Kozaishō), commits suicide. In *Michimori*, a nō play written by Iami and revised by Zeami, the ghosts of Michimori and Kozaishō describe their last meeting and deaths [9:9, 11:3; 5:14, 7:2, 7:3, 7:6, 7:12, 7:13, 7:19, 9:6, 9:18, 9:19, 10:4].

MICHINOBU: Kōno no Michinobu (1156–1223) of Iyo Province in Shikoku. After changing to the Genji side, Michinobu foils repeated attempts by the Heike and their allies to punish him for disloyalty and helps the Genji at the battle of Dan-no-ura. After the Genpei war, Michinobu is rewarded by the Kamakura shogunate but ultimately is exiled to Hiraizumi for his support of Emperor GoDaigo in the Jōkyū rebellion [6:7, 11:7; 6:6, 9:6, 11:2, 11:6].

MICHIZANE: Sugawara no Michizane (845–903), minister of the right under Emperor Daigo. He fell victim to a fellow minister's slander and was forced to accept a post in distant Dazaifu (Kyushu). He later is worshiped as the deity of the Kitano Shrine [10:7; 2:4, 3:16, 8:2].

MIONOYA NO JŪRŌ: warrior serving under Yoshitsune. He has a lucky escape in an encounter with Kagekiyo at Yashima [11:5].

MITSUMORI: Tezuka [no] Tarō Mitsumori, warrior from Shinano Province serving under Yoshinaka. He takes Sanemori's head at the battle of Shinohara and is one of the last of Yoshinaka's retainers to fall at Awazu [7:8; 9:4].

MITSUYOSHI: Fujiwara no Mitsuyoshi (1132–1183), senior courtier. He loses his title of commander of the Military Guards of the Right in Kiyomori's coup d'état of 1179. Mongaku visits him in Fukuhara in 1180 to obtain from Retired Emperor GoShirakawa an edict authorizing Yoritomo to attack the Heike, as Mongaku recalls later [3:16, 5:10, 12:7].

MIURA NO SUKE: *see* Yoshizumi.

MIURA TARŌ: Miura no Ishizakon no Tarō, Genji warrior [11:8].

MOCHIHITO, PRINCE (1151–1180): second son of Retired Emperor GoShirakawa. He is also known as Prince Takakura. After he is persuaded by Yorimasa to give his name to the anti-Taira revolt of 1180, Prince Mochihito is killed after Yorimasa is defeated at the battle of Uji [4:11, 5:14; 4:3, 4:5–8, 4:10, 4:12–14, 5:1, 6:4].

MONGAKU: religious name of Endō Moritō (1139–1203), Buddhist monk. The Kakuichi version credits "a religious awakening" for making him leave lay life at the age of nineteen, whereas other variants relate the story of how he accidentally kills Kesa Gozen, a married woman whom he loves. Mongaku becomes known as Saint Mongaku (Mongaku Shōnin) for his unstinting—and historically documented—efforts to rebuild Jingo-ji and other temples that had fallen into ruin. Exiled to Izu in 1180, he meets Yoritomo and incites him to revolt against the Heike, obtaining for him the support of Retired Emperor GoShirakawa. Mongaku intercedes on behalf of the last Heike heir, Koremori's son Rokudai, saving him from execution. After Yoritomo's death, Mongaku is exiled to the island of Oki, where he dies [12:9; 5:8–10, 12:2, 12:7, 12:8].

MORIKATA: Emi no Jirō Morikata (1157–1185), Heike samurai commander. Active at the battle of Yashima, he is killed at the battle of Dan-no-ura [11:5; 9:8].

MORIKUNI (1113?–1186): police lieutenant and father of the Taira commander Etchū no Zenji Moritoshi. He is a senior adviser to both Kiyomori and Shigemori. Morikuni later protests when Kiyomori orders that an unsuccessful general be put to death [2:6; 2:3, 2:7, 5:12, 6:10].

MORINAGA: Gotōbyōe Morinaga, foster brother of Taira no Shigehira, whom he deserts at the battle of Ichi-no-tani. His cowardice is remembered in the war tale *Chronicle of Great Peace (Taiheiki)* [9:15].

MORITOSHI: Etchū no Zenji Moritoshi (d. 1184), Heike samurai commander. He is killed at the battle of Ichi-no-tani [9:9, 9:12; 7:2, 7:4, 9:13].

MORITSUGI: Etchū no Jirōbyōe Moritsugi (d. 1197), son of Moritoshi and Heike samurai commander throughout the conflict. Moritsugi survives the battle of Dan-no-ura and is not captured and executed until long afterward [4:11, 11:3, 11:5, 11:7; 7:2, 7:14, 7:19, 8:9, 9:10, 10:14, 11:11, 12:9].

MOROMORI (d. 1184): grandson of Taira no Kiyomori, son of Shigemori, and younger brother of Koremori. He is killed at the battle of Ichi-no-tani [9:18, 10:1; 7:14, 7:19, 9:8, 10:10, 10:13].

MOROSHIGE: Onda no Moroshige, Genji warrior from Musashi Province. He is killed by Tomoe [9:4].

MOTOKIYO: Shinbyōe Motokiyo (d. 1221), retainer of Minamoto no Yoshitsune. He is executed by his own son during the Jōkyū rebellion [11:3, 11:5; 11:1].

MOTOMICHI: Fujiwara no Motomichi (1160–1233), son-in-law of Taira no Kiyomori. He serves as regent (*sesshō* and *kanpaku*) during the Genpei war (1179–1183, 1184–1186) and again afterward [5:14; 1:5, 3:15–17, 3:19, 5:1, 5:11, 5:13, 7:13, 8:1, 8:2, 8:11, 9:5].

MUNEMITSU: Yuasa no Shichirōbyoe Munemitsu of Kii Province. He recognizes Koremori in Kumano [10:10].

MUNEMOCHI: Kano no Suke Munemochi of Izu Province, in whose custody Shigehira is placed when in Kamakura. A confident of Yoritomo's, Munemochi appears in the chronicle *Mirror of the East (Azuma kagami)* and in *The Tale of the Soga (Soga monogatari)* [10:7].

MUNEMORI (1147–1185): third son of Taira no Kiyomori. He becomes the head of the Taira clan after his father's death in 1181, but repeatedly makes errors of judgment. After allowing himself to be captured at the battle of Dan-no-ura, Munemori is brought to Kamakura with his son Kiyomune and later is executed [1:5, 2:6, 6:7, 7:8, 9:9, 10:7, 11:3, 11:8; 1:12, 1:15, 2:3,

2:11, 3:4, 3:11, 3:18, 3:19, 4:1, 4:4–6, 4:13, 4:14, 5:12, 6:8, 6:10, 6:12, 7:4, 7:7, 7:12, 7:13, 7:15, 7:19, 7:20, 8:1, 8:3, 8:4, 8:6, 8:11, 9:6, 9:7, 9:17, 10:2–4, 10:6, 10:9, 10:11, 10:13, 10:15, 11:2, 11:6, 11:7, 11:10, 11:11, 11:13, 11:16–18].

MUNETAKA: Yoichi Munetaka (Nasu no Yoichi), Genji archer from Nasu in Shimotsuke Province [11:4; 11:5].

MUNETŌ: Abe no Munetō, northern Japanese "barbarian" (*ebisu*). With his elder brother Sadatō, he challenges imperial authority in the "former Nine Years' War." In 1062 he and his brother are defeated in battle by Yoriyoshi. Munetō surrenders and is exiled to Dazaifu (Kyushu) [10:12; 1:11, 5:5, 7:5].

MUTSURU: Gengo Uma-no-jō Mutsuru of the Watanabe League [11:10].

NAGATSUNA: Takahashi no Hangan Nagatsuna (d. 1183), Taira warrior at the battle of Uji. He later participates in the northern war against Yoshinaka, dying in the battle of Shinohara [4:11; 7:2, 7:7].

NAHA NO TARŌ: Taira warrior at the battle of Uji [4:11].

NAOIE: Kumagae Kojirō Naoie (1169–1221), son of Naozane and Genji warrior in Yoshitsune's rear attack force. He is wounded in a challenge to the Heike position at the battle of Ichi-no-tani (9:16; 9:7, 9:10).

NAOZANE: Kumagae Naozane (1141–1208), Genji warrior from Musashi Province. Naozane reluctantly takes the life of Atsumori, an act that leads him to turn to a religious life. He is first under the command of Noriyori at the battle of Uji and then under Yoshitsune. Naozane is the first warrior to attack the Heike position at Ichi-no-tani. During the night attack, his son Kojirō Naoie is injured. Several variants describe how Naozane returns Atsumori's head and belongings to his father, with additional episodes illustrating his bravery and concern for his son's safety. He was a popular subject of later legend, prose, and nō and kabuki plays [9:16; 9:2, 9:7, 9:10, 9:16].

NARICHIKA: Major Counselor Fujiwara no Narichika (1138–1177), principal Shishi-no-tani conspirator and father of Naritsune. On two earlier occasions, Narichika is involved in failed plots but is saved from severe punishment by his close relationship with Retired Emperor GoShirakawa and members of the Taira family: his sister was married to Shigemori; his daughter, to Koremori; and his son Naritsune, to Norimori's daughter. For his part in the Shishi-no-tani plot, Narichika is sent into exile and subsequently is executed on Kiyomori's orders. After his death, his resentful spirit is blamed for problems suffered by Empress Kenreimon'in in her pregnancy. In an effort to pacify the spirit, Narichika's exiled son Naritsune is pardoned and allowed to return from exile [2:6, 3:1; 1:12, 1:13, 2:3–5, 2:8–11, 3:7, 3:15, 3:18, 4:3, 7:14].

NARIHIRA: Ariwara no Narihira (825–880), Heian-period poet [7:20].

NARITSUNE (d. 1202): Tanba Lesser Captain and son of Fujiwara no Narichika, a Shishi-no-tani conspirator. After the conspiracy is discovered,

Naritsune is brought to Kiyomori for questioning. His father-in-law, Norimori, intercedes on his behalf, saving him from execution. Exiled to Kikai-ga-shima, he and Yasuyori spend their time on the island in prayer, in contrast to their fellow exile Shunkan. After their pardon, Naritsune and Yasuyori return to the capital, stopping on the way to see his father's place of exile in Bizen. Reunited with his family in 1179, Naritsune lived for more than thirty years, rising in the court hierarchy. A different account of Naritsune's life in exile is found in some later works. In one variant of *The Tales of the Heike*, Naritsune has a child by the daughter of a fisherman (*Genpei jōsuiki*, book 9). His relationship with the fisherman's daughter is central to a puppet play by Chikamatsu Monzaemon (*The Heike and the Isle of Women* [*Heike nyogo no shima*], 1719 [kabuki version, 1720]) [2:10, **2:15, 3:1**; 2:4, 2:5, 2:9, 3:2, 3:3, 3:7–9].

NIIDONO: *see* Tokiko.

NITTA: Priest Nitta of Kōzuke [**4:11**].

NOBUTAKA: Fujiwara no Nobutaka (1126–1179), senior noble. One of his wives was Kiyomori's daughter; another was a nobleman's daughter who bore Emperor Takakura several children, including the future emperor GoToba. The nobleman's daughter is thought to be the one who calls on Kenreimon'in in her first refuge [1:5, **Initiates 2, 4**; 1:5, 8:1].

NOBUTSUNA: Tashiro no Kanja Nobutsuna of Izu Province, Genji warrior of imperial descent. He serves with Yoshitsune's forces at the battles of Mikusa, Yashima, and Dan-no-ura. Soon after the battle of Dan-no-ura, Nobutsuna receives a letter from Yoritomo warning him not to obey Yoshitsune's orders (*Mirror of the East* [*Azuma kagami*], entry of 1185.4.29) [**11:3**; 9:7, 9:8, 11:5].

NOBUYORI: Fujiwara no Nobuyori (1131–1159). Together with Yoshitomo, Nobuyori instigates the Heiji rebellion in 1159, succeeding in bringing about the death of his rival Shinsei. On Kiyomori's return, the rebellion is crushed and Nobuyori is executed [1:1; 1:3, 1:12, 2:6, 3:18, 5:5, 11:18].

NORIMORI (1128–1187): son of Taira no Tadamori, younger brother of Kiyomori, father of Michimori and Noritsune, and consultant and middle counselor. When his son-in-law Naritsune is implicated in the Shishino-tani conspiracy, Norimori intervenes to save his life. He sends food to Naritsune in exile and is later instrumental in obtaining a pardon. Norimori takes little part in the fighting. The tale describes him as drowning himself at Dan-no-ura, but historical sources show him surviving the battle [**2:15, 3:1**; 1:15, 2:5, 2:9, 3:3, 3:4, 3:7, 7:12, 7:19, 9:6, 9:7, 9:19, 11:10].

NORITSUNE (1159/1160?–1184/1185?): son of Taira no Tsunemori, elder brother of Michimori, nephew of Kiyomori, and governor of Noto

Province (Lord Noto). Noritsune leads the Heike forces to victory on several occasions but is unable to halt Yoshitsune's surprise attack on Ichi-no-tani. Active at the battle of Yashima, he takes his own life at Dan-no-ura after failing to engage Yoshitsune in single-handed combat. The Kakuichi account of Noritsune's flight from Ichi-no-tani, leading role in subsequent battles, and death at Dan-no-ura is fictional: two major historical sources, the chronicle *Mirror of the East* (*Azuma kagami*) and the diary by the nobleman Kanezane, confirm that Noritsune was in fact killed at the battle of Ichi-no-tani in 1184 [9:9, 11:3; 7:13, 7:19, 8:7, 9:6, 9:10, 9:12, 9:18, 9:19, 11:5, 11:6, 11:10].

NORIYORI (d. 1193): son of Minamoto no Yoshitomo, half brother of Yoritomo and Yoshitsune, and governor of Mikawa Province. He is known as Gama (or Kaba) no kanja after his birthplace. In the campaigns of books nine through eleven, Noriyori acts as the senior commander in chief of the Genji forces and Yoshitsune, the junior commander, but Noriyori's own achievements fall far short of Yoshitsune's. After the end of the war, he is unable to allay Yoritomo's suspicions and finally is put to death [11:7; 8:11, 9:1–3, 9:5, 9:7, 9:11, 10:1, 10:14, 10:15, 11:1, 11:17, 12:5].

NUN OF THE SECOND RANK: *see* Tokiko.

ŌGO: Ōgo no Saburō Sanehide, Taira warrior at the battle of Uji [4:11; 10:14].

ŌMURO: Taira warrior at the battle of Uji [4:11].

ONO: Empress Dowager Ono, consort of Emperor GoReizei (r. 1045–1068) [**Initiates 3**].

ONODERA: Onodera [no] Zenji Tarō Michitsuna, Taira warrior at the battle of Uji [4:11; 9:7].

RETIRED EMPEROR: most of the references to "the retired emperor" are to GoShirakawa. Other retired emperors mentioned by name are GoToba, Takakura, and Toba.

ROKUDAI: son of Taira no Koremori. After the fall of the Heike, his mother tries to hide him, but he is discovered by Hōjō Tokimasa. He is saved from execution by Mongaku, who obtains a pardon from Yoritomo on condition that Rokudai take religious orders. Despite Yoritomo's suspicions, he survives past the age of thirty, to the year 1203 or later. Rokudai is finally put to death on orders of the lord of Kamakura. Depending on when the execution took place (and the evidence in the *Heike* variants and the chroniclers is contradictory), this lord is either Yoritomo (who died in 1199) or one of his successors, Yoriie or Sanetomo. Rokudai is the last direct male heir of Heike, ending the line of six generations from Masamori through Tadamori, Kiyomori, Shigemori, and Koremori to Rokudai [**10:10, 10:12, 12:9**; 7:14, 7:19, 10:1, 12:7, 12:8].

ROKUYATA: *see* Tadazumi.

SABURŌ: *see* Yoshimori (1).

SADAMORI: Taira military commander and leader of a successful campaign against the rebel Masakado. Masakado is Sadamori's cousin and responsible for his father's death. Tales about Sadamori can be found in *Tales of Times Now Past* (*Konjaku monogatari shū*), 29:15, 29:25 [10:10; 1:11, 5:11, 5:12, 10:4].

SADAMOTO: Ōe no Sadamoto (d. 1034), mid-Heian-period poet. He went to China around 1003, dying there in 1034. As a Buddhist prelate, he was known as Jakushō [**Initiates 3**].

SADATŌ: Abe no Sadatō (1019–1062), northern Japanese "barbarian" (*emishi*). With his brother Munetō, he challenges imperial authority in the "former Nine Years' War." He dies after being captured in battle by Yoriyoshi. A *Tale of Mutsu* (*Mutsu waki*) is a narrative account of the war [**10:12**; 1:11, 5:5, 7:5].

SADAYOSHI: Taira no Sadayoshi, governor of Chikugo Province and, later, of Higo Province. Books two and three describe Sadayoshi as attending both Shigemori and Kiyomori, performing errands and providing advice, as his father, Iesada, had done for Kiyomori and Tadamori. Although he later conducts a successful military campaign in Kyushu, he does not accompany the Heike on their flight from the capital [**2:6**; 2:3, 2:4, 2:7, 3:11, 3:12, 6:11, 7:13, 7:19, 10:13].

SAIKŌ: religious name of Fujiwara Moromitsu (d. 1177), Buddhist monk close to Retired Emperor GoShirakawa. One of the chief Shishi-no-tani conspirators also responsible for maligning the Tendai abbot Meiun, Saikō is tortured and executed on Kiyomori's orders. The account of the Heiji rebellion (1159) describes him as taking the tonsure when accompanying Shinsei on his flight from the capital [**2:6**; 1:9, 1:12, 1:13, 2:1, 2:3, 2:4, 2:6, 3:1, 4:2].

SAITŌGO: son of Saitō Bettō Sanemori. Sanemori leaves behind Saitōgo and his brother Saitōroku when he goes to fight in the Hokuriku campaign. Koremori puts the brothers in charge of his son Rokudai when he flees the capital with the other Heike. When the heads of the Heike taken at the battle of Ichi-no-tani are paraded through the streets of the capital, the brothers go to see if Koremori's head is among them [**12:9**; 7:14, 10:1, 12:7, 12:8].

SAITŌROKU: younger brother of Saitōgo. After Rokudai is captured, he acts as a messenger, bringing news to the boy's mother [**12:9**; 7:14, 10:1, 12:7, 12:8].

SANEHIRA: Toi no Jirō Sanehira, commander of the Genji army. An easterner of Heike descent, he joins forces with Yoritomo in 1180. Sanehira serves in the armies of both Yoshitsune and Noriyori and performs important duties for Yoritomo. Some variants of *The Tales of the Heike* describe his role in helping Yoritomo escape by boat to Awa after the defeat at

Ishibashiyama in 1180. A different account is given in the nō play *Seven Warriors in Flight (Shiki ochi)*. After the Genpei war, Sanehira is sent by Yoritomo on important missions and is in the vanguard when Yoritomo goes to the capital in 1190 [**9:4, 9:9, 9:16, 10:5**; 5:4, 7:1, 9:7, 9:8, 9:10, 9:11, 9:16, 10:2, 10:14, 11:7, 11:13, 11:17].

SANEMORI: Nagai no Saitō Bettō Sanemori (1126?–1183), eastern warrior from Musashi Province. He fights on Yoshitomo's side in the Hōgen and Heiji rebellions (1156, 1159). After Yoshitomo's defeat, he is absorbed into the victors' army, serving Shigemori. When the Genji revolt in 1180, he decides to continue in his service to the Heike. At Fuji River, his tales of the fierce eastern warriors alarm the Heike forces, and they flee without fighting. His shame at joining in the panic leads him to participate in the Hokuriku campaign, despite his age and his realization that the Heike are bound to be defeated. Sanemori is survived by his sons Saitōgo and Saitōroku, whom he leaves to serve Koremori and Rokudai. In Zeami's nō play *Sanemori*, the spirit of the warrior appears and recounts his own death [**6:7**; 5:11, 7:7, 7:8, 7:14].

SANEMOTO: Gotō[byōe] Sanemoto, experienced Genji warrior serving under Yoshitsune [**11:3–5, 11:8, 12:9**; 11.1].

SANESADA (also read JITTEI or SHITTEI): Fujiwara no Sanesada (1139–1191), Tokudai-ji minister of the left. Sanesada is a nobleman with close connections to the imperial family and a model of courtly elegance. His progress up the hierarchy is slowed by the Heike dominance over official appointments. When disappointed, however, he shows more patience and political savvy than does Narichika, with whom he is explicitly contrasted. He remains with Retired Emperor GoShirakawa when the Heike flee the capital and later accompanies him to Ōhara [**Initiates 3, 5**; 1:12, 2:11, 3:4, 5:1, 5:2, 8:1, 8:11, 10:1, 10:15].

SAZUKU: warrior on Prince Mochihito's side at the battle of Uji [**4:11**].

SECOND NUN: *see* Tokiko.

SEIWA, EMPEROR (850–880, r. 858–878): members of the "Seiwa Genji" traced their ancestry to Emperor Seiwa's son Prince Sadasumi (Rokusonō), who was given the Genji name [**11:3**; 1:8, 1:16, 8:2].

SENJU-NO-MAE: entertainer sent to Shigehira by Yoritomo [**10:7**].

SHIGEHIRA (1156–1185): fourth son of Taira no Kiyomori, captain of the third rank, and leader in the Heike's attacks on Uji and Nara. Captured at Ichino-tani, he is brought as a prisoner to Kamakura. Held responsible for the destruction of the Nara temples, Shigehira is later handed over to the monks for execution. The important role of Shigehira in many of the Taira's military successes is played down in the Kakuichi version, which credits his victories at Sunomata (1181) and Mizushima (1184) to his older brother Tomomori [**4:11, 5:14, 9:15, 10:5, 10:7**; 1:15, 2:3, 3:3, 4:16, 5:12, 6:10, 6:12, 7:12, 7:13, 7:19, 8:9, 10:1–4, 10:6, 10:8, 10:11, 10:13, 10:15, 11:17, 11:19].

SHIGEKAGE: Yosōbyōe Shigekage, accompanies Koremori from Yashima and drowns with him [10:8, 10:10].

SHIGEMORI (1138–1179): eldest son of Taira no Kiyomori, "Lord Komatsu." He is depicted as a virtuous minister who attempts to curb the excesses of the ruler but with only limited success. The narrative also contrasts Shigemori and his half brother Munemori, who is portrayed as much inferior. Shigemori suffers from poor health, dying in his early forties. Predicting that his father's sins will lead to the decline of the Taira, he contributes to Buddhist temples in Japan and China. After Shigemori dies, his father's behavior goes unchecked [1:5, 2:6, 2:7, 3:1, 10:10, 10:12, 12:9; 1:9, 1:11–13, 1:15, 1:16, 2:4, 2:5, 2:8, 2:10, 2:11, 2:16, 3:3, 3:4, 3:6, 3:11–15, 3:18, 4:6, 5:10, 6:10, 10:11, 10:14].

SHIGEYOSHI: Awa no Minbu Shigeyoshi, trusted vassal of the Heike from Awa in Shikoku Province. He comes to the aid of the Heike when they take refuge in Yashima but loses confidence in their cause after his son is captured by a clever Genji ruse. Although his change of heart is suspected on the eve of the battle of Dan-no-ura, no action is taken, and his betrayal weakens the Heike at a crucial point in the battle. According to some versions of the narrative, the Genji victors, far from rewarding Shigeyoshi, bring him to Kamakura as a prisoner. After debating whether to execute or pardon him, they put him to death for his treachery to his hereditary lords, burning him alive, according to the Enkyō variant [11:8; 6:8, 9:17, 10:14, 11:2, 11:6, 11:7, 11:11].

SHIMA-NO-SENZAI: with Waka-no-mai, the first *shirabyōshi* dancer [1:6].

SHINSEI: Fujiwara no Michinori (d. 1159), known as (lay) Priest Shinsei (or Shinzei) after taking the tonsure. A scholar in the service of Emperor Go-Shirakawa, Shinsei's influence at court is resented by Nobuyori, one of the ringleaders of the Heiji rebellion (1159). After the attempted coup d'état, Shinsei flees the city but is captured and executed. He is one of the subjects of *The Tales of Hōgen* (*Hōgen monogatari*), an earlier war tale about the Hōgen rebellion (1156) [**Initiates 3**; 1:12, 1:13, 2:4, 3:15, 8:2, 8:11].

SHIRŌ OF KŌZUKE: Nifu no Shirō, Genji warrior from Kōzuke Province [11:5].

SHIRŌ OF MIONOYA: Mionoya no Shirō, Genji warrior from Musashi Province [11:5].

SHUNCHŌ: warrior on Prince Mochihito's side at the battle of Uji [4:11; 4:10].

SHUNKAN: one of the main Shishi-no-tani conspirators and the Hosshō-ji administrator. Shunkan is banished to Kikai-ga-shima, where he refuses to join his fellow exiles in religious practices. He is left on the island after Kiyomori explicitly omits him from the pardon granted to Yasuyori and Naritsune. Shortly before his death, his servant Ariō brings him news of his wife and daughter. This episode inspired later works, including the nō play *Shunkan* and Chikamatsu Monzaemon's puppet (later kabuki) play *The Heike and the Isle of Women* (*Heike nyogo no shima*) [2:10, 3:1, 3:2, 3:8, 3:9; 1:12, 1:13, 2:3, 2:15, 3:3, 3:6, 3:18].

SHUNKAN'S DAUGHTER [3:8, 3:9].

SHUNZEI (also read TOSHINARI): Fujiwara no Shunzei (1114–1204), major poet and critic, author of poetic treatises, and compiler of *Senzaishū*, the seventh imperial anthology of poetry [7:16].

SUESHIGE: Hirayama Mushadokoro no Sueshige, Genji warrior from Musashi Province [9:9; 9:2, 9:7, 9:10].

SUKEKANE: Anhōgan (or Anhangan) Sukekane, police commissioner. He is sent to arrest Koremori's son Rokudai [12:9].

SUKEMORI: second son of Taira no Shigemori. He takes his own life at the battle of Dan-no-ura. An important episode in book one relates how he shows great discourtesy to the regent [1:11, 4:2, 7:12, 7:14, 7:19, 8:4, 9:8, 10:1, 10:13, 10:14, 11:10].

TADAKIYO (d. 1185): governor of Kazusa Province and samurai commander. He participates in the Heike attack at the battle of Uji and is held responsible for the failure of the Heike army to engage the Genji at Fuji River. According to the tale, he dies of grief after the death of his son Tadatsuna, but historical sources record that he survives the war and is executed in the capital [4:11; 5:11–13, 7:9].

TADAMITSU: Kazusa no Gorōbyōe Tadamitsu (d. 1192), elder brother of Akushichibyōe Kagekiyo and Heike vassal. He is active as samurai commander in all major campaigns and continues to resist the Genji after the battle of Dan-no-ura [4:11; 7:2, 8:9, 9:10, 10:14, 11:11, 12:9].

TADAMORI (1096–1153): son of Taira no Masamori and father of Kiyomori, Tsunemori, Norimori, Yorimori, and Tadanori. According to a story told in section 6:10, Kiyomori is not his son but Emperor Shirakawa's. Although it is uncertain whether this is true, Emperor Shirakawa and his successor Toba are important to Tadamori's advancement and to the Heike's rising fortunes [1:1, 1:2, 1:3, 9:16; 1:5, 2:3, 4:8, 6:10].

TADANARI: superintendent of the Kangaku-in academy. He fails to calm the Kōfuku-ji monks' anger [5:14].

TADANOBU: Satō Saburōbyōe Tadanobu (1161–1186), Genji warrior of Fujiwara descent from Ōshū Province (northern Japan), younger brother of Tsuginobu, and one of Minamoto no Yoshitsune's closest retainers. According to the later legends, when Yoshitsune is pursued by Yoritomo's men in the mountains of Yoshino, Tadanobu enables him to escape and then takes his own life. Tadanobu is featured in nō, *jorūri*, and kabuki plays [11:3, 11:5, 11:7; 9:7].

TADANORI (1144–1184): son of Taira no Tadamori, younger brother of Kiyomori, governor of Satsuma Province, attendant of Retired Emperor Toba, pupil of the poetry master Fujiwara no Shunzei, and deputy commander in chief of several military campaigns. Tadanori dies at the battle of Ichi-no-tani. His parting from Shunzei and his death in battle are the subject of the nō plays *Tadanori* and *Shunzei Tadanori* [1:3, 4:11, 7:16, 9:14; 4:16, 5:11, 5:13, 7:2, 7:4, 7:13, 7:19, 8:3, 9:18].

TADATSUNA (1): Ashikaga no Matatarō Tadatsuna, Heike warrior from Shi-motsuke Province. His feat in fording the Uji River in 1180 is remembered by the Genji warriors when crossing the same river in 1184 [4:11, 9:2; 4:12].

TADATSUNA (2): Kazusa no Tarō Tadatsuna, Heike samurai commander and son of Tadakiyo, governor of Kazusa. His death in 1183 during the northern campaign against Yoshinaka is said to have caused his father to die of grief [4:11, 7:9; 7:2].

TADAYORI: Ichijō no Jirō Tadayori (d. 1184) of Kai Province, Genji leader. He is awarded Suruga Province by Yoritomo and leads the final attack on Yoshinaka but is later executed on Yoritomo's orders [9:4; 5:12, 9:2, 9:5].

TADAZUMI: Okabe no Rokuyata Tadazumi, Genji warrior of the eastern Inomata League. He takes Tadanori's head at the battle of Ichi-no-tani. According to *The Tales of Hōgen* (*Hōgen monogatari*) and *The Tales of Heiji* (*Heiji monogatari*), he served Yoshitomo in the Hōgen and Heiji rebellions (1156, 1159) [9:14].

TAJIMA: warrior on Prince Mochihito's side at the battle of Uji [4:11; 4:10].

TAKAFUSA (1148–1209): Reizei major counselor, Fujiwara courtier, and son-in-law of Taira no Kiyomori. He suffers from love for Kogō. His wife sends letters and provisions to Kenreimon'in in Ōhara. Takafusa was a political survivor, rising to high rank after the conflict. A noted poet, he contributed to several imperial anthologies. His personal poetry collection survives, as does a series of poems describing his love for an unnamed lady thought to be Kogō. Other episodes of his life are recorded in an illustrated scroll of short tales about courtiers of the period (*Heike kinda-chi sōshi*) [**Initiates 2, 4**; 1:5, 4:1, 4:2, 6:3, 6:4].

TAKAIE: Shō no Takaie, Genji warrior of the eastern Kodama League. He captures Shigehira at the battle of Ichi-no-tani. In the historical record, Takaie is credited with killing Taira no Tsunemasa at the battle of Ichi-no-tani [**9:15**; 9:7].

TAKAKURA, EMPEROR (1161–1181, r. 1168–1180): son of Emperor GoShi-rakawa, and father of Emperors Antoku and GoToba. He takes Kiyomori's daughter Kenreimon'in as his consort. After being forced by Kiyomori to resign in favor of Antoku, he dies the following year. Despite reigning for the unusually long period of twelve years, Emperor Takakura could wield little influence in a court dominated by the rivalry between Kiyo-mori and GoShirakawa. The narrative describes his early death as having been brought on by successive shocks: Kiyomori's treatment of his father, the rebellion of his half brother Prince Takakura (Mochihito), and the destruction of the Nara temples. Book six begins with a series of tales about his death, life, and character [1:5, 3:1, 5:14, 12:9; 1:10, 1:12, 1:16, 2:1, 3:15, 3:18, 3:19, 4:1–3, 4:6, 4:7, 4:13, 5:1, 5:11, 5:13, 6:1–5, 8:1, 10:4, 12:3].

TAKAKURA, PRINCE: *see* Mochihito, Prince.

TAKEHISA: Washio no Shōji Takehisa, hunter in the mountains behind Ichi-no-tani. His son Kumaō joins Yoshitsune's men [9:9].

TAKESATO: retainer of Taira no Koremori. He is ordered by Koremori to report his death to his wife and children [10:8, 10:10; 10:13].

TAKIGUCHI, PRIEST (TAKIGUCHI NYŪDŌ): *see* Tokiyori.

TAMEHISA: Ishida no Jirō Tamehisa of Miura in Sagami Province, Genji warrior. His arrow kills Yoshinaka. His role in Yoshinaka's death is confirmed by *Mirror of the East (Azuma kagami)*, entry of 1184.1.20 [9:4].

TAMETOMO: eighth son of Minamoto no Tameyoshi and a famous archer. Exiled after the Hōgen rebellion (1156), Tametomo features prominently in *The Tales of Hōgen (Hōgen monogatari)* and in a historical romance by Takizawa Bakin (1767–1848) [11:5; 7:13].

TANBA LESSER CAPTAIN: *see* Naritsune.

TANKAI: *see* Fuhito.

TANZŌ: superintendent of the Kumano Shrine in Kii. He gives military support first to the Heike and then to the Genji. After Kiyomori's death, rumors say that he has changed sides, but he is depicted as making his final decision only on the eve of the battle of Dan-no-ura, when he contributes "more than two hundred boats" to the Genji fleet. He later aids Yoritomo by attacking pockets of Heike resistance. Historical sources show that he changed sides at the outset of the war, in the Eighth Month of 1180 when Yoritomo began his revolt. Descended from nobleman Fujiwara no Morosuke (908–960), Tanzō's family had served as shrine administrators for generations [6:7, 11:7; 4:3, 4:4, 12:9].

TASHIRO NO KANJA: *see* Nobutsuna.

TEZUKA NO BETTŌ: retainer of Kiso no Yoshinaka. One Heike variant identifies him as Mitsumori's nephew [7:8].

TEZUKA TARŌ: *see* Mitsumori.

THIRD-RANK LADY OF ECHIZEN: *see* Kozaishō.

TOBA, EMPEROR (1103–1156, r. 1107–1123): son of Emperor Horikawa and father of Emperors Sutoku, Konoe, and GoShirakawa. Retired emperor for twenty-eight years, his death precipitated the Hōgen rebellion. Emperor Toba was the patron of Tadamori [1:2, 2:6, 9:16; 1:3, 1:6–8, 1:13, 1:14, 2:1, 3:5, 3:15, 4:8, 4:10, 6:10, 6:12, 8:2].

TOI (NO JIRŌ): *see* Sanehira.

TOJI: *shirabyōshi* dancer and mother of Giō and Ginyo [1:6].

TŌJICHI OF MIONOYA: Mionoya no Tōjichi, Genji warrior from Musashi Province [11:5].

TOKIKO (d. 1185): Nun of the Second Rank (Nii no ama, Niidono) and wife of Taira no Kiyomori. Kiyomori marries her in 1142 or earlier, after the death of his first wife, Shigemori's mother. Tokiko bears him numerous children, including Munemori, Tomomori, Shigehira, and Tokuko (Kenreimon'in). She is unsuccessful in her attempts to obtain Shigehira's release from captivity. She drowns herself at Dan-no-ura with her grandchild, the former emperor Antoku. Tokiko's siblings were closely connected with the imperial family and the Taira. Her brother Tokitada was an influential adviser to the Taira. One sister became Emperor GoShirakawa's consort and the mother of the future sovereign Takakura. Two others married Kiyomori's sons Shigemori and Munemori. Tokiko took religious orders in 1168, following Kiyomori's death. She was awarded the second rank (*nii*) after her daughter Kenreimon'in became Emperor Takakura's consort [6:7, **11:9, Initiates** 1, 4; 3:3, 4:3, 7:19, 8:1, 10:4, 10:6, 10:9, 10:13, 11:1, 11:2].

TOKITADA: Major Counselor Taira no Tokitada (1127–1189). Although Tokitada is only distantly related to Kiyomori, on a separate branch of the Heike family, he becomes one of his most trusted advisers through Kiyomori's marriage to his younger sister Tokiko (later the Nun of the Second Rank) but is banished to Noto Province after being captured at the battle of Dan-no-ura [11:10; 1:4, 1:10, 1:16, 3:4, 4:1, 5:1, 7:13, 7:19, 8:2, 8:4, 8:11, 10:3, 10:4, 11:11, 11:13, 11:15, 12:3].

TOKIYORI: Saitō Tokiyori, later Priest Takiguchi, samurai in Taira no Shigemori's Komatsu mansion. After his father forbids him to marry the low-ranking Yokobue, he takes the tonsure. He settles on Mount Kōya, where Shigemori's son Koremori comes to him for spiritual help [10:8, **10:12, 12:9;** 10:9, 10:10].

TOKUKO: *see* Kenreimon'in.

TOMOE: "woman attendant" of Kiso no Yoshinaka from Shinano Province. Both mistress and valued warrior, she is among the last of Yoshinaka's retainers to remain with him at the end. The Nagato variant depicts Tomoe in earlier battles, leading more than one thousand riders. She is described in the *Genpei jōsuiki* variant as the daughter of Kiso no Chūzō Kanetō, the man who adopted Yoshinaka after his own father died, making her the sister of Higuchi Kanemitsu and Imai no Kanehira and a foster sister of Yoshitsune, as well as his mistress. (The *Genpei tōjōroku* variant identifies Kanemitsu as her father.) Heike texts, later prose tales, and dramatic works give varying accounts of what happened to her later, often beginning with her flight to the Kantō region and marriage to the Kamakura general and politician Wada Yoshimori. Tomoe is also credited with giving birth to Yoshimori's son, the famous strongman Asaina Yoshihide, although the chronology rules this out. She is also said to have died at the age of ninety-one as a nun, having taken religious vows after the Hōjō's destruction of the Miura family [9:4].

TOMOKATA: Jirō Taifu Tomokata, "a minor overseer of the Fukui estate in Harima." With the Taira army during its attack of the Nara temples, he lights the fire that begins the conflagration that destroys the Buddhist temples [**5:14**; 3:4].

TOMOMORI (1152–1185): second son of Taira no Kiyomori and Tokiko (Nun of the Second Rank) and "the new middle counselor." Among his male relatives, Tomomori is depicted as the most experienced and reliable leader in battle, winning notable victories in book eight. He does not hesitate to voice uncomfortable truths, most memorably at the battle of Dan-no-ura, where he calmly accepts his fate—and his family's—with the words "I have seen all I need to see" [**1:5**, **4:11**, **11:7–9**; 1:15, 2:3, 4:12, 5:13, 6:10, 7:4, 7:12, 7:13, 7:15, 8:4, 8:7, 8:11, 9:11, 9:17, 10:4, 10:11, 10:15, 11:1, 11:10, 11:11, 11:18, 12:9].

TOMOTOKI: Moku no [m]uma-no-jō Tomotoki, formerly in Shigehira's service. He returns to aid his former master in captivity, arranging for Shigehira to have a last meeting with a lover and preparing a statue of Amida for him to worship at his execution [**10:5**; 10:2, 11:19].

TSUGINOBU: Satō Saburōbyōe Tsuginobu (or Tsugunobu) (1158–1185), Genji warrior of Fujiwara descent from Ōshū Province (northern Japan), older brother of Tadanobu, and one of Minamoto no Yoshitsune's closest retainers, mourned by him at his death in Yashima. On Yoshitsune's departure from Hiraizumi, his protector Fujiwara no Hidehira assigns the two brothers to his service. In the Kakuichi version, Tsuginobu dies sorry only not to have seen his "lord gain his rightful place in the world," a significant change from the earlier Yasaka variant, which stresses instead his wish to have seen once more his "aged mother left behind in Ōshū" [**11:3**; 9:7, 11:1].

TSUNEMORI: son of Taira no Tadamori, younger brother of Kiyomori, father of Atsumori, and master of the Palace Repair Office. He dies with his brother Norimori at the battle of Dan-no-ura. Little more than a name in the Kakuichi version, he is more prominent in the *Genpei jōsuiki* variant, where he receives keepsakes of his son from Naozane, a theme taken up by nō playwrights [**9:16**, **11:10**; 7:12, 7:19, 8:3, 9:17].

UBUKATA NO JIRŌ: Taira warrior at the battle of Uji [**4:11**].

WAKA-NO-MAI: *shirabyōshi* dancer [1:6].

WATANABE LEAGUE (WATANABE-TŌ): an association of locally based warriors (*bushidan*) based at the seaport of Watanabe in Settsu Province (present-day Osaka city). The league traced its origins through the famous samurai Watanabe Tsuna through Minamoto Tōru to Emperor Saga, and it had close links to the Genji from the time of Minamoto no Mitsunaka (d. 997) and his son Yorimitsu or Raikō (d. 1021). Many of its members fought at the battle of Uji. Their personal names are typically written with a single character like Kiō, Tonō, and Mitsuru [**4:12**, **11:10**; 4:6].

WIFE: of Koremori [10:8, 10:10, 10:12]; of Nobutaka [**Initiates 1, 4**]; of Shunkan [3:9]; of Takafusa [**Initiates 1, 4**].

WIFE OF KIYOMORI: *see* Tokiko.

WIFE OF MICHIMORI: *see* Kozaishō.

YAMABUKI: woman attendant of Kiso no Yoshinaka [9:4].

YAMAGAMI: Taira warrior at the battle of Uji [4:11].

YASUKUNI: Murakami no Hangan Yasukuni, Genji warrior serving under Yoshitsune [9:12; 9:7].

YASUTSUNA: native of Suruga Province who executes Rokudai [12:9].

YASUYORI: Hei-hōgan (Taira police lieutenant) Yasuyori. Implicated in the Shishi-no-tani conspiracy, he is exiled to Kikai-ga-shima with Shunkan and Naritsune. On his way to the island, he takes religious vows. Throughout his exile, he leads Naritsune in prayer to the Kumano deities. One of the prayer stupas they cast in the water is brought to the capital and arouses the sympathy even of Kiyomori. Pardoned, he becomes a recluse and edits the Buddhist anthology *A Collection of Buddhist Treasures* (*Hōbutsushū*) [**2:10, 2:15, 3:2, 3:9**; 1:12, 2:3].

YOICHI (1): Asari no Yoichi, skilled archer of the Genji of Kai Province. [11:8].

YOICHI (2): *see* Munetaka.

YOKOBUE: lesser maid-in-waiting (*zōshi*) to Kenreimon'in. After her former lover, Tokiyori, takes the tonsure and refuses to meet her, she enters a nunnery in Nara and dies soon afterward. Many variants describe her as throwing herself into the Ōi River. The best-known version of the story of Yokobue and Tokiyori (the Takiguchi novice) is the medieval *Tale of Yokobue* (*Yokobue no sōshi*) [10:8].

YORIMASA: Minamoto no Yorimasa (1104–1180), of the third rank. A veteran warrior, he fights in the Hōgen and Heiji rebellions, first on Yoshitomo's side in support of Emperor GoShirakawa (1156) and then aiding Kiyomori against Yoshitomo (1159). When Yorimasa is over seventy, he persuades Prince Mochihito to lend his name to a revolt against the Heike. The reasons given are essentially personal: his son has been humiliated by Kiyomori's son Munemori. Yorimasa gains the support of the Miidera monks, who fight alongside his men at the battle of Uji. But the Kōfuku-ji monks arrive too late to prevent defeat, and Yorimasa commits *seppuku* in the Byōdō-in after reciting a final poem. The extended Yorimasa sequence in book four ends with the retelling of two highlights from his life—unusual feats of archery in the imperial service—but ends with condemnation: Yorimasa's "pointless rebellion" led to his destruction and to the prince's death [**4:11**; 1:11, 1:15, 4:3–6, 4:10, 4:12, 4:14, 4:15, 5:9, 7:10, 11:19].

YORIMORI (1131–1186): son of Taira no Tadanori and the Ike Nun and Ike major counselor. After the Heiji rebellion (1159), his mother begs for

Yoritomo to be exiled rather than executed. This may be one reason why Yorimori is kept at a distance by his half brother Kiyomori. When the Heike flee the capital in 1183, he decides to stay behind, trusting in Yoritomo's promises of protection. His family regards him as a traitor, but when the Genji win the war, he is the only senior member of the Heike to escape execution or banishment [**Initiates 5**; 1:15, 3:4, 3:6, 4:2, 4:13, 5:1, 7:12, 7:19, 10:9, 10:13].

YORITOMO (1147–1199): third son of Minamoto no Yoshitomo and half brother of Noriyori and Yoshitsune. After his father and older brothers Akugenda and Tomonaga die in the Heiji rebellion (1159), Yoritomo is captured in 1160. Spared execution, he lives as an exile in Izu, gaining the support of his erstwhile captor Hōjō Tokimasa and marrying his daughter Masako. In 1180 Yorimasa and his allies attack Heike supporters in the east but suffer a major defeat at Ishibashiyama. With a small group of survivors, Yoritomo escapes to Awa (present-day Chiba), then returns to Sagami, and sets up his headquarters in Kamakura, where he spends much of the remainder of the war. His cousin Yoshinaka and his half brothers Yoshitsune and Noriyori bring him victory in the war. The Kakuichi version is highly selective in its treatment of Yoritomo, saying little about how he gains the support of eastern warriors and omitting all but a mention of the battle of Ishibashiyama, which the other variants describe at great length. Mongaku is given a central role in persuading Yoritomo to join the revolt. Although he is eager to avenge his father's death, Yoritomo wants his actions to be authorized by an imperial edict. The narrative legitimizes his war against the Heike by a convenient fiction: having him receive an imperial appointment as shogun at a date nine years earlier than the historical one, 1183 rather than 1192. The Kakuichi version does not disguise the ferocity with which Yoritomo consolidates his position during and after the war, most strikingly through the elimination of his own kin, but in the case of his persecution of Yoshitsune, much of the blame is shifted to Kagetoki and his slanders [6:7, **9:12**, **10:5**, **10:7**, **11:7**, **12:9**; 3:17, 4:3, 5:3, 5:4, 5:6, 5:7, 5:10–12, 6:5, 6:6, 6:10, 6:12, 7:1, 7:2, 7:7, 7:12, 7:19, 8:4–6, 8:10, 8:11, 9:1, 9:3–5, 9:9, 9:10, 10:3, 10:4, 10:6, 10:13, 10:14, 11:1, 11:10, 11:14, 11:15, 11:17, 11:18, 12:2–8].

YORIYOSHI: Minamoto no Yoriyoshi (988–1075) of Iyo Province. Successful in his northern wars against Abe Munetō and Sadatō, Yoriyoshi becomes the governor of Izu Province, founding a Hachiman shrine in Kamakura and expanding the influence of the Genji warriors in the east. In basing his headquarters in Kamakura and rebuilding the Hachiman shrine, Yoritomo is consciously emulating this ancestor [**10:12**; 1:11, 7:5].

YOSHIHIRA: Kamakura no Akugenda Yoshihira (d. 1160), eldest son of Minamoto no Yoritomo. He dies in the Heiji rebellion [**10:10**; 6:5].

YOSHIHISA: name given by Yoshitsune to Kumaō, son of the hunter Washio no Shōji Takehisa. He becomes Yoshitsune's retainer and dies with him many years later in Ōshū [9:9].

YOSHIMORI (1): Ise no Saburō Yoshimori (d. 1185), trusted warrior serving under Yoshitsune. The tale last mentions him fighting at the battle of Dan-no-ura. He dies the same year in a battle at Mount Suzuka in Ise Province [11.3, 11.5, 11.7, 11.8; 9:7, 11:1, 11:2, 11:6, 11:10].

YOSHIMORI (2): Wada [no Kotarō] Yoshimori (1147–1213), Genji warrior and member of the Miura family of Sagami Province [11:8; 9:7].

YOSHINAKA: Kiso no Yoshinaka (1154–1184), cousin of Minamoto no Yoritomo and Yoshitsune. Victor of a campaign against the Heike in the northwest (book seven), he occupies the capital after the Heike flee but later is killed on Yoritomo's orders. In the episode translated here, Yoshinaka is generally referred to respectfully as Lord Kiso, whereas in those sections that mock his lack of courtly manners and political understanding, he is called simply Kiso [9:4, **Initiates 4**; 4:3, 4:14, 6:5, 6:6, 6:11, 6:12, 7:1–19, 8:1, 8:2, 8:4–11, 9:1–5, 10:13, 10:15, 11:1, 11:17, 12:4].

YOSHITOMO: Minamoto no Yoshitomo (1123–1160), father, by different women, of Akugenda Yoshihira, Tomonaga, Yoritomo, Yoshitsune, and Noriyori, among others. Feeling insufficiently rewarded for the part he played in ending the Hōgen rebellion (1156), Yoshimoto joins Fujiwara no Nobuyori in instigating the Heiji rebellion (1159). After his defeat, Yoshitomo flees to Owari, where he is betrayed and killed. It takes twenty years for the Genji to recover from their loses in the two short conflicts. In the first, Yoshitomo's father, Tameyoshi, and many of his brothers are on the losing side and are executed. After the second, Yoshitomo and his elder two sons are killed. Yoshitomo's head is publicly exhibited in the capital. In the Kakuichi version, Mongaku twice brings to Yoritomo what he claims to be Yoshitomo's skull [1:7, 2:6, 4:3, 4:10, 5:7, 5:10, 10:1, 10:4, 11:18, 12:2].

YOSHITSUNE (1159–1189): son of Minamoto no Yoshitomo and Lady Tokiwa, half brother of Yoritomo and Noriyori, commander of Genji forces, and victor at Ichi-no-tani, Yashima, Dan-no-ura, and other battles. According to the narrative, Kagetoki's "slander" of Yoshitsune causes Yoritomo to distrust him. The history of the young "Ushiwaka" is freely retold and reinvented in The Tale of Yoshitsune (Gikeiki), including his years at the Kurama-ji temple, his journey to northern Japan, and his acceptance by Fujiwara no Hidehira. The Tales of the Heike does not explain how Yoshitsune came to command an army. When we meet him, he is already an experienced general [9:9, 9:12, 10:5, 11:3–5, 11:7, 11:8; 4:3, 8:11, 9:1–3, 9:5, 9:7, 9:8, 10:1, 10:5, 10:14, 10:15, 11:1, 11:2, 11:6, 11:10–13, 11:15–18, 12:3–5, 12:8].

YOSHITSURA: Sawara no Jūrō Yoshitsura, Genji warrior from Miura in Sagami Province serving under Yoshitsune [9:12; 9:7].

YOSHIYUKI: Yoshiyuki of Aki Province, sent by Munemori as a messenger to other Heike commanders [9:9].

YOSHIZUMI: Miura no Suke Yoshizumi (1127–1200). Although Heike by descent, Yoshizumi's family joins the Genji in their revolt. Yoritomo gives him the honor of receiving the Fukuhara edict from the imperial messenger. When Kagetoki and Yoshitsune nearly come to blows, Yoshizumi steps in to restrain Yoshitsune [11:7; 8:5, 9:7, 10:14].

YOSŌBYŌE: *see* Shigekage.

YUKIMORI (d. 1185): grandson of Taira no Kiyomori; son of Motoyori, who dies young; and director of the stables of the left. Yukimori dies at the battle of Dan-no-ura with his cousins Sukemori and Arimori [4:11; 2:3, 7:13, 7:19, 10:14, 11:10].

YUKITSUNA: Tada no Kurando Yukitsuna of the Genji of Settsu Province. He is present at the meeting of the Shishi-no-tani conspirators where anti-Heike sentiments are voiced. One of the chief conspirators then gives him cloth and tells him to use it to equip the warriors. Afraid of being discovered, Yukitsuna reveals to Kiyomori what was said at the meeting. When Yorimasa circulates a call to arms listing the Genji warriors in every region, Yukitsuna is explicitly mentioned as a traitor [3:1; 1:12, 1:13, 2:3, 4:3].

BIBLIOGRAPHY

The bibliography suggests resources for those who want to explore further the world of *The Tales of the Heike*.

Complete Translations of *The Tales of the Heike*

Kitagawa, Hiroshi, and Bruce T. Tsuchida. *The Tale of the Heike*. With a foreword by Edward G. Seidensticker. 2 vols. Tokyo: University of Tokyo Press, 1975.

McCullough, Helen Craig. *The Tale of the Heike*. Translated with an introduction. Stanford, Calif.: Stanford University Press, 1988.

Sadler, A. L. "The *Heike monogatari*." *Transactions of the Asiatic Society of Japan* 46, no. 2 (1918): 1–278; 49, no. 1 (1921): 1–354.

Includes a translation of a related text, "The Book of Swords," 325–354.

Sieffert, René. *Le Dit des Heiké*. Le Cycle épique des Taïra et des Minamoto. Paris: Publications orientalistes de France, 1978.

Variant Texts of *Heike monogatari*

Texts of the *Heike monogatari* are available in widely differing variants, as many as one hundred according to some counts. Ten of the major versions are listed here. This translation is based on the variant of Akashi no Kakuichi, which was made for recitation rather than reading. Variants are grouped into "lineages" of "recited texts" (*kataribon*) and "read texts" (*yomihon*) or, alternatively, "abbreviated" texts (*ryakuhon*) and "expanded" texts (*kōhon*), respectively.

Enkyō-bon *Heike monogatari*.

An early text of *Heike monogatari* of the "read" lineage. Its colophons indicate that an exact copy was made in 1419 and 1420 of an original dated Enkyō 2–3 (1309–1310). "Enkyō" is sometimes read "Engyō" or "Enkei."

Feique no monogatari.

A romanized version in colloquial Japanese printed in 1592 at the Jesuit *collegio* (seminary) at Amakusa in Kyushu and used as a language textbook for European missionaries.

Genpei jōsuiki (Genpei seisuiki).

A late variant of the "read" lineage, important to later reception.

Genpei tōjōroku.

A variant of the "read" lineage resembling the Enkyō-bon. Some books are missing. Additions focus on the Taira in eastern Japan, especially the Chiba family. It is dated in the colophon to 1337 (Kenmu 4).

Hyakunijukku-bon *Heike monogatari*.

A variant of the "recited" lineage. There are six known manuscripts, but with the text edited so that each of its twelve books has 10 sections (*ku*), for a total of 120 sections. Like the Yashiro-bon, it has no separate "Initiates' Book" (Kanjō no maki).

Kakuichi-bon *Heike monogatari*.

The main example of the "recited" lineage. It owes its final form to Akashi no Kakuichi, leader of the Ichikata school of reciters, who had a disciple write down an official version in 1371, of which six copies (*beppon*) survive. Most Japanese editions are based on either the former Takano Collection manuscript, now at the University of Tokyo, or a manuscript at Ryūkoku University in Kyoto. Section names and divisions in the two manuscripts differ, and the University of Tokyo text (the version translated here) contains many short phrases and a few long passages not present in the Ryūkoku manuscript.

Nagato-bon *Heike monogatari*.

A variant of the "read" lineage.

Rufubon *Heike monogatari*.

A "vulgate" (*rufubon*) text found in different forms in Edo-period printed editions. The first complete English translation was of a *rufubon* text.

Shibugassenjō-bon *Heike monogatari*.

A variant written entirely in Chinese characters. Books two, four, and eight are missing. The fact that its account is often shorter or simpler than those of other versions was once regarded as evidence for its being closer to a lost archetype, but it is now usually thought to be a simplified edition of a more detailed version. Although the title refers to "four conflicts," the longer subtitle makes clear that this work deals with only the Genpei war (1180–1185) and not with the earlier Hōgen (1156) and Heiji (1159) rebellions or with the later Jōkyū rebellion (1221).

Yashiro-bon *Heike monogatari*.

A variant of the "recited" lineage. Chapters (*maki*) four and nine did not survive. Compared with the Kakuichi version, this account is often simpler and shorter, leading some scholars to see it as an "archaic" stage in the evolution of recited texts. Other scholars argue for later abridgments.

Yōshi-bon *Heike monogatari*.

A Muromachi-period variant for recitation.

Primary Sources and Related Works

Azuma kagami (*Mirror of the East*).

A chronicle of the period between 1180 and 1266 from the perspective of Kamakura. It was compiled in the late thirteenth century based on court diaries, temple records, and other documents from Kyoto as well as records from Kamakura itself. For a partial translation, see Minoru Shinoda, *The Founding of the Kamakura Shogunate, 1180–1185, with Selected Translations from the Azuma Kagami* (New York: Columbia University Press, 1960).

Benkei monogatari (*The Tale of Benkei*).

A medieval tale about Yoshitsune's retainer Benkei. For a complete translation into French, see René Sieffert, *Histoire de Benkei* (Paris: Publications orientalistes de France, 1995).

Gikeiki (The Tale of Yoshitsune).

An account of episodes in the life of Yoshitsune, largely omitting his part in the Genpei war already described in *Heike monogatari*. For a translation, see Helen Craig McCullough, *Yoshitsune: A Fifteenth-Century Japanese Chronicle* (Tokyo: University of Tokyo Press, 1966).

Gukanshō.

A historical account covering all of Japanese history, with particular attention to the "military age" (*musa no yo*), beginning with the Hōgen rebellion (1156), as well as historical and political reflections. It was largely completed in 1220 by Jien (1155–1225), the abbot of Tendai-ji from 1184 and the younger brother of Kujō Kanezane (1149–1207). Both the "recited" and the "read" text lineages of *Heike monogatari* are believed to have used the account in *Gukanshō*. See Delmer Brown and Ichirō Ishida, *The Future and the Past: A Translation and Study of the Gukanshō, an Interpretative History of Japan Written in 1219* (Berkeley: University of California Press, 1979).

Gyokuyō.

The diary of the nobleman Kujō Kanezane, in sixty-six volumes covering the period between 1164 and 1200, and one of the main contemporary sources confirming the accuracy of the details in the *Heike* variants.

Heiji monogatari.

The tale of the Heiji rebellion of 1159 in three chapters (*maki*). It is important for understanding the development of "war tales" (*gunki-mono*) and the background of the conflict described in *Heike monogatari*, as many characters appear in both works. *Heiji monogatari* was also the subject of an early illustrated scroll. For a complete translation of books one and two, as well as excerpts from book three, see Edwin O. Reischauer and Joseph K. Yamagiwa, *Translations from Early Japanese Literature* (Cambridge, Mass.: Harvard University Press, 1951), 271–351. An appendix contains a complete translation of the text of the *Heiji monogatari emaki*.

Heiji monogatari emaki.

An illustrated scroll of the Heiji revolt, from the Kamakura period. It originally was thought to consist of ten scrolls, of which three complete ones have survived: *The Burning of Sanjō Palace* (Museum of Fine Arts,

Boston), *Shinzei* (Seikado Art Museum, Tokyo), and *The Removal of the Imperial Family to Rokuhara* (Tokyo National Museum).

Heike monogatari emaki.

An early Edo scroll, in the collection of the Hayashibara Art Museum in Okayama, all of whose thirty-six *kan* have survived. This scroll illustrates more scenes than does any other illustrated version of the *Heike*. The narrative text included is similar to the "vulgate" versions in Edo-period printed editions.

Hōgen monogatari.

The tale, in various versions, of the Hōgen rebellion of 1156 in three chapters (*maki*). For a translation and study of the Rufubon *Hōgen monogatari*, with translated excerpts from other variants, see William R. Wilson, *Hōgen monogatari: Tale of the Disorder in Hōgen*, Monumenta Nipponica Monograph (Tokyo: Sophia University Press, 1971).

Kanmon gyoki.

The diary of the imperial prince Gosukōin (1372–1456), valuable for its frequent mention of performances by *Heike* reciters.

Kenreimon'in ukyō no daibushū.

An important diary by a court lady of the Genpei period. For a translation, see Phillip Tudor Harries, *The Poetic Memoirs of Lady Daibu* (Stanford, Calif.: Stanford University Press, 1980).

Mai no hon.

A collection printed in the Kan'ei period (1624–1643) of some forty-five libretti (*daihon*) of the *kōwaka-mai* performance tradition, more than half of which concern the Genpei war, including the Hōgen and Heiji periods. Many pieces deal with Minamoto no Yoshitsune (for example, *Izumigajō*). Those closely related to the Kakuichi version include *Atsumori*, *Tsukishima*, *Iōnoshima* (related to the Kikai-ga-shima story), *Mongaku*, *Kiso ganjo*, and *Nasu no Yoichi*. Some others have as their source "read" *Heike* variants such as Nagato-bon and Enkyō-bon. See James T. Araki, *The Ballad-Drama of Medieval Japan* (Berkeley: University of California Press, 1964; Rutland, Vt.: Tuttle, 1978).

Masukagami (The Clear Mirror).

An account of Japanese history beginning at the end of the Genpei war in 1185 and covering the period up to the fall of Kamakura in 1333. It was compiled in the late fourteenth century. For a translation, see George W. Perkins, *The Clear Mirror: A Chronicle of the Japanese Court During the Kamakura Period (1185–1333)* (Stanford, Calif.: Stanford University Press, 1998).

Meigetsuki (Clear Moon Chronicle).

The diary of the poet and critic Fujiwara no Teika (1162–1241). The diary begins with the Second Month of 1180 and continues until the Twelfth Month of 1236. A much quoted phrase is Teika's comment when news of Yoritomo's revolt reached the capital in the Ninth Month of 1180: "The campaign of the 'red flags' [Taira] against the 'barbarians' [Genji] is no concern of mine."

Mōko shūrai [ekotoba] (Scrolls of the Mongol Invasions).

An illustrated account of the Mongol invasions in the late thirteenth century. For a translation, with an interpretative essay and reproductions, see Thomas D. Conlan, *In Little Need of Divine Intervention: Takezaki Suenaga's Scrolls of the Mongol Invasions of Japan* (Ithaca, N.Y.: East Asia Program, Cornell University, 2001).

Mutsuwaki.

An early battle chronicle. See Helen Craig McCullough, "A Tale of Mutsu," *Harvard Journal of Asiatic Studies* 25 (1964–1965): 178–211.

Sankaiki.

The diary of Nakayama Tadachika. The earliest entry is dated 1151; the last, 1194. Entries are missing for many months and for some entire years, but the diary is still of great value for the period covered by the *Heike monogatari.*

Shōkyūki (also read *Jōkyūki*) *(An Account of the Shōkyū Era).*

An account of a conflict in 1221. See William H. McCullough, "*Shōkyū ki*: An Account of the Shōkyū War of 1221," *Monumenta Nipponica* 19, nos. 1–2 (1964): 163–215; 19, nos. 3–4 (1964): 420–455.

Shōmonki (Record of Masakado).

A major precursor of the war tale *(gunki-mono)* genre. For a translation, see Judith N. Rabinovitch, *Shōmonki: The Story of Masakado's Rebellion* (Tokyo: Sophia University Press, 1986).

Soga monogatari (The Tale of the Soga).

A medieval narrative of the Soga brothers and their revenge on their father's killer. It is set in Kamakura and the surrounding area in the period after the Genpei war. For a translation, see Thomas J. Cogan, *The Tale of the Soga Brothers* (Tokyo: University of Tokyo Press, 1987).

Taiheiki (Chronicle of Great Peace).

The principal war narrative after *Heike monogatari*, covering the years between 1318 and 1386, regarding the fall of the Kamakura shogunate, Emperor GoDaigo's Kenmu restoration, and the establishment of the Northern and Southern Courts. The narrative includes references to the battles of the Genpei war, as well as to the recitation of the *Heike* narrative. For a translation of volumes one through twelve, see Helen Craig McCullough, *The Taiheiki: A Chronicle of Medieval Japan* (New York: Columbia University Press, 1959).

Tsurezuregusa (Essays in Idleness).

A miscellany by Kenkō, in which section 226 describes the circumstances under which Kenkō believed *Heike monogatari* to have been written. For a translation, see Donald Keene, *Essays in Idleness: The Tsurezuregusa of Kenkō* (New York: Columbia University Press, 1967).

Yokobue sōshi (The Tale of Yokobue).

A Muromachi-period work giving an expanded account of the story of Tokiyori (Takiguchi novice) and Yokobue. See Yoshiko Dykstra and Yuko Kurata, "The *Yokobue-sōshi*: Conflicts Between Social Convention, Human Love and Religious Renunciation," *Japanese Religions* 26 (2001): 117–129.

General Studies

Akamatsu, Toshihide. "The Prototype of the *Heike-Monogatari*." In *Proceedings of the Twenty-seventh Congress of Orientalists*, 555–556. Ann Arbor, Mich.: Harrassowitz, 1967.

Alberizzi, Valerio Luigi. "*Wakan konkōbun e buntai* della lingua giapponese classica: Metodologia di analisi." *Asiatica Venetiana* 5 (2000): 3–19.

Bialock, David T. *Eccentric Spaces, Hidden Histories: Narrative, Ritual, and Royal Authority from The Chronicles of Japan to The Tale of the Heike*. Stanford, Calif.: Stanford University Press, 2007.

Bialock, David T. "Heike monogatari." In *Medieval Japanese Writers*, edited by Steven D. Carter, 73–84. Vol. 203 of *Dictionary of Literary Biography*. Detroit: Gale Research, 1999.

Butler, Kenneth Dean, Jr. "The *Heike monogatari* and the Japanese Warrior Ethic." *Harvard Journal of Asiatic Studies* 29 (1969): 93–108.

Butler, Kenneth Dean, Jr. "The Textual Evolution of the *Heike monogatari*." *Harvard Journal of Asiatic Studies* 26 (1966): 5–51.

Ehmcke, Franziska, and Heinz-Dieter Reese, eds. *Von Helden, Mönchen und schönen Frauen: Die Welt des japanischen Heike Epos*. Cologne: Boehlau, 2000.

Hasegawa, Tadashi. "The Early Stages of the *Heike monogatari*." *Monumenta Nipponica* 22 (1967): 65–81.

Moeshart, Herman J. "Women in the *Heike monogatari*." In *Women in Japanese Literature*, edited by Erika G. de Poorter, 27–38. Leiden: Center for Japanese and Korean Studies, 1981.

Morrison, Clinton D. "Context in Two Episodes from *Heike monogatari*." In *The Distant Isle: Studies and Translations of Japanese Literature in Honor of Robert H. Brower*, edited by Thomas Hare, Robert Borgen, and Sharalyn Orbaugh, 321–336. Ann Arbor: Center for Japanese Studies, University of Michigan, 1996.

Oyler, Elizabeth Ann. "Giō: Women and Performance in the *Heike monogatari*." *Harvard Journal of Asiatic Studies* 64 (2004): 341–366.

Plutschow, Herbert. *Chaos and Cosmos: Ritual in Classical Japanese Literature*. Leiden: Brill, 1990.

Plutschow, Herbert. "The Placatory Nature of *The Tale of the Heike*: Additional Documents and Thoughts." In *Currents in Japanese Culture: Translations and Transformations*, edited by Amy Vladeck Heinrich, 71–80. New York: Columbia University Press, 1997.

Schneider, Roland. "Pinsel, Schwert und Mönchsgewand: Das *Heike monogatari* als literarisches Werk." In *Von Helden, Mönchen und schönen Frauen: Die Welt des japanischen Heike Epos*, edited by Franziska Ehmcke and Heinz-Dieter Reese, 11–32. Cologne: Boehlau, 2000.

Varley, H. Paul. "Warriors as Courtiers: The Taira in *Heike monogatari*." In *Currents in Japanese Culture: Translations and Transformations*, edited by Amy Vladeck Heinrich, 53–70. New York: Columbia University Press, 1997.

Watson, Michael. "Genre, Convention, Parody, and the Middle Style: *Heike monogatari* and Chaucer." *Poetica* 44 (1995): 23–40.

Watson, Michael. "Theories of Narrative and Their Application to the Study of *Heike monogatari*." In *Observing Japan from Within*, edited by James Baxter, 91–122. Kyoto: Nichibunken kenkyūjō, 2004.

Yamashita, Hiroaki. "The Structure of 'Story-telling' (*katari*) in Japanese War Tales with Special Reference to the Scene of Yoshitomo's Last Moments." *Acta Asiatica* 37 (1976): 47–69.

Historical and Cultural Context

Adolphson, Mikael S. *The Gates of Power: Monks, Courtiers, and Warriors in Premodern Japan*. Honolulu: University of Hawai'i Press, 2000.

Blacker, Carmen. "The Exiled Warrior and the Hidden Village." *Folklore* 95, no. 2 (1985): 139–150.

Brown, Delmer M., and Ichirō Ishida. *The Future and the Past: A Translation and Study of the Gukanshō, an Interpretative History of Japan Written in 1219.* Berkeley: University of California Press, 1979.

Brownlee, John S. *Political Thought in Japanese Historical Writing: From Kojiki (712) to Tokushi Yoron (1712).* Waterloo, Ont.: Wilfred Laurier University Press, 1991.

Conlan, Thomas. *The Violent Order of Fourteenth-Century Japan.* Ann Arbor: Center for Japanese Studies, University of Michigan, 2003.

Farris, William Wayne. *Heavenly Warriors: The Evolution of Japan's Military, 500–1300.* Cambridge, Mass.: Harvard University Press, 1992.

Friday, Karl. *Hired Swords: The Rise of Private Warrior Power in Early Japan.* Stanford, Calif.: Stanford University Press, 1992.

Friday, Karl. *Samurai, Warfare, and the State in Early Medieval Japan.* London: Routledge, 2004.

Friday, Karl. "Teeth and Claws: Provincial Warriors and the Heian Court." *Monumenta Nipponica* 43, no. 2 (1988): 153–185.

Groemer, Gerald. "The Guild of the Blind in Tokugawa Japan." *Monumenta Nipponica* 56, no. 3 (2001): 349–380.

Hurst, Cameron. "Insei." In *The Cambridge History of Japan*, vol. 2, *Heian Japan*, edited by Donald H. Shively and William H. McCullough, 576–643. Cambridge: Cambridge University Press, 1999.

Mass, Jeffrey. "The Genpei War." In *The Cambridge History of Japan*, vol. 3, *Medieval Japan*, edited by Kozo Yamamura, 47–66. Cambridge: Cambridge University Press, 1990.

McCullough, William H., and Helen C. McCullough. *A Tale of Flowering Fortunes: Annals of Japanese Aristocratic Life in the Heian Period.* 2 vols. Stanford, Calif.: Stanford University Press, 1980.

Minobe, Shigekatsu. "The World View of *Genpei jōsuiki.*" *Japanese Journal of Religious Studies* 9, nos. 2–3 (1982): 213–234.

Ruch, Barbara. "The Other Side of Culture in Medieval Japan." In *The Cambridge History of Japan*, vol. 3, *Medieval Japan*, edited by Kozo Yamamura, 500–543. Cambridge: Cambridge University Press, 1990.

Shinoda, Minoru. *The Founding of the Kamakura Shogunate, 1180–1185, with Selected Translations from the Azuma Kagami.* New York: Columbia University Press, 1960.

Souyri, Pierre François. *The World Turned Upside Down: Medieval Japanese Society.* Translated by Käthe Roth. New York: Columbia University Press, 2001.

Takeuchi, Rizō. "The Rise of the Warriors." In *The Cambridge History of Japan*, vol. 2, *Heian Japan*, edited by Donald H. Shively and William H. McCullough, 644–709. Cambridge: Cambridge University Press, 1999.

Varley, H. Paul. *Warriors of Japan as Portrayed in the War Tales*. Honolulu: University of Hawai'i Press, 1994.

Musical Recitation

De Ferranti, Hugh. "Composition and Improvisation in Satsuma *biwa*." In *Musica Asiatica*, edited by Allan Marrett, 6:102–127. Cambridge: Cambridge University Press, 1991.

Komoda Haruko. *Heike on ongaku: Tōdō no dentō*. Tokyo: Daiichi shobō, 2003.

An important synthesis of the history of *Heike* recitation and its scholarship, followed by a detailed analysis of the features of both vocal and *biwa* music. The CD contains a recording of performances by Imai Tsutomu, *kengyō* (holder of highest rank) in the Nagoya line of reciters.

Malm, William P. *Traditional Japanese Music and Musical Instruments*. New ed. Tokyo: Kōdansha International, 2000.

The CD contains four tracks of music with *biwa*: *mōsō biwa* (blind *biwa* monk) chant, a *biwa* performance by Takeyama Kōgo of the opening lines of the opening "Gion shōja" section (*Heike* 1:1), a performance of an excerpt from the "Atsumori" piece in the Satsuma *biwa* tradition (*Heike* 9:16), and a Chikuzen *biwa* performance of the "Ōgi no mato" piece (Nasu no Yoichi story of *Heike* 11:8).

Ruch, Barbara. "Medieval Jongleurs and the Making of a National Literature." In *Japan in the Muromachi Age*, edited by John W. Hall and Takeshi Toyoda, 279–309. Berkeley: University of California Press, 1977.

Rutledge, Eric. "Orality and Textual Variation in the *Heike monogatari*: Part One: The Phrase and Its Formulaic Nature." In *Heike biwa: Katari to ongaku*, edited by Kamisangō Yūkō, 360–340. Kasukabe City: Hitsuji shobō, 1993.

Tokita, Alison. "The Reception of the *Heike monogatari* as Performed Narrative: The Atsumori Episode in *heikyoku*, *zato biwa* and *satsuma biwa*." *Japanese Studies* 23, no. 1 (2003): 59–85.

Ueda, Makoto, ed. *Literary and Art Theories in Japan*. 1967. Reprint, Ann Arbor: Center for Japanese Studies, University of Michigan, 1991.

Contains an introduction to and a translation of a description of *Heike* recitation from *Saikai yoteki shū*.

Reception in Drama

Some thirty-three nō plays—more than one-tenth of the current repertoire—are based on *Heike monogatari*. Many others outside the repertoire have survived as well.

Araki, James. *The Ballad-Drama of Medieval Japan*. Berkeley: University of California Press, 1964.

Contains a translation of the "Atsumori" narrative from the *kōwaka-mai* performance tradition.

Brazell, Karen W. "Subversive Transformations: Atsumori and Tadanori at Suma." In *Currents in Japanese Culture: Translations and Transformations*, edited by Amy Vladeck Heinrich, 35–52. New York: Columbia University Press, 1997.

Brazell, Karen W., ed. *Traditional Japanese Theater: An Anthology of Plays*. New York: Columbia University Press, 1998.

Contains translations of *Heike*-related material from the nō, *kōwaka-mai*, puppet, and kabuki traditions.

Brazell, Karen W., ed. *Twelve Plays of the Nō and Kyōgen Theaters*. Cornell University East Asia Papers, no. 50. Ithaca, N.Y.: East Asia Program, Cornell University, 1988.

Contains *Heike*- and *Gikeiki*-related plays.

Keene, Donald, ed. *Twenty Plays of the Nō Theatre*. New York: Columbia University Press, 1970.

Nippon gakujutsu shinkōkai, ed. *Japanese Noh Drama*. 3 vols. Tokyo: Nippon gakujutsu shinkōkai, 1955–1959.

Shimazaki, Chifumi. *Battle Noh: In Parallel Translations with an Introduction and Running Commentaries*. Vol. 2 of *The Noh*. Tokyo: Hinoki shoten, 1987.

Shimazaki, Chifumi. *Troubled Souls from Japanese Noh Plays of the Fourth Group: Parallel Translations with Running Commentary*. Cornell University East Asia Series, no. 95. Ithaca, N.Y.: East Asia Program, Cornell University, 1998.

Shimazaki, Chifumi. *Warrior Ghost Plays from the Japanese Noh Theater: Parallel Translations with Running Commentary*. Cornell University East Asia Series, no. 60. Ithaca, N.Y.: East Asia Program, Cornell University, 1993.

Shimazaki, Chifumi. *Women Noh: In Parallel Translations with an Introduction and Running Commentaries*. Vol. 3 of *The Noh*. Tokyo: Hinoki shoten, 1987.

Tyler, Royall. *Japanese Nō Dramas*. London: Penguin, 1992.

Tyler, Royall, trans. *Granny Mountains: A Second Cycle of Nō Plays*. Cornell University East Asia Series, no. 18. Ithaca, N.Y.: East Asia Program, Cornell University, 1978.

Reception in the Visual Arts

Collcutt, Martin. "An Illustrated Edition of the *Tale of the Heike (Heike monogatari)* in the Gest Library Rare Books Collections." *Gest Library Journal* 4, no. 1 (1991): 9–26.

Ford, Barbara. "Tragic Heroines of the *Heike monogatari* and Their Representation in Japanese Screen Painting." *Orientations* 28, no. 2 (1997): 40–47.

Hutt, Graham, ed. *Heike Monogatari*. Vol. 4 of *Japanese Book Illustration*. New York: Abaris Books, 1982.

Reproduces all illustrations from the 1656 (Meireki 2) woodblock edition of *Heike monogatari*.

Meech-Pekarik, Julia. *The Hogen and Heiji Battle Screens in the Metropolitan Museum of Art*. Jacksonville, Fla.: Jacksonville Art Museum, 1984.

Sadler, A. L., trans. *The Ten Foot Square Hut and Tales of the Heike: Being Two Thirteenth-Century Japanese Classics, the "Hojoki" and Selections from "The Heike Monogatari."* 1928. Reprint, Tokyo: Tuttle, 1972.

Includes reproductions from seventeenth-century printed editions of *Heike*.

Modern Reception

Many narrative and dramatic works have been inspired by characters or episodes from *Heike monogatari*. Akutagawa Ryūnosuke, Hanada Kiyoteru, Inoue Yasushi, Kikuchi Kan, Kinoshita Junji, Kōda Rohan, Mori Ōgai, Murō Saisei, Nagai Kafū, Nagai Michiko, Sakaguchi Ango, Setouchi Harumi, Shiba Ryōtarō, Shimamura Hōgetsu, Tayama Katai, and Yamazaki Masakazu are among the many writers since the Meiji period who based narratives or dramatic pieces on *Heike* episodes or characters. The steady flow of new works continues to the present. In the postwar period, many multivolume versions of the *Heike* story have appeared; for example:

Hashimoto Osamu, *Sōchō Heike monogatari*, 8 vols. (1998–2001).

Miyao Tomiko, *Miyaobon Heike monogatari*, 4 vols. (2001).

Morimura Seiichi, *Heike monogatari*, 6 vols. (1998–2000).
Yoshikawa Eiji, *Shin Heike monogatari*, 13 vols. (1950–1973).

In addition, many *manga* (comic book) versions of *Heike monogatari* seem intended to both educate and entertain, combining pictures and dialogue with informative footnotes and quotations from the original. *Manga* like these bear the name of a distinguished scholar on the title page, attesting that the text and pictures have been checked for accuracy. Far freer adaptations are available as well, some with a science-fiction touch.

Film

The Tales of the Heike is a popular subject for television specials, drama series, and feature films, although the direct source is more often the work of a modern popularizer than any version of the original. Yoshitsune is a perennial favorite. Information about many of these films and their current availability can be found on the Internet Movie Database (http://us.imdb.com) and similar Web sites. Examples include:

Heike monogatari (1993–1995).

NHK TV series with puppets, based on Yoshikawa Eiji's version.

Jigokumon (*Gate of Hell*, 1953). Directed by Kinugasa Teinosuke, with Hasegawa Kazuo as Endō Moritō, Kyō Machiko as Lady Kesa, Watanabe Isao as her husband Wataru, and Senda Koreya as Kiyomori.

The story of why Mongaku took religious orders, based on Kikuchi Kan's story "Kesa no otto" (Kesa's Husband, 1923). It begins at the height of the Heiji rebellion. *Jigokumon* was the winner of various international film prizes, including the Grand Prize at the Cannes Film Festival (1956).

Kaidan (1964). Directed by Kobayashi Masaki, with music by Takemitsu Tōru.

Based on Lafcadio Hearn's *Kwaidan: Stories and Studies of Strange Things* (1892). The longest section is the final one, "Miminashi Hōichi," about the blind acolyte who plays the *biwa* for the souls of the Heike who drowned at Dan-no-ura. *Kaidan* was awarded the Special Jury Prize at the Cannes Film Festival and is widely available outside Japan. English titles include *Kwaidan* and *Ghost Stories*.

Minamoto Kurō Yoshitsune (1962). Directed by Matsuda Teiji.
Minamoto Yoshitsune (1955). Directed by Hagiwara Ryō.
Shin Heike monogatari (1955). Directed by Mizoguchi Kenji, with Ichikawa Raizō VIII as Taira no Kiyomori.

Based on Yoshikawa Eiji's novel of the same name. English titles include *Legend of the Taira Clan* and *New Tales of the Taira Clan*.

Shin Heike monogatari (1972).

NHK *Taiga* TV series, based on Yoshikawa Eiji's novel of the same name.

Shin Heike monogatari: Shizuka to Yoshitsune (1956). Directed by Shima Kōji.

The third of three films based on Yoshikawa Eiji's best-seller.

Shin Heike monogatari: Yoshinaka o meguru sannin no onna (1956). Directed by Kinugasa Teinosuke, with the same actors as in *Jigokumon*, including Hasegawa Kazuo as Kiso no Yoshinaka and Kyō Machiko as Tomoe.

Yoshitsune (2005).

NHK *Taiga* TV series. An earlier NHK series on Yoshitsune was broadcast in 1966.

OTHER WORKS IN THE COLUMBIA ASIAN STUDIES SERIES

Translations from the Asian Classics

Major Plays of Chikamatsu, tr. Donald Keene 1961

Four Major Plays of Chikamatsu, tr. Donald Keene. Paperback ed. only. 1961; rev. ed. 1997

Records of the Grand Historian of China, translated from the Shih chi of Ssu-ma Ch'ien, tr. Burton Watson, 2 vols. 1961

Instructions for Practical Living and Other Neo-Confucian Writings by Wang Yangming, tr. Wing-tsit Chan 1963

Hsün Tzu: Basic Writings, tr. Burton Watson, paperback ed. only. 1963; rev. ed. 1996

Chuang Tzu: Basic Writings, tr. Burton Watson, paperback ed. only. 1964; rev. ed. 1996

The Mahābhārata, tr. Chakravarthi V. Narasimhan. Also in paperback ed. 1965; rev. ed. 1997

The Manyōshū, Nippon Gakujutsu Shinkōkai edition 1965

Su Tung-p'o: Selections from a Sung Dynasty Poet, tr. Burton Watson. Also in paperback ed. 1965

Bhartrihari: Poems, tr. Barbara Stoler Miller. Also in paperback ed. 1967

Basic Writings of Mo Tzu, Hsün Tzu, and Han Fei Tzu, tr. Burton Watson. Also in separate paperback eds. 1967

The Awakening of Faith, Attributed to Aśvaghosha, tr. Yoshito S. Hakeda. Also in paperback ed. 1967

Reflections on Things at Hand: The Neo-Confucian Anthology, comp. Chu Hsi and Lü Tsu-ch'ien, tr. Wing-tsit Chan 1967

The Platform Sutra of the Sixth Patriarch, tr. Philip B. Yampolsky. Also in paperback ed. 1967

Essays in Idleness: The Tsurezuregusa of Kenkō, tr. Donald Keene. Also in paperback ed. 1967

The Pillow Book of Sei Shōnagon, tr. Ivan Morris, 2 vols. 1967

Two Plays of Ancient India: The Little Clay Cart and the Minister's Seal, tr. J. A. B. van Buitenen 1968

The Complete Works of Chuang Tzu, tr. Burton Watson 1968

The Romance of the Western Chamber (Hsi Hsiang chi), tr. S. I. Hsiung. Also in paperback ed. 1968

The Manyōshū, Nippon Gakujutsu Shinkōkai edition. Paperback ed. only. 1969

Records of the Historian: Chapters from the Shih chi of Ssu-ma Ch'ien, tr. Burton Watson. Paperback ed. only. 1969

Cold Mountain: 100 Poems by the T'ang Poet Han-shan, tr. Burton Watson. Also in paperback ed. 1970

Twenty Plays of the Nō Theatre, ed. Donald Keene. Also in paperback ed. 1970

Chūshingura: The Treasury of Loyal Retainers, tr. Donald Keene. Also in paperback ed. 1971; rev. ed. 1997

The Zen Master Hakuin: Selected Writings, tr. Philip B. Yampolsky 1971

Chinese Rhyme-Prose: Poems in the Fu Form from the Han and Six Dynasties Periods, tr. Burton Watson. Also in paperback ed. 1971

Kūkai: Major Works, tr. Yoshito S. Hakeda. Also in paperback ed. 1972

The Old Man Who Does as He Pleases: Selections from the Poetry and Prose of Lu Yu, tr. Burton Watson 1973

The Lion's Roar of Queen Śrīmālā, tr. Alex and Hideko Wayman 1974

Courtier and Commoner in Ancient China: Selections from the History of the Former Han by Pan Ku, tr. Burton Watson. Also in paperback ed. 1974

Japanese Literature in Chinese, vol. 1: *Poetry and Prose in Chinese by Japanese Writers of the Early Period*, tr. Burton Watson 1975

Japanese Literature in Chinese, vol. 2: *Poetry and Prose in Chinese by Japanese Writers of the Later Period*, tr. Burton Watson 1976

Scripture of the Lotus Blossom of the Fine Dharma, tr. Leon Hurvitz. Also in paperback ed. 1976

Love Song of the Dark Lord: Jayadeva's Gītagovinda, tr. Barbara Stoler Miller. Also in paperback ed. Cloth ed. includes critical text of the Sanskrit. 1977; rev. ed. 1997

Ryōkan: Zen Monk-Poet of Japan, tr. Burton Watson 1977

Calming the Mind and Discerning the Real: From the Lam rim chen mo of Tsoṇ-kha-pa, tr. Alex Wayman 1978

The Hermit and the Love-Thief: Sanskrit Poems of Bhartrihari and Bilhaṇa, tr. Barbara Stoler Miller 1978

The Lute: Kao Ming's P'i-p'a chi, tr. Jean Mulligan. Also in paperback ed. 1980

A Chronicle of Gods and Sovereigns: Jinnō Shōtōki of Kitabatake Chikafusa, tr. H. Paul Varley 1980

Among the Flowers: The Hua-chien chi, tr. Lois Fusek 1982

Grass Hill: Poems and Prose by the Japanese Monk Gensei, tr. Burton Watson 1983

Doctors, Diviners, and Magicians of Ancient China: Biographies of Fang-shih, tr. Kenneth J. DeWoskin. Also in paperback ed. 1983

Theater of Memory: The Plays of Kālidāsa, ed. Barbara Stoler Miller. Also in paperback ed. 1984

The Columbia Book of Chinese Poetry: From Early Times to the Thirteenth Century, ed. and tr. Burton Watson. Also in paperback ed. 1984

Poems of Love and War: From the Eight Anthologies and the Ten Long Poems of Classical Tamil, tr. A. K. Ramanujan. Also in paperback ed. 1985

The Bhagavad Gita: Krishna's Counsel in Time of War, tr. Barbara Stoler Miller 1986

The Columbia Book of Later Chinese Poetry, ed. and tr. Jonathan Chaves. Also in paperback ed. 1986

The Tso Chuan: Selections from China's Oldest Narrative History, tr. Burton Watson 1989

Waiting for the Wind: Thirty-six Poets of Japan's Late Medieval Age, tr. Steven Carter 1989

Selected Writings of Nichiren, ed. Philip B. Yampolsky 1990

Saigyō, Poems of a Mountain Home, tr. Burton Watson 1990

The Book of Lieh Tzu: A Classic of the Tao, tr. A. C. Graham. Morningside ed. 1990

The Tale of an Anklet: An Epic of South India—The Cilappatikāram of Iḷaṅkō Aṭikaḷ, tr. R. Parthasarathy 1993

Waiting for the Dawn: A Plan for the Prince, tr. and introduction by Wm. Theodore de Bary 1993

Yoshitsune and the Thousand Cherry Trees: A Masterpiece of the Eighteenth-Century Japanese Puppet Theater, tr., annotated, and with introduction by Stanleigh H. Jones, Jr. 1993

The Lotus Sutra, tr. Burton Watson. Also in paperback ed. 1993

The Classic of Changes: A New Translation of the I Ching as Interpreted by Wang Bi, tr. Richard John Lynn 1994

Beyond Spring: Tz'u Poems of the Sung Dynasty, tr. Julie Landau 1994

The Columbia Anthology of Traditional Chinese Literature, ed. Victor H. Mair 1994

Scenes for Mandarins: The Elite Theater of the Ming, tr. Cyril Birch 1995

Letters of Nichiren, ed. Philip B. Yampolsky; tr. Burton Watson et al. 1996

Unforgotten Dreams: Poems by the Zen Monk Shōtetsu, tr. Steven D. Carter 1997

The Vimalakirti Sutra, tr. Burton Watson 1997

Japanese and Chinese Poems to Sing: The Wakan rōei shū, tr. J. Thomas Rimer and Jonathan Chaves 1997

Breeze Through Bamboo: Kanshi of Ema Saikō, tr. Hiroaki Sato 1998

A Tower for the Summer Heat, Li Yu, tr. Patrick Hanan 1998

Traditional Japanese Theater: An Anthology of Plays, Karen Brazell 1998

The Original Analects: Sayings of Confucius and His Successors (0479–0249), E. Bruce Brooks and A. Taeko Brooks 1998

The Classic of the Way and Virtue: A New Translation of the Tao-te ching of Laozi as Interpreted by Wang Bi, tr. Richard John Lynn 1999

The Four Hundred Songs of War and Wisdom: An Anthology of Poems from Classical Tamil, The Puṟanāṉūṟu, ed. and tr. George L. Hart and Hank Heifetz 1999

Original Tao: Inward Training (Nei-yeh) and the Foundations of Taoist Mysticism, by Harold D. Roth 1999

Lao Tzu's Tao Te Ching: A Translation of the Startling New Documents Found at Guodian, by Robert G. Henricks 2000

The Shorter Columbia Anthology of Traditional Chinese Literature, ed. Victor H. Mair 2000

Mistress and Maid (Jiaohongji), by Meng Chengshun, tr. Cyril Birch 2001

Chikamatsu: Five Late Plays, tr. and ed. C. Andrew Gerstle 2001

The Essential Lotus: Selections from the Lotus Sutra, tr. Burton Watson 2002

Early Modern Japanese Literature: An Anthology, 1600–1900, ed. Haruo Shirane 2002

The Sound of the Kiss, or The Story That Must Never Be Told: Pingali Suranna's Kala-purnodayamu, tr. Vecheru Narayana Rao and David Shulman 2003

The Selected Poems of Du Fu, tr. Burton Watson 2003

Far Beyond the Field: Haiku by Japanese Women, tr. Makoto Ueda 2003

Just Living: Poems and Prose by the Japanese Monk Tonna, ed. and tr. Steven D. Carter 2003

Han Feizi: Basic Writings, tr. Burton Watson 2003

Mozi: Basic Writings, tr. Burton Watson 2003

Xunzi: Basic Writings, tr. Burton Watson 2003

Zhuangzi: Basic Writings, tr. Burton Watson 2003

The Awakening of Faith, Attributed to Aśvaghosha, tr. Yoshito S. Hakeda, introduction by Ryuichi Abe 2005

Modern Asian Literature

Modern Japanese Drama: An Anthology, ed. and tr. Ted. Takaya. Also in paperback ed. 1979

Mask and Sword: Two Plays for the Contemporary Japanese Theater, by Yamazaki Masakazu, tr. J. Thomas Rimer 1980

Yokomitsu Riichi, Modernist, Dennis Keene 1980

Nepali Visions, Nepali Dreams: The Poetry of Laxmiprasad Devkota, tr. David Rubin 1980

Literature of the Hundred Flowers, vol. 1: Criticism and Polemics, ed. Hualing Nieh 1981

Literature of the Hundred Flowers, vol. 2: Poetry and Fiction, ed. Hualing Nieh 1981

Modern Chinese Stories and Novellas, 1919–1949, ed. Joseph S. M. Lau, C. T. Hsia, and Leo Ou-fan Lee. Also in paperback ed. 1984

A View by the Sea, by Yasuoka Shōtarō, tr. Kären Wigen Lewis 1984

Other Worlds: Arishima Takeo and the Bounds of Modern Japanese Fiction, by Paul Anderer 1984

Selected Poems of Sŏ Chŏngju, tr. with introduction by David R. McCann 1989

The Sting of Life: Four Contemporary Japanese Novelists, by Van C. Gessel 1989

Stories of Osaka Life, by Oda Sakunosuke, tr. Burton Watson 1990

The Bodhisattva, or Samantabhadra, by Ishikawa Jun, tr. with introduction by William Jefferson Tyler 1990

The Travels of Lao Ts'an, by Liu T'ieh-yün, tr. Harold Shadick. Morningside ed. 1990

Three Plays by Kōbō Abe, tr. with introduction by Donald Keene 1993

The Columbia Anthology of Modern Chinese Literature, ed. Joseph S. M. Lau and Howard Goldblatt 1995

Modern Japanese Tanka, ed. and tr. Makoto Ueda 1996

Masaoka Shiki: Selected Poems, ed. and tr. Burton Watson 1997

Writing Women in Modern China: An Anthology of Women's Literature from the Early Twentieth Century, ed. and tr. Amy D. Dooling and Kristina M. Torgeson 1998

American Stories, by Nagai Kafū, tr. Mitsuko Iriye 2000

The Paper Door and Other Stories, by Shiga Naoya, tr. Lane Dunlop 2001

Grass for My Pillow, by Saiichi Maruya, tr. Dennis Keene 2002

For All My Walking: Free-Verse Haiku of Taneda Santōka, with Excerpts from His Diaries, tr. Burton Watson 2003

The Columbia Anthology of Modern Japanese Literature, ed. J. Thomas Rimer and Van C. Gessel, vol. 1, 2005

Studies in Asian Culture

The Ōnin War: History of Its Origins and Background, with a Selective Translation of the Chronicle of Ōnin, by H. Paul Varley 1967

Chinese Government in Ming Times: Seven Studies, ed. Charles O. Hucker 1969

The Actors' Analects (Yakusha Rongo), ed. and tr. Charles J. Dunn and Bungō Torigoe 1969

Self and Society in Ming Thought, by Wm. Theodore de Bary and the Conference on Ming Thought. Also in paperback ed. 1970

A History of Islamic Philosophy, by Majid Fakhry, 2d ed. 1983

Phantasies of a Love Thief: The Caurapañcāśikā Attributed to Bilhaṇa, by Barbara Stoler Miller 1971

Iqbal: Poet-Philosopher of Pakistan, ed. Hafeez Malik 1971

The Golden Tradition: An Anthology of Urdu Poetry, ed. and tr. Ahmed Ali. Also in paperback ed. 1973

Conquerors and Confucians: Aspects of Political Change in Late Yüan China, by John W. Dardess 1973

The Unfolding of Neo-Confucianism, by Wm. Theodore de Bary and the Conference on Seventeenth-Century Chinese Thought. Also in paperback ed. 1975

To Acquire Wisdom: The Way of Wang Yang-ming, by Julia Ching 1976
Gods, Priests, and Warriors: The Bhṛgus of the Mahābhārata, by Robert P. Goldman
    1977
Mei Yao-ch'en and the Development of Early Sung Poetry, by Jonathan Chaves
    1976
The Legend of Semimaru, Blind Musician of Japan, by Susan Matisoff 1977
Sir Sayyid Ahmad Khan and Muslim Modernization in India and Pakistan, by Hafeez
    Malik 1980
The Khilafat Movement: Religious Symbolism and Political Mobilization in India, by
    Gail Minault 1982
The World of K'ung Shang-jen: A Man of Letters in Early Ch'ing China, by Richard
    Strassberg 1983
The Lotus Boat: The Origins of Chinese Tz'u Poetry in T'ang Popular Culture, by
    Marsha L. Wagner 1984
Expressions of Self in Chinese Literature, ed. Robert E. Hegel and Richard C. Hess-
    ney 1985
Songs for the Bride: Women's Voices and Wedding Rites of Rural India, by W.G.
    Archer; ed. Barbara Stoler Miller and Mildred Archer 1986
The Confucian Kingship in Korea: Yŏngjo and the Politics of Sagacity, by JaHyun
    Kim Haboush 1988

Companions to Asian Studies

Approaches to the Oriental Classics, ed. Wm. Theodore de Bary 1959
Early Chinese Literature, by Burton Watson. Also in paperback ed. 1962
Approaches to Asian Civilizations, ed. Wm. Theodore de Bary and Ainslie T. Embree
    1964
The Classic Chinese Novel: A Critical Introduction, by C.T. Hsia. Also in paperback
    ed. 1968
Chinese Lyricism: Shih Poetry from the Second to the Twelfth Century, tr. Burton
    Watson. Also in paperback ed. 1971
A Syllabus of Indian Civilization, by Leonard A. Gordon and Barbara Stoler Miller
    1971
Twentieth-Century Chinese Stories, ed. C.T. Hsia and Joseph S.M. Lau. Also in
    paperback ed. 1971
A Syllabus of Chinese Civilization, by J. Mason Gentzler, 2d ed. 1972
A Syllabus of Japanese Civilization, by H. Paul Varley, 2d ed. 1972
An Introduction to Chinese Civilization, ed. John Meskill, with the assistance of
    J. Mason Gentzler 1973
An Introduction to Japanese Civilization, ed. Arthur E. Tiedemann 1974
Ukifune: Love in the Tale of Genji, ed. Andrew Pekarik 1982
The Pleasures of Japanese Literature, by Donald Keene 1988

A Guide to Oriental Classics, ed. Wm. Theodore de Bary and Ainslie T. Embree; 3d edition ed. Amy Vladeck Heinrich, 2 vols. 1989

Introduction to Asian Civilizations

Wm. Theodore de Bary, General Editor
Sources of Japanese Tradition, 1958; paperback ed., 2 vols., 1964. 2d ed., vol. 1, 2001, compiled by Wm. Theodore de Bary, Donald Keene, George Tanabe, and Paul Varley; vol. 2, 2005, compiled by Wm. Theodore de Bary, Carol Gluck, and Arthur E. Tiedemann
Sources of Indian Tradition, 1958; paperback ed., 2 vols., 1964. 2d ed., 2 vols., 1988
Sources of Chinese Tradition, 1960, paperback ed., 2 vols., 1964. 2d ed., vol. 1, 1999, compiled by Wm. Theodore de Bary and Irene Bloom; vol. 2, 2000, compiled by Wm. Theodore de Bary and Richard Lufrano
Sources of Korean Tradition, 1997; 2 vols., vol. 1, 1997, compiled by Peter H. Lee and Wm. Theodore de Bary; vol. 2, 2001, compiled by Yŏngho Ch'oe, Peter H. Lee, and Wm. Theodore de Bary

Neo-Confucian Studies

Instructions for Practical Living and Other Neo-Confucian Writings by Wang Yang-ming, tr. Wing-tsit Chan 1963
Reflections on Things at Hand: The Neo-Confucian Anthology, comp. Chu Hsi and Lü Tsu-ch'ien, tr. Wing-tsit Chan 1967
Self and Society in Ming Thought, by Wm. Theodore de Bary and the Conference on Ming Thought. Also in paperback ed. 1970
The Unfolding of Neo-Confucianism, by Wm. Theodore de Bary and the Conference on Seventeenth-Century Chinese Thought. Also in paperback ed. 1975
Principle and Practicality: Essays in Neo-Confucianism and Practical Learning, ed. Wm. Theodore de Bary and Irene Bloom. Also in paperback ed. 1979
The Syncretic Religion of Lin Chao-en, by Judith A. Berling 1980
The Renewal of Buddhism in China: Chu-hung and the Late Ming Synthesis, by Chün-fang Yü 1981
Neo-Confucian Orthodoxy and the Learning of the Mind-and-Heart, by Wm. Theodore de Bary 1981
Yüan Thought: Chinese Thought and Religion Under the Mongols, ed. Hok-lam Chan and Wm. Theodore de Bary 1982
The Liberal Tradition in China, by Wm. Theodore de Bary 1983
The Development and Decline of Chinese Cosmology, by John B. Henderson 1984
The Rise of Neo-Confucianism in Korea, by Wm. Theodore de Bary and JaHyun Kim Haboush 1985

Chiao Hung and the Restructuring of Neo-Confucianism in Late Ming, by Edward T. Ch'ien 1985

Neo-Confucian Terms Explained: Pei-hsi tzu-i, by Ch'en Ch'un, ed. and tr. Wing-tsit Chan 1986

Knowledge Painfully Acquired: K'un-chih chi, by Lo Ch'in-shun, ed. and tr. Irene Bloom 1987

To Become a Sage: The Ten Diagrams on Sage Learning, by Yi T'oegye, ed. and tr. Michael C. Kalton 1988

The Message of the Mind in Neo-Confucian Thought, by Wm. Theodore de Bary 1989